THE COMPUTER MUSEUM GUIDE TO THE BEST SOFTWARE FOR KIDS

THE COMPUTER MUSEUM GUIDE TO THE BEST SOFTWARE FOR KIDS

More Than 200 Reviews for Windows™, Macintosh® & DOS Computers Including the Best CD-ROMs

CATHY MIRANKER & ALISON ELLIOTT

HarperPerennial
A Division of HarperCollinsPublishers

The Authors and Publisher in preparing this book have made their best efforts to obtain accurate information from sources believed to be reliable. However, the Authors and Publisher make no warranties of any kind, express or implied, with regard to the accuracy, adequacy, or completeness of any information contained herein and are not responsible for any errors or omissions and are not liable for any loss of profit or any other commercial damages or any other damages arising from the use of this book, the information it contains, and the program listings in the book.

The authors and publisher have attempted to distinguish trademarks throughout this book by following the capitalization style used by the manufacturer.

THE COMPUTER MUSEUM GUIDE TO THE BEST SOFTWARE FOR KIDS. Copyright © 1995 by Cathy Miranker and Alison Elliott. All rights reserved. Printed in the United States of America. No part of this book may be used or reproduced in any manner whatsoever without written permission except in the case of brief quotations embodied in critical articles and reviews. For information address HarperCollins Publishers, Inc., 10 East 53rd Street, New York, NY 10022.

HarperCollins books may be purchased for educational, business, or sales promotional use. For information, please write: Special Markets Department, HarperCollins Publishers, Inc., 10 East 53rd Street, New York, NY 10022.

FIRST EDITION

Designed by Jessica Shatan

Library of Congress Cataloging-in-Publication Data

Miranker, Cathy (Catherine Wedge)
   The Computer Museum guide to the best software for kids : more than 200 reviews for Windows™, Macintosh® & DOS computers including the best CD-ROMs / Cathy Miranker & Alison Elliott.
      p. cm.
   Includes index.
   ISBN 0-06-273376-1 (pb : alk. paper)
    1. Children's software—Evaluation.   I. Elliott, Alison, 1953– .   II. Computer Museum (Boston, Mass.)   III. Title.
QA76.76.C54M57   1995
005.36—dc20   95-14950

95 96 97 98 99 ❖/RRD 10 9 8 7 6 5 4 3 2

*With thanks to our families and friends,
the children and parents who helped us test the best software,
and to our colleagues at The Computer Museum
and in the education and software communities.*

CONTENTS

A Letter from The Computer Museum   ix
Getting the Most from the *Guide*   xi

THE BEST LISTS   2

The Best for Your 2–3-Year-Old   2
The Best for Your 4–5-Year-Old   3
The Best for Your 6–7-Year-Old   4
The Best for Your 8–9-Year-Old   5
The Best for Your 10–12-Year-Old   6
The Best of the New & Notable Titles   7

THE BEST TITLES   8

1 • Playing to Learn   8
2 • Creative Pursuits   29
    Arts & Animation 30
    Wordplay & Storytelling 50
3 • Reading   67
    Stories on Screen 68
    Reading Basics 78
4 • Math   94
    Math Explorations 96
    Skills & Drills 110
5 • Explorations for Curious Kids   121
    ...Around the World 122
    ...Back in Time 132
    ...Into Science, Nature & Beyond 149
6 • Fun & Games   168
7 • Information, Please!   188

8 • Productivity	198
9 • New & Notable	212

MORE BEST LISTS   235

The Best Simulation Programs	235
The Most Challenging Programs	236
The Best Video-Game-Meets-Education Programs	237
The Best Homework Helpers	238
The Best Programs for Kids & Parents to Use Together	239
The Best Programs for Siblings to Share	240
Glossary	241

INDEXES   245

Titles	245
CD-ROM Titles	249
Floppy Titles	253
Publishers	255
Titles by Age	261
Titles by Rating	275
Titles by Subject	279

A LETTER FROM THE COMPUTER MUSEUM

The *Computer Museum Guide to the Best Software for Kids* was conceived to fill a need at The Computer Museum. After a day of exploration, more and more families would end their visit to the museum with a question: What software should we get for our children? And with 1,500 visitors some days, that was getting to be a lot of questions!

We also realized that this need extended far beyond the Museum and its home in Boston. Indeed, millions of families around the country were investing in computers for their kids and asking exactly the same question. Like our visitors, they too could benefit from knowledgeable, objective advice on how to make the most of their kids' computer experience. And so we decided to use our experience in bringing kids and computers together to develop a guide to the best in children's software.

For more than 10 years, The Computer Museum has been dedicated to helping children and adults explore the impact of computing on our lives. The Museum is filled with dynamic, hands-on exhibits that let people discover how computing technology works and experiment with the many different ways computers are used. Even if you've never visited us at Museum Wharf in Boston, one of our best-known exhibits may be familiar to you and your children. It's The Walk-Through Computer, a working computer that's so large people can actually walk inside for an up-close look at computing technology. Featured on *Sesame Street* and other television programs, The Walk-Through Computer is also the subject of a video shown to tens of thousands of students every year.

Over the years we've been creating exhibits at the Museum, we've come to know a lot about computers and kids. How they inspire children to learn. How they encourage kids to ask questions, to explore, to experiment and to see what happens.

With this in mind, we asked authors Alison Elliott and Cathy Miranker to help us apply the Museum's perspective to the rapidly expanding universe of children's software. Our authors have done an exemplary job of sifting through hundreds and hundreds of titles. In researching and organizing the *Guide*, they've drawn on their collective experience that spans education, journalism, the computer industry, and parenting. They've consulted educational specialists, multimedia experts, developers of both software and hardware. And they've worked closely with children and parents.

The result is an informative, insightful set of reviews. Reviews you can trust. Reviews you can use to find the right software for your children.

As you explore the world of children's software, keep the Museum in mind. In fact, we'd like *you* to help create reviews for the next edition of the *Guide*. We would value your opinion on which programs work for your kids, which programs don't, and why. Contact our authors by e-mail at guide@tcm.org or by regular mail at 3145 Geary Blvd., San Francisco, CA 94118. And for updates on new and noteworthy software not included in this edition of the *Guide*, check The Computer Museum World Wide Web page at http://www.tcm.org.

OLIVER STRIMPEL
Executive Director,
The Computer Museum

GETTING THE MOST FROM THE *GUIDE*

Welcome to *The Computer Museum Guide to the Best Software for Kids*. If you're looking for a compendium filled with summaries of every software program created for kids, read no further. You won't find that in this book. But if you want concise, thoughtful advice on which programs will be right for your kids, this *Guide* can help.

From a universe of more than a thousand titles, we chose some 200 programs for this *Guide*. Within this highly selective group, you'll find products that present a wide variety of subjects and skills. Products that are fun—and educational. Products that work for children between the ages of 2 and 12 (and sometimes even for the whole family).

Almost all are available for both Windows and Macintosh computers. Most are available as CD-ROMs. Each one has something to recommend it. But some are better than others, and we tell you why.

If you've heard about a product but you don't see it in the *Guide to the Best*, odds are that we evaluated it and decided it didn't make the grade. (Contact us via e-mail at guide@tcm.org to ask about titles you don't see here.) Or, if it's quite new, you may find it listed in the "New & Notable" section of the *Guide*.

HOW WE FIND THE BEST

What's best about the software in this *Guide*? Every product was measured against three criteria—learning, looks, and longevity—as well as the Museum's perspective on how kids learn best. To this evaluation we added the real-world assessments of kids and parents based on their experience with the titles on their home computers. Our ratings—ranging from 1 to 4 stars—represent our opinion about how well a product measures up to these standards.

As we evaluated software, we constantly asked questions about the qualities we considered essential. We invite you to use our checklist when you take a look at products recommended in the *Guide*.

Learning
- Does this program fit your child's developmental needs and interests?
- Does it invite active participation, exploration and self-directed discovery?
- Does it challenge your child to think, to make choices and decisions that alter the outcome? And to learn from those choices?
- Does this program use the computer to create a unique experience (or does it merely re-create an experience children can have off the computer)?

Looks
- Is the program's design and use of animation, sound and video appropriate to the age of the players?
- Does it have a distinctive look and feel? A sense of humor?
- Is it easy for a child to figure out how it works?

Longevity
- Once the novelty factor wears off, do kids continue to play this program over and over again?
- Does it present an experience that's different and more challenging each time your child uses the program?
- Does it provide the satisfaction of discovery and mastery, of getting better at solving a puzzle, winning a game or completing a quest?
- Does it strike a good balance between familiar pleasures and new challenges?

HOW TO USE THIS GUIDE

We designed the *Guide* to help you find what you're looking for quickly.

You can search for software based on your child's age, for example, by looking in the "Best Lists." These lists recommend a good mix of software for children ages 2–3, 4–5, 6–7, 8–9, and 10–12. You can also find every title appropriate for different age ranges in the "Age Index" at the back of the book.

You can head for particular subject areas by looking in the "Best Titles" chapters. These chapters group products by such topics as "Playing to Learn," "Creative Pursuits," "Explorations for Curious Kids," and "Fun & Games." At the beginning of each chapter, you'll find a list of programs reviewed, the *Guide*'s rating and recommended age range, along with the page where the review appears. The "Subject Indexes" at the back of the book also list every title in the *Guide*.

You can zero in on star ratings by checking the "Rating Indexes" for lists of 4-, 3-, 2-, and 1-star products. Other indexes list titles by format (CD-ROM or floppy) or by publisher. Additional "Best Lists" suggest the best homework helpers, the most challenging programs, the best programs for kids and parents to use together, among others. And any and all of these routes through the *Guide* give you the page number where you'll find a full product review.

Turn the page to see what you'll find in every review.

1. The title and its star rating. Wherever possible, reviews and ratings are based on the latest release of a product.

2. A paragraph that says it all: what's good (or bad) about the program, what it does, and what we think about it.

3. A more detailed description of what's in the program.

4. The most realistic age range for the program. Our recommendation often differs from the software developer's, reflecting the experience of our test families.

5. Separate ratings for the key criteria we use to assess software, plus a capsule description of the kind of learning, looks and longevity that characterize the program.

6. Computer platform (Macintosh or Windows system) and software format (floppy disk or CD-ROM). Reviews that cover multiple programs often provide additional details within the text. Publishers often upgrade their products, so check with them or The Computer Museum Store ([617] 426-2800 x307) for the latest versions available.

7. Approximate street price, provided by the software publisher. Subject to frequent change.

8. Publisher's name and phone number. Since the *Guide* doesn't address software/hardware compatibility issues in detail, we suggest you call the publisher to check whether a particular program will work with your computer system. A publisher's technical support department will also help you with installation or performance problems.

9. Still unsure if you want to buy the program? A concluding thought is intended to help you make the decision.

① Odell Down Under

★ ★ ★

② *Odell Down Under* **transforms 9-year-olds into sharks. In this fast-paced simulation, kids become inhabitants of Australia's Great Barrier Reef and learn what it takes to survive.**

③ Although they can choose from more than 60 sea creatures, kids invariably start out as sharks. (Is this a reflection of our competitive culture? A sophisticated instinct for survival? Or kids showing their true colors as vicious beasts?) Players can also create a fish and experiment with the impact of different attributes (speed, size, coloration, defense strategies like poison or electric shocks) in their quest for survival. Staying alive—and moving up the food chain—is not easy, and kids must learn quickly from experience (or the help of the field guide) in order to live long enough to become Reef Ruler.

This game is especially fun to play with friends, siblings or parents. And, naturally, there's an added attraction when your kid gets to eat you.

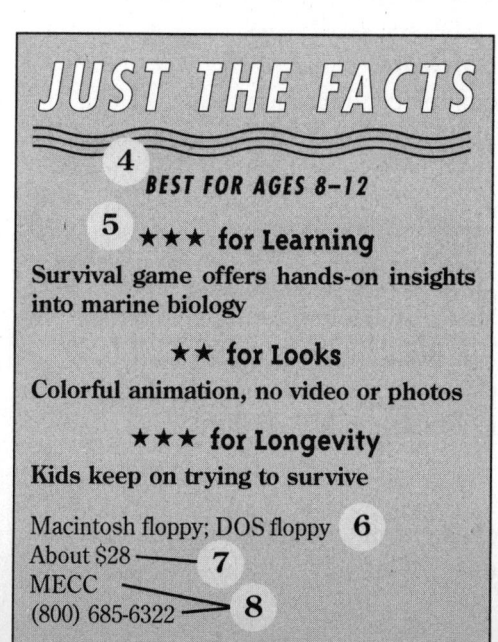

⑨ The bottom line: A good marine life simulation game from the same folks who brought you the *Trail* titles (*Oregon, Amazon, Yukon*).

JUST THE FACTS

④ **BEST FOR AGES 8-12**

⑤ ★★★ **for Learning**
Survival game offers hands-on insights into marine biology

★★ **for Looks**
Colorful animation, no video or photos

★★★ **for Longevity**
Kids keep on trying to survive

Macintosh floppy; DOS floppy ⑥
About $28 ⑦
MECC
(800) 685-6322 ⑧

BEFORE YOU BUY:
MORE TIPS FOR BUYING THE BEST SOFTWARE

As you use the *Guide* to identify software programs that suit your child, there are a couple of other issues to consider before heading out to make your purchase.

How Many Titles to Buy, How Often

Building a software library for your children is a lot like buying books, toys or games. The collection grows the way your kids do, sometimes in spurts, sometimes little by little. If you're just getting started, we suggest you first consult the Best List corresponding to your child's age. Each list recommends a well-rounded mix of programs covering the most appropriate subject areas for every age range. Introduce them, one at a time, over the course of 12 or 18 months. Then, depending on your child's development and interest in the computer (and your software budget), you can select additional titles to match particular needs (math practice, for example) or current passions (wild animals, perhaps).

Always install software and familiarize yourself with it *before* you show a program to your child. Stick around the first few times your kids use a new program to make sure they've figured it out. And periodically you may want to put some children's programs away for a month or so. That way your kids will approach the software with a fresh perspective when you reintroduce it.

Choosing Floppy Disk or CD-ROM Software

Your choice depends upon your computer configuration. You can run CD-ROMs only if you have a CD-ROM drive. Many of the products in the *Guide* are available as either floppy disks or CD-ROMs. But most new children's software is available on CD-ROM only. Unless you have a CD-ROM-equipped computer, your choices in children's software will become more and more limited.

If you're interested in a program that's available both as a CD-ROM and as a floppy disk, we'd opt for the CD-ROM. In many cases, CD-ROM versions have richer sound, graphics, animation and video than their floppy counterparts. They also take up less space on your hard drive.

Finding the Software You Want

We recommend many excellent programs from small, little known companies. You may not see some of these titles if you shop in discount or super stores. The reason: with so many more software products these days, shelf space is hard to come by—and often filled with products from bigger companies with larger advertising budgets. If you can't find a program you want, simply call The Computer Museum Store at (617) 426-2800 x307 to order one of the best. (You can also send the Store e-mail at store@tcm.org.) The Store can also suggest other helpful books and products that explain how computers, operating systems, networks and on-line services, or particular programs, work.

Know Your Computer System

Before you buy software, read the fine print on the software package to make sure your computer is up to the program's requirements. Or review the program's requirements when you call The Computer Museum Store. Installing children's software—even for the most seasoned computer users—is not always child's play. Every parent has trouble from time to time. (We sometimes did!) If you have trouble installing or running a program, don't hesitate to contact the software publisher's technical service department via the phone numbers listed in the *Guide*.

Stay Involved

The computer is a great resource for parent-child activity. Little kids love to sit on your lap while they play. Older kids love to beat you at games. And kids 10 and up will be eager students of your word processing, calendar, address book, or spreadsheet programs—if you show them the ropes. Whatever your children's ages, you are their most important audience for the artwork and stories they create, the math challenges and simulations they master, and the many other activities they'll explore on the computer.

From time to time, ask your kids to show you what they are doing at the computer. You'll learn if they've figured out how to use all the software you've invested in. You'll learn what they like. And, by watching or playing by their side, you'll gain insights into how they learn and think.

THE COMPUTER MUSEUM GUIDE TO THE BEST SOFTWARE FOR KIDS

THE BEST LISTS

THE BEST FOR YOUR 2-3-YEAR-OLD

RATINGS	TITLES
★★★★	**Just Grandma and Me** (Page 71)
★★★★	**Kid Pix 2** (Page 32)
★★★★	**Millie's Math House** (Page 100)
★★★★	**Putt Putt Saves the Zoo** (Page 176)
★★★	**Zurk's Learning Safari** (Page 14)
★★	**The Playroom** (Page 22)

THE BEST FOR YOUR 4-5-YEAR-OLD

RATINGS	TITLES
★★★★	**AlphaBonk Farm** (Page 12)
★★★★	**Circus!** (Page 10)
★★★★	**Freddi Fish and the Case of the Missing Kelp Seeds** (Page 174)
★★★★	**Little Monster at School** (Page 72)
★★★★	**Sammy's Science House** (Page 150)
★★★	**Davidson's Kid Works Deluxe** (Page 62)

THE BEST FOR YOUR 6-7-YEAR-OLD

RATINGS	TITLES
★★★★	**Arthur's Teacher Trouble** (Page 71)
★★★★	**At Bat** (Page 178)
★★★★	**Kid Pix Studio** (Page 34)
★★★★	**Math Workshop** (Page 98)
★★★★	**Where in the World Is Carmen Sandiego? Jr. Detective Edition** (Page 128)
★★★	**Storybook Weaver Deluxe** (Page 58)

THE BEST FOR YOUR 8-9-YEAR-OLD

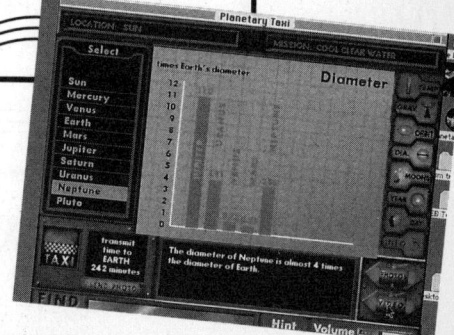

RATINGS	TITLES
★★★★	**The Amazing Writing Machine** (Page 52)
★★★★	**Flying Colors** (Page 36)
★★★★	**Imagination Express** (Page 54)
★★★★	**Planetary Taxi** (Page 152)
★★★★	**Star Act** (Page 56)
★★★	**Explorapedia** (Page 190)

THE BEST FOR YOUR 10-12-YEAR-OLD

RATINGS	TITLES
★★★★	**Art Explorer** (Page 40)
★★★★	**Myst** (Page 170)
★★★★	**Oregon Trail II** (Page 134)
★★★★	**SimCity 2000** (Page 172)
★★★★	**What's the Secret?** (Page 154)
★★★★	**Where in the World Is Carmen Sandiego?** (Page 124)

THE BEST OF THE NEW & NOTABLE TITLES

AGE	TITLES
6–48 months	**Baby ROM** (Page 212)
3–6 years	**Curious George Comes Home** (Page 220)
4–8 years	**Pantsylvania** (Page 215)
6–10 years	**Bumptz Science Carnival** (Page 228)
8–12 years	**Top Secret Decoder** (Page 217)
9 years & up	**The Lost Mind of Dr. Brain** (Page 230)

•ONE•

THE BEST TITLES: PLAYING TO LEARN

Early Learning Titles Including ABCs, Counting & More

Kids are always playing. Playing tag, playing house, playing ball, playing space aliens, playing games. It's spontaneous. And it's essential—because that's how children learn. And as the name of this section suggests, Playing to Learn programs let kids learn naturally—by playing.

Playing to Learn titles are great for getting little kids started on the computer. The best are unhurried in their approach, giving kids the freedom to poke around appealing environments that are filled with different things to do. They're rich in activities that sharpen the senses and cultivate a spirit of curiosity and inquiry. Equally important, kids can easily navigate around these programs on their own, moving from activity to activity simply by clicking. So, as they play, they're also developing competence, self-esteem, and a habit of success.

Learning through play is not for little kids only. Several titles in this section, as well as elsewhere in the *Guide*, give older kids this same kind of freedom to explore, discover, and learn for themselves.

THE BEST TITLES: PLAYING TO LEARN • 9

RATINGS	TITLES	AGES
★★★★	Circus! (Pages 10-11)	4–8
★★★★	AlphaBonk Farm (Pages 12-13)	3–5
★★★	Zurk's Learning Safari (Pages 14-15)	2–5
★★★	Zurk's Rainforest Lab (Pages 16-17)	5–9
★★★	Thinkin' Things Collection 1 (Pages 18-19)	3–8
★★★	Thinkin' Things Collection 2 (Pages 20-21)	6–12
★★	The Playroom (Pages 22-23)	2–4
★★	The Backyard (Pages 24-25)	3–5
★★	My First Incredible Amazing Dictionary (Pages 26-27)	2–4
★	Richard Scarry's How Things Work in Busytown (Page 28)	3–5

Circus!

★ ★ ★ ★

The best mix of intuitive learning and exuberance we've seen. *Circus!* **invites children into the world of a one-ring circus, where they can participate in backstage and bigtop activities, enjoy catchy music and discover hidden surprises.**

Almost everywhere kids click, there are silly antics to watch. But there's plenty of opportunity to get into the act, too—eight different acts, in fact. Seemingly simple, these circus acts pose a real imaginative challenge for kids (and adults). You think it's easy measuring out the right combination of kazoom powder (for height) and shazzam powder (for speed) to blast a clown out of a cannon in just the right direction to snatch a parrot off a trapeze? Figure it out, and the hapless human cannonball will stop barreling through the tent, and your kids will learn something about physics, too.

Teaching the baby elephants to waltz is also harder than it looks. And, unless your kids have a perfect eye for complex sequences, freeing the clowns that Rex the magician traps in a fiendish cylinder may take hours of clicking and experimenting.

For the youngest players there are plenty of innocent pleasures.

JUST THE FACTS

BEST FOR AGES 4–8

★★★★ **for Learning**
Exploration and problem-solving challenges; skills include pattern recognition, sequencing, estimation

★★★★ **for Looks**
Exceptional graphics, animation and original music

★★★ **for Longevity**
Kids return time and again

Macintosh CD-ROM; Windows CD-ROM
About $50
Voyager
(800) 446-2001

In the clown's camper backstage they can toy with theatrical makeup to create dozens of different clown faces or dress up circus performers for the big parade. In the Music Tent they can strike up a tune on the instruments, and watch as magic emerges with every note!

The bottom line: Spirited fun with strong appeal for kids across a wide age range.

AlphaBonk Farm

★ ★ ★ ★

As parents of preschoolers, we thought we'd seen the ABCs covered in every conceivable way. But *AlphaBonk Farm* surprised and charmed us with a delightfully different tour of the alphabet.

AlphaBonk Farm presents a farmyard alphabet through an inventive combination of photographs and bold graphics, quirky animations and ridiculous rhymes, twangy banjo music and alphabetically inspired "fun facts." Kids start in the Picture Show, an alphabetically arranged slide show of farm-life photographs. Whenever an image takes their fancy, they can click to stop the show for a longer look.

The Gigglebone Gang of characters guides kids to other activities. Click on Velma the swine to hear brief tales about farm life and bits of "dazzling data." Click on Clyde the parrot to hear funny rhymes that reinforce letter sounds: "*O*utside you can smell the barnyard stink. Your mouth drops *o*pen and your eyes go blink." (Rich in preschool humor, this program has plenty of kid-pleasing references to "unmentionables" like underwear and manure.)

Click on our kids' favorite, Bunji the frog, to jump into *AlphaBonk Farm*'s distinctive

JUST THE FACTS

BEST FOR AGES 3–5

★★★ **for Learning**
A novel look at the ABCs; skills include letter recognition, rhyming, auditory and visual discrimination

★★★★ **for Looks**
Highly original blend of photos, graphics and sound

★★★ **for Longevity**
Lots to do so kids keep coming back

Worth Noting
If your kids like the Gigglebone Gang, try the Gang's second adventure in *Pantsylvania* (see Page 215).

Macintosh CD-ROM; Windows CD-ROM
About $35
Headbone Interactive
(800) 267-4709

games. In Seek and Find, kids search a black-and-white line drawing for objects that begin with certain letters—like *d*ilapidated truck, *D*oberman, *d*andelion. Find them all and the picture is transformed into glorious color. Even more engaging are the 13 offbeat Poke 'N Prod activities. In the I Scream for Ice Cream Parlor, kids concoct towering ice cream cones with all the trimmings. In the X-Ray Lab, they examine the innards of different animals. And in U's Upside Down Room, they help ripen an *u*nripe peach and *u*se *u*tensils to cut it open.

The bottom line: Enormous fun—and a great way to learn the sight and sounds of letters.

Zurk's Learning Safari

★ ★ ★

Using *Zurk's Learning Safari* is like playing inside a beautifully crafted children's book.

Serene watercolor illustrations and lively original music create an African backdrop for five exploration and learning games. Our favorite is Alphabet Soup, a hide-and-seek game kids play with Zurk, a funny little fellow who's a cross between the Michelin tire man and the Pillsbury doughboy. In pursuit of Zurk, kids see letters transform into animals whose names start with that letter. Without deliberately teaching letter recognition, this activity encourages kids to pick up that knowledge. We're convinced that 3-year-old Katie learned to identify and write letters just by playing with *Zurk's*.

Young children also enjoy helping a lost lion cub named Maya find her way home by clicking on animals in several richly illustrated scenes. Kids will also find a well executed set of puzzles (the pieces snap convincingly into place) and a camouflage game where they hide animals in their natural habitats—and make *you* search for them.

Zurk's does not stress specific skills. Instead, it provides a set

---

JUST THE FACTS

BEST FOR AGES 2–5

★ ★ ★ **for Learning**
Hands-on ways to learn concepts; skills include letter, shape and pattern recognition

★ ★ ★ ★ **for Looks**
Original watercolors and music are a delight

★ ★ ★ **for Longevity**
Plenty of fun for preschoolers but less compelling once they've mastered all its challenges

Macintosh CD-ROM or floppy; Windows CD-ROM or floppy
About $30
Soleil
(415) 494-0114

of imaginative activities that allow children to play with letters, shapes, patterns and numbers. Its storybook look and gentle pace are just right for preschoolers.

The bottom line: An imaginative, well-balanced introduction to kindergarten skills.

Zurk's Rainforest Lab

★ ★ ★

A nice successor to *Zurk's Learning Safari* for older kids. In this unhurried, picture-book quality program, kids can explore and make discoveries about life science, sharpening their thinking skills as they play.

At first, *Zurk's Rainforest Lab* struck us as too tame, and we wondered whether kids would stick with it long enough to absorb its implicit lessons. But we soon discovered that they do.

The heart of the product is Jungle Discovery, a stunning watercolor canvas depicting scores of rainforest dwellers. As kids scroll from the understory to the floor to the canopy, they can hear the animals' names (and realistic sound effects), read about them, or hear text read to them. They can also snap pictures for a photo album. Older kids can then write captions, comments or made-up stories. *Zurk's* provides a different "story starter" every time kids play. And we've found even reluctant writers like making log entries in their album.

Gaining familiarity with exotic rainforest creatures is useful (but not required) for the Seek & Sort game, where the challenge is to classify a dozen or more animals according to species. (Creating graphs of the sorted animals is a nice touch, encouraging kids to look at what they achieved in a

JUST THE FACTS

BEST FOR AGES 5–9

★★★ **for Learning**
Hands-on activities let kids explore math and science concepts; skills include classification, beginning geometry, pattern recognition, graphing

★★★★ **for Looks**
Original watercolors and music are a delight

★★★ **for Longevity**
Different challenges as kids grow

Macintosh CD-ROM; Windows CD-ROM
About $30
Soleil
(415) 494-0114

different way.) Kids who can't yet read enjoy an Egg Hunt that sends them through the rainforest in search of colored eggs. (A strange juxtaposition, but it works.)

Pattern Puzzles seems at first to be simply a game where kids use geometric shapes to complete or create tangram-like puzzles. But play with the "rotate" buttons, and kids will see that it also provides an exceptionally clear, visual introduction to geometric concepts.

The bottom line: *Zurk's* **is a rich learning resource with opportunities for both creative play and challenging problem-solving. Both nonreaders and readers will have plenty of fun with this program.**

Thinkin' Things Collection 1

★ ★ ★

Cute critters, flying colors and loony music take kids beyond letters and numbers to develop skills critical to thinking and learning.

Thinkin' Things has six colorful activities that exercise young minds by encouraging them to observe and compare attributes, figure out a rule and test their guess, hone listening skills as they try to remember and repeat musical patterns and more. And in the software's playful settings, abstract concepts are always transformed into whimsical challenges.

Take our favorite, the Fripple Shop. These colorful, doodle-like creatures sport a variety of patterns, hairstyles and eyeglasses, and kids must choose the Fripple that fits a customer's request. For example: "I like purple or spots but not straight hair, please." Click the correct Fripple, and it wobbles happily out the door. With the Fripples, even 3-year-olds can practice Boolean (and, or, not) logic!

Older children will get a lot of mileage from the open-ended pos-

JUST THE FACTS

BEST FOR AGES 3–8

★★★ **for Learning**
Challenging thinking games, genuinely different; skills include pattern recognition, classification, visual and auditory memory

★★★★ **for Looks**
Imaginative, age-appropriate graphics

★★★ **for Longevity**
Best for little children and for older kids with musical and artistic interests

Worth Noting
Thinkin' Things Collection 2 **and** *3* **are similar sets of games for older kids.**

Macintosh CD-ROM or floppy; Win/DOS CD-ROM or floppy
About $45
Edmark
(800) 691-2985

sibilities of the Blox games and Flying Spheres, where they experiment with music and movement in three-dimensional space. The other games in *Thinkin' Things*—Toony Loon, Oranga Banga and Feathered Friends—are also as engaging as they are thought-provoking.

The bottom line: A great program for nurturing the many facets of children's learning—musical, visual, mathematical, verbal, auditory—and for gaining insight into how your child learns best.

Thinkin' Things Collection 2

★ ★ ★

More challenging games from the creators of *Thinkin' Things Collection 1*, **this time for the elementary school-age crowd.**

Featuring many characters from the first *Thinkin' Things* (the Fripples, Toony Loon, and Oranga Banga), this collection gives kids a real intellectual workout. Frippletration, for example, puts auditory and visual memory to the test with one of the toughest, most inventive games of concentration we've seen. Kids can both create rhythmic patterns and test their ear for rhythm in Oranga Banga's Band game. Another musical game, Toony's Tunes, invites children to make up melodies or learn to play up to 15 familiar tunes.

Best of all are Snake Blox and 2–3D Blox, which provide a bold, new twist in on-screen creativity. In these colorful, kinetic environments, kids can explore two- and three-dimensional space, experiment with optical effects and manipulate visual images. The payoff (besides fun, of course) is an increase in visual perception and spatial awareness, as well as a greater willingness to experiment. Adults may be daunted by these games: the tools and wealth of variables are complex and a bit

JUST THE FACTS

BEST FOR AGES 6–12

★★★ **for Learning**
Challenging thinking and creativity games; skills include spatial awareness, auditory and visual memory, patterning

★★★ **for Looks**
Imaginative graphics

★★★ **for Longevity**
Different challenges as kids grow

Worth Noting
Use all the *Thinkin' Things* programs with your children for insights into how they learn.

Macintosh CD-ROM or floppy; Win/DOS CD-ROM or floppy
About $45
Edmark
(800) 691-2985

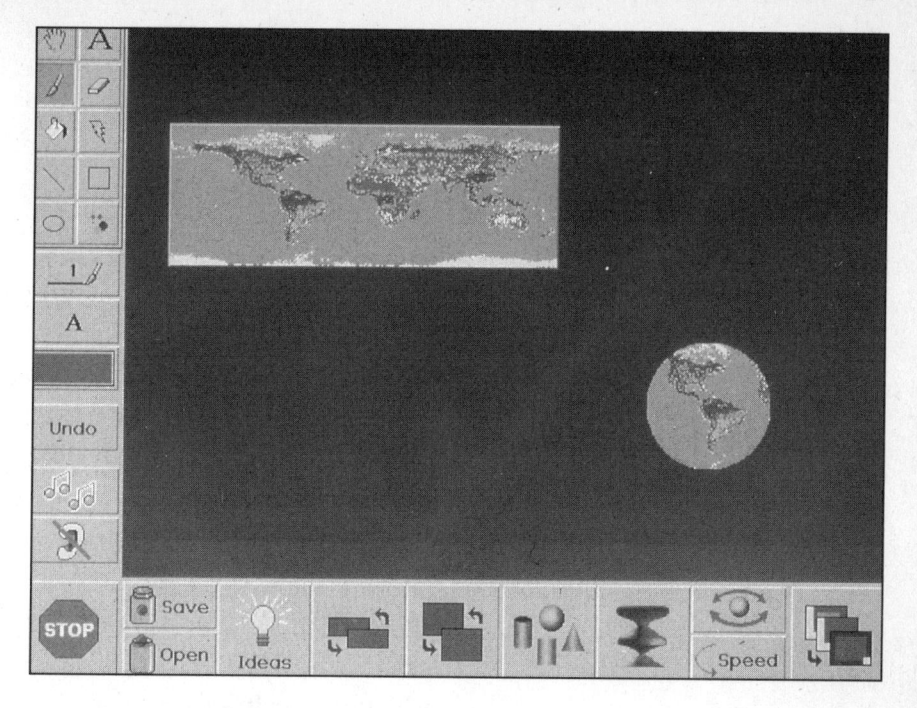

overwhelming. Children, on the other hand, prove to be surprisingly confident explorers.

As kids grow older, they'll find new challenges in these open-ended games. And some of the games, particularly Frippletration, can be enjoyed by children as young as 4 or 5, especially if they play with an adult or older sibling. Fripple fans will find another wonderful set of challenges in *Thinkin' Things Collection 3* (ages 8–12).

The bottom line: Unique games and broad age appeal, but some of the activities may be too abstract for some kids.

The Playroom

★ ★

The Playroom set a standard in 1989 for kid-friendly design and playful learning activities that has been widely imitated ever since. In fact, it's hard to find a kid's program that doesn't borrow from *The Playroom*'s innovations.

Although it lacks the graphic flair and personality of more recent titles, *The Playroom* is still a good first program for preschoolers. With a simple click of the mouse, they can explore a child's room filled with playful activities and surprises. Through the mouse hole lies a counting game; beneath the book, a hands-on encounter with the ABCs. There are no menus to maneuver, no ticking clocks to beat, and no reading required (though prereading skills are gently and skillfully encouraged).

We recommend the new CD-ROM version of *The Playroom*. It adds animation, music and upscale graphics while retaining the unhurried flavor of the original. The title's eight activities are easy to play and right on target for their preschool audience. Clicking on the playroom clock, for example, takes kids into "clock-time" where they can move the

JUST THE FACTS

BEST FOR AGES 2–4

★★★ for Learning
Age-appropriate click-discover-and-learn games; skills include letter and number recognition, counting, telling time

★★ for Looks
Lacks graphic flair and personality; CD-ROM version is better

★★ for Longevity
Not as much staying power as newer programs

Worth Noting
Part of the *Active Mind* series covering reading, math and science.

Macintosh floppy; DOS, Windows floppy; Windows CD-ROM
About $30–$40
Broderbund
(800) 521-6263

hands on a clock's jolly face, hear the time announced by a friendly frog or walrus, see the time in numbers and words, and watch what happens at that time of day. (Noon is lunchtime; 8 p.m. is bath time.) There's no explicit lesson in telling time, but the activity is so appealing that the concepts stick with kids. Other games introduce letters and their sounds, numbers and counting. And some are just pure fun.

The bottom line: *The Playroom* **has deeply satisfying activities for very young children, but lacks the graphic flair and personality of newer programs.**

The Backyard

★ ★

More original learning games from the creators of *The Playroom*. This time, kids get to poke around a backyard and beyond (including Antarctica, a tropical rainforest and the desert).

The Backyard is rich in click-and-discover activities—eight in all. Some are whimsical, like creating silly faces for a scarecrow or a pumpkin. Others are highly original, like the dig-for-treasure game that turns kids loose in a sandbox with a simple map and a tiny bulldozer. (Especially popular with preschool boys, the bulldozer emits satisfying noises as it drives and digs.)

The program goes far afield in its ambitious introduction to different habitats: the desert, Antarctica and the rainforest ("where you can bet, it's always hot and very wet"). Through trial-and-error clicking, children can figure out the right environment for creatures like a crab-eater seal, kangaroo rat, or arrow poison frog. As it snaps into its habitat, like a piece into a puzzle, each animal makes itself at home: the frog scuttles up and down a tree, the elf owl hides in a hole in the cactus. A nice touch, these creatures turn up again in a board-game activity where players read dice and count spaces in order to place each animal (with all its proper parts) in its preferred habitat. While we liked the program's attempt to instill envi-

JUST THE FACTS

BEST FOR AGES 3–5

★★★ **for Learning**
Rich in click-and-discover activities; skills include parts-to-whole recognition, mapping, counting, classification

★★ **for Looks**
Nothing special

★★ **for Longevity**
Not as much staying power as similar programs

Macintosh floppy; DOS, Windows floppy
About $30
Broderbund
(800) 521-6263

ronmental awareness, these games weren't as compelling for children as the *Backyard*'s other activities.

The bottom line: Innovative games but less staying power than *The Playroom*.

My First Incredible Amazing Dictionary

★ ★

A wonderful way for little children and parents to explore words together, through pictures, animations, and sound effects.

Based on the Dorling Kindersley book, this dictionary is one of the best looking we've ever seen. The entries are big and colorful, as are the corresponding photographs and illustrations. Definitions are simple and appropriate for the 2–4-year-old set; the accompanying animations and sound effects are fun and informative. And kids can instantly tour the alphabet by clicking letters or words or pictures.

Clicking the letter K, for example, reveals illustrated K words like kick, karate, kangaroo and kiss. Click on kiss, and kids see the word itself in big blue letters, watch a little girl plant a kiss on a friend's cheek, hear the sound of a smacker and listen to a short definition. The program uses pictures to lead kids from kiss to lips to other "face" words like eye, nose and chin.

Amazing Dictionary works best for very young children. But

JUST THE FACTS

BEST FOR AGES 2–4

★★ **for Learning**
An appealing way to play with words; skills include letter recognition, sight words, beginning spelling

★★★★ **for Looks**
Photorealistic pictures and clear text; distinctive DK Multimedia design

★★ **for Longevity**
Good for browsing together, more looking than doing

Macintosh CD-ROM; Windows CD-ROM
About $30
DK Multimedia
(800) 225-3362

revisit the product with your 7- or 8-year-old to use the spelling games. They actually help teach spelling rather than just quiz kids.

The bottom line: Well designed and beautiful to look at, but your kids will get more from this program if you use it together.

Richard Scarry's How Things Work in Busytown

★

The best part of *How Things Work in Busytown* is driving tractors, bulldozers, helicopters and garbage trucks across the computer screen. But the program's wooden movements and long, repetitive sequences interfere with the fun.

In *Busytown*, kids get lots of practice following directions and sequencing events. They can grow wheat, run a flour mill and help the baker make rolls and pretzels. They can drive a garbage truck, sort trash at the recycling center, construct a road or build machines at the assembly plant.

There are two levels of play in *Busytown*, easy and advanced. The easy level provides flashing stars to show kids what comes next. At the advanced level, kids use trial and error, memory or verbal cues to determine the next action.

The software faithfully re-creates familiar Richard Scarry characters like Huckle the Cat, Hilda Hippo and Lowly the Worm. But these don't behave in a lifelike manner: everyone and everything in *Busytown* moves in a rigid, linear way. So the title "feels" more like a dated video game than a contemporary children's program.

The bottom line: Best for fans of Richard Scarry books and kids who love trucks.

JUST THE FACTS

BEST FOR AGES 3–5

★ **for Learning**
Lots to do but not much challenge; skills include sequencing, following directions

★ **for Looks**
Dated video game-style graphics

★ **for Longevity**
Seems to have more staying power for boys than girls

Macintosh CD-ROM or floppy; DOS CD-ROM or floppy
About $50
Viacom New Media
(800) 469-2539

•TWO•
THE BEST TITLES: CREATIVE PURSUITS

Just as an assortment of good books, toys and art supplies stimulate imaginative play, so does the variety of software in this section we call "Creative Pursuits."

You'll find programs here to appeal to the youngest children (who find that simply doodling rainbow-colored lines—and erasing them—is good fun), to independent-minded preteens (who can produce theatrical scripts or practice animation skills) and to those in between.

Using Arts & Animation and Wordplay & Storymaking software may strike some parents as more fun than educational. But in important ways these titles also lay the groundwork for learning. They provide subtle encouragement for kids to explore and experiment, to envision and express what's in their mind's eye, to appreciate the importance of reading and writing, and to recognize the need for the skills and information that will in turn let them produce richer creations.

More than most titles in this *Guide*, creativity programs have tremendous longevity. Because they're open-ended and flexible, and challenging to so many of the senses, they can lead in new directions with practically every use. (To prove the point, try putting a particular program "away" for a few months and see what happens when your child rediscovers it. Though it may be familiar, because of the passage of time and developmental changes in your child, it's likely to be perceived as newly rich with possibilities.)

ARTS & ANIMATION

Freehand Art, Coloring, Design, Painting, Animation, Crafts and Slide Shows

Make room on your refrigerator door—and add some chairs near the computer for on-screen showings, too. When you introduce your kids to Arts & Animation programs, you'll be giving them new outlets for creative expression.

We're not suggesting that software replace scissors, paint, clay, glue or papier-mâché. But it is an appealing and innovative addition. The titles in this section provide an encouraging start for little kids (or hesitant artists) because they make it easy to get going and fun to clean up, start over or try something different. As kids gain confidence and skill, these programs provide endless (and zany) possibilities, not just for "printable" artwork but also for animated "productions."

With Arts & Animation programs, the "process" of making something is as satisfying as the finished product. Exploring scores of tools and experimenting with their effects can engross children for hours. The results can be pretty spectacular, too.

RATINGS	TITLES	AGES
★★★★	Kid Pix 2 & Kid Pix Fun Pack (Pages 32-33)	3–10
★★★★	Kid Pix Studio (Pages 34-35)	3–12
★★★★	Flying Colors (Pages 36-37)	5–12
★★★★	Kid Cuts (Pages 38-39)	3–8
★★★★	Art Explorer (Pages 40-41)	8–12
★★	Amazing Animation (Pages 42-43)	5–12
★★	Magic Theatre (Pages 44-45)	6–12
★★	Kids World (Page 46)	5–10
★	Fine Artist (Page 47)	8–12
★	Crayola Amazing Art Adventure (Page 48)	3–6
★	Crayola Art Studio (Page 48)	6–9

If you choose your family's creativity programs wisely, you may not need a specialized printing title like *Print Shop*. For example, your kids can print personalized calendars using *Kid Desk* or *Keroppi*. They can print greeting cards and invitations with *Bailey's Book House* or *Kid Cuts*. Journal entries, poems, and more can be written with *The Amazing Writing Machine*. Banners and buttons made with *Fine Artist*. In fact, every single title in the "Wordplay & Storymaking" and "Arts & Animation" sections has built-in print capabilities of some sort.

But for families with special printing needs—if you handle publicity for the cub scout troop, for example, or your child is coordinating rehearsals for the school play—a standalone product may be the way to go. Broderbund's *Print Shop Deluxe CD Ensemble* provides thousands of kid-oriented design elements for creating banners, signs, greeting cards, certificates, calendars, newsletters, postcards, letterhead, envelopes, business cards and more. (Available as a Macintosh or Windows CD-ROM, $80.) *Print Artist* (available on DOS or Windows floppy, $50, or Windows CD-ROM, $60, from Maxis), is easy enough for kids to use but we think its graphics have more adult appeal than *Print Shop*'s. It also lets you preview special effects before you apply them.

Kid Pix 2
Kid Pix Fun Pack

★ ★ ★ ★

The granddaddy of computer art programs for kids, and (thanks to frequent updates) still one of the best. If we had to recommend only one (floppy-based) software program, *Kid Pix 2* would be it.

The reason: Not only is it an incredibly well-stocked, on-screen studio for creating noisy, zany, colorful artwork. It's also a great canvas for on-screen wordplay, math games and fun family activities, too.

The *Kid Pix* people (starting with art professor Craig Hickman, who first devised it for his 3-year-old son, and the Broderbund folks who keep adding ever more appealing features) invented many of the tools that are now standard fare in most children's art titles. Like noisy art supplies. Crazy brushes that paint zigzags, bubbles, footprints and more. Erasers that let you blast your whole design to smithereens. Talking ABCs. And, of course, stamps, hundreds of stamps.

There are countless ways to play with *Kid Pix 2*. Exploring the product is a great adventure in itself whether or not your child even gets around to making a picture. For very young children still learning to mouse around, try Hidden Pictures—the screen

JUST THE FACTS

BEST FOR AGES 3–10

★★★★ **for Learning**
Encourages kids to explore and experiment

★★★★ **for Looks**
Lively, original graphics

★★★★ **for Longevity**
Endless possibilities

Worth Noting
Letter stamps are read aloud in English and Spanish.

Macintosh floppy; DOS, Windows floppy
About $40
Broderbund
(800) 521-6263

seems blank until kids start erasing, and then bit by bit, they'll uncover a surprise. Kids can stamp their way to wonderful artwork, and add or record sounds to accompany the picture. They can draw and paint freehand. They can click the Draw Me feature for a story-starter like this: "I'm a beautiful fairy princess—with a sparkly fish tail—and I love to dance. Draw me." They can make a slide show out of their artwork. They can play Wacky TV movies.

Compared to other products, however, *Kid Pix 2* does have some drawbacks. The small toolbar and tiny color palette can frustrate little kids, the many pull-down menus may be puzzling for prereaders and the stamps can get fuzzy-looking when kids enlarge them.

The bottom line: The best, floppy-based art product, with terrific opportunities for graphic arts, word play, number games and musical fun.

Kid Pix 2 can be a terrific source of family fun and learning games. Try playing hangman with *Kid Pix 2*. (If your kids don't beat you at the game, they'll certainly enjoy making a gruesome effigy on the scaffold!) Try painting randomly numbered dice across the screen then asking your child to color the ones that add up to her age. Use stamps to send coded messages (a butterfly for B, etc.). Draw swirling lines of letters with the ABC brush and ask your preschooler to draw boxes around the letters in her name. Or sketch a figure with the dot-to-dot tool and let your kindergartner connect the numbers.

If your kids have an insatiable appetite for stamps (ours certainly do), consider *Kid Pix Fun Pack* (available on Macintosh, DOS and Windows, floppy, $20). It's an add-on product that makes hundreds of additional hidden pictures, stamps and ColorMe pictures (line drawings kids can color in) available to *Kid Pix* users.

Kid Pix Studio

★ ★ ★ ★

This is the *Kid Pix* to buy if you have a CD-ROM drive in your computer. It includes the classic *Kid Pix* art tools (old and lots of new), plus a host of wildly original ways to play with sound and animation. Kids can spend hours just exploring the possibilities.

Hats off (again) to Craig Hickman, the creator of *Kid Pix*. This time he's let his imagination loose in the world of multimedia. The result: irresistible new opportunities for creative fun.

Take the Digital Puppet activity, for example. First, kids choose a character—a dragon, a dancing princess, or our favorite, an elf named Doofus. Then they tap the keyboard (anywhere will do). Each letter causes an action—a kick, a wink, a wave—and keystrokes can be combined and saved as 30-second animations.

With Stampimator and Moopies, kids can animate wacky brushes, hundreds of *Kid Pix* stamps, or black-and-white photographs. Making mischief with photos is especially fun: we embellished a real dog with a trickle of blue tears while a hand-drawn cat padded past. And every creation can be combined with wonderful backgrounds, music, or original art and then printed, viewed on-screen, or linked together as a slide show.

The Pick A Sound option goes beyond the standard beeping

JUST THE FACTS

BEST FOR AGES 3–12

★★★★ **for Learning**
Encourages kids to explore and experiment

★★★★ **for Looks**
Great *Kid Pix* graphics plus lots of special effects

★★★★ **for Longevity**
Spans simple coloring to inventive animations

Macintosh CD-ROM; Windows CD-ROM
About $45
Broderbund
(800) 521-6263

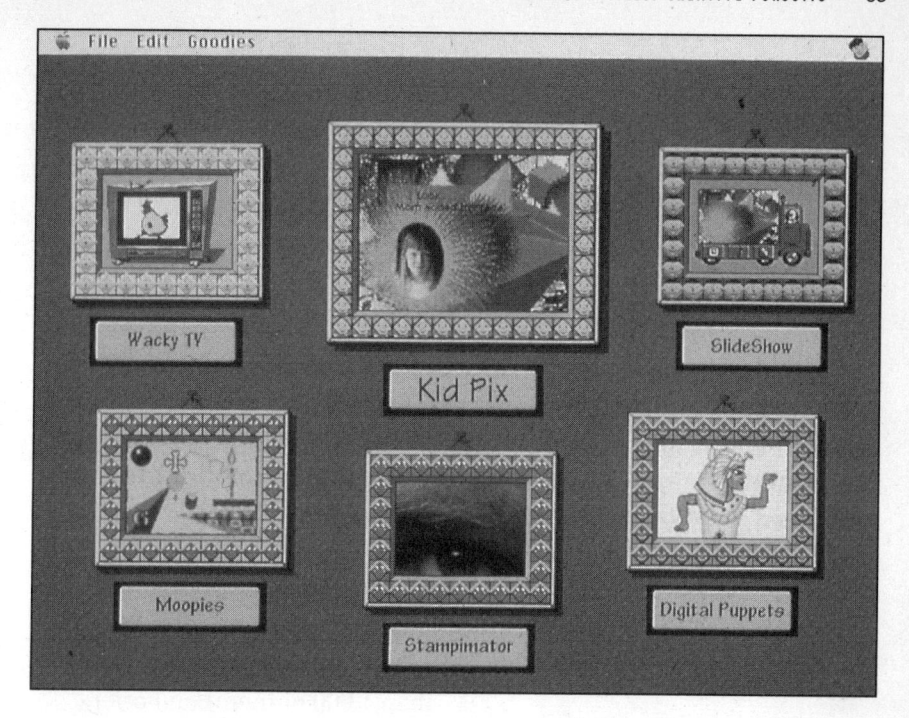

horns and ringing doorbells; it gives kids more than 80 musical snippets to enliven their animated creations. Among the options: "Four Toptations," "Reggae Bob," and "Arabian Nights." In addition, kids can record their own narration or sound effects, or import sounds from another CD.

Kid Pix Studio is not without limitations, however. The art and animation workspace is confined to a 3" x 4" box in the middle of the screen. Enlarging stamps makes them look jaggy. Kids need to use pull-down menus to get around the program. Still, we think the mix of innovative animation and top-notch painting tools makes *Kid Pix Studio* the best CD-ROM art program to choose if you can buy only one.

The bottom line: The best CD-ROM art product, with terrific opportunities for experimenting with multimedia elements as well as great graphic arts tools.

Flying Colors

★ ★ ★ ★

Flying Colors **has one of the most imaginative and captivating features we've seen in a children's art program: colors that shimmer and glitter and sparkle. Kids feel as if they're really seeing what's in their mind's eye. Plus, they'll get years of fun from the program's versatile tools.**

In addition to "cycling colors" (as the feature is known), *Flying Colors* includes an exceptional set of fanciful yet crisply drawn stamps (more than 1,000 of them) and offers add-on disks with hundreds of others. We particularly like the "building-block" stamps—architectural elements, components for space ships, anatomical parts and so on—because they give kids the power to construct something truly personal, not just a click-and-drag creation.

The program also offers vivid, kid-pleasing background canvases: the ocean floor, a castle interior, outer space scenes, a cave, the countryside, a moonscape, a desert. Many others are available on add-on disks.

Flying Colors is a great product to grow with. If you select the Small Kid mode, it's easy enough for 4- and 5-year-olds. This setting sensibly eliminates the text-based

---

JUST THE FACTS

BEST FOR AGES 5–12

★★★★ **for Learning**
Great opportunities to explore and create

★★★★ **for Looks**
Well-designed art tools make for great results

★★★★ **for Longevity**
Endless possibilities

Worth Noting
You can buy add-on disks with more backgrounds and stamps, including Fashion Faces, Funny Faces, Tropical, Food, Machines, Dinosaurs, Maps, Animals and Japanese *Art Packs.*

Macintosh CD-ROM or floppy; Windows CD-ROM or floppy
About $40
Davidson
(800) 545-7677

menu bar and offers a simplified, smaller but still satisfactory range of drawing, painting and writing tools. For older, computer-savvy kids, the Advanced setting adds controls for effects like opacity and brightness, providing opportunities for even richer artistic creations.

The bottom line: Its unique, shimmery colors make *Flying Colors* **a good addition, or successor, to the** *Kid Pix* **products.**

Kid Cuts

★ ★ ★ ★

As soon as your kids reach scissors-wielding age, consider *Kid Cuts*, a crafts program that works with the *Kid Pix* products. We've never seen a computer product that better satisfies every child's need to cut and fold and paste and color and play-act.

Kid Cuts is a set of crafts projects that starts on the computer. Kids click through a huge range of activities, including making cards, paper airplanes and crazy hats; then they select a project, color it, print and go to work.

When your children hit their mask phase, *Kid Cuts* has the makings for masks. When the paper doll addiction strikes, there are paper dolls. There are puppets for play-acting. Animals for staging a circus. Knights and damsels for playing castle. Puzzles to color and cut.

Amazingly, Molly at 5 was just as engrossed in *Kid Cuts* as Emily at 8. Even more amazing, they sometimes played together, devising their own projects like party favors and Halloween decorations.

Kid Cuts, like all the *Kid Pix* products, makes use of text-based, pull-down menus for printing, saving, moving from activity to activity and quitting.

JUST THE FACTS

BEST FOR AGES 3–8

★★★★ **for Learning**
Arts and crafts projects galore

★★★★ **for Looks**
Great *Kid Pix* graphics plus lots more

★★★★ **for Longevity**
This will take care of many rainy days

Worth Noting
You need *Kid Pix* to run *Kid Cuts*. A color printer adds to the fun but it's not required.

Macintosh floppy; DOS floppy
About $30
Broderbund
(800) 521-6263

Most of the menu choices are accompanied by pictures to show what each option means. But nonreaders may initially need some parental help.

The bottom line: Perfect for rainy-day activities. This software doesn't just provide hours of fun—we're talking years.

Art Explorer

★ ★ ★ ★

Art Explorer is *Kid Pix* grown up. It's a wonderful way for older kids to experiment with near-professional tools and create sophisticated computer artwork. Another plus: It was obviously designed to have features with special appeal for boys.

Art Explorer tailors adult drawing and painting tools to the 10-year-old taste for alien creatures, ghoulish monsters and super-heroes. There are also plenty of preadolescent sound effects (which thankfully can be turned off).

Here's a sampling of the title's innovative touches: hundreds of colors—we counted 41 shades of blue alone! Rainbow color blends. Colors that change with the addition of tints and dyes. Brush strokes that range from charcoal to pastel chalk, calligraphy pens to finger-painted smears. There's also a wild and wonderful collection of special visual effects including five kinds of bubbles, kaleidoscopes, sprinkles and glitter.

Like most creativity titles, *Art Explorer* provides a rich assortment of backgrounds and stamps.

JUST THE FACTS

BEST FOR AGES 8–12

★★★★ **for Learning**
Encourages kids to explore and experiment

★★★★ **for Looks**
A more grown-up design than similar programs; CD-ROM has more stamps and backgrounds

★★★★ **for Longevity**
Sophisticated tools last till kids get adult titles

Worth Noting
Stamp collection has a decidedly boy bent: strange space vehicles, monsters, mad scientists, dinosaurs, super heroes, cowboys. Some girls may be happier with the stamps in *Flying Colors*.

Macintosh floppy or CD-ROM; Windows floppy
About $40
Adobe/Aldus
(800) 888-6293

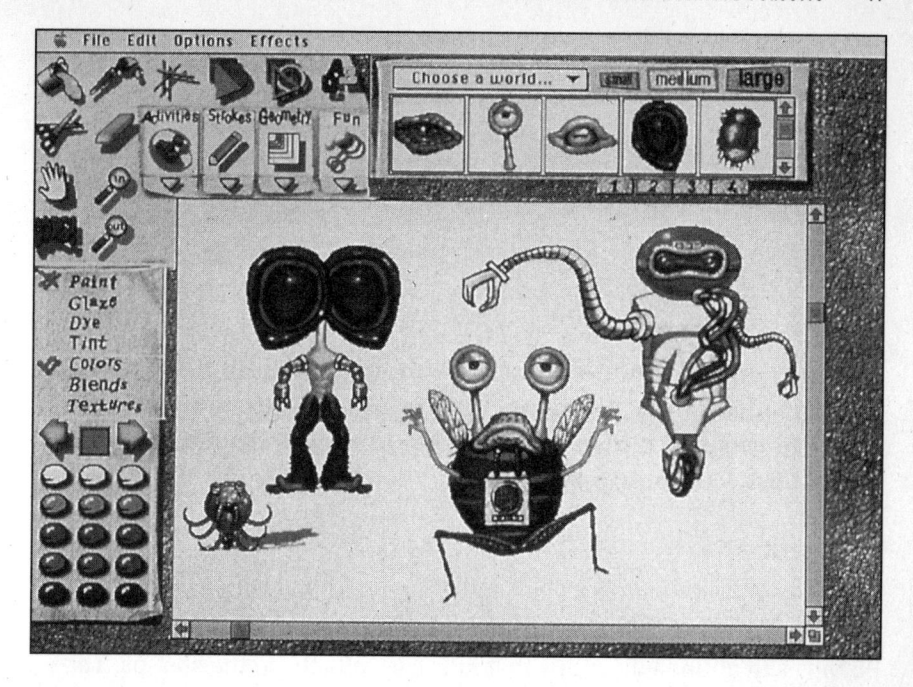

One nice touch is the many stamps that are silhouettes kids can change using the title's art tools. The body-parts stamps are especially fun for letting kids build their own versions of space creatures, funky cavemen and whatever else their imagination dictates.

The bottom line: A wealth of near-professional tools and teen-oriented stamps makes *Art Explorer* **a good choice for older children.**

Amazing Animation

★ ★

Amazing on two counts: First, its simplicity and immediate satisfactions mean even beginners can make a "movie" on their first try. And second, it turns out to be quite sophisticated and capable of fairly complex productions.

Amazing Animation is a click-and-drag toolkit for building animated pictures and cartoons. It provides background scenes, an assortment of stamps and abundant sounds that kids can "attach" to the stamps. To create a scene, kids click on a background and drag stamps around the screen. The software captures the motion and plays it back. Before long, kids can see aliens plodding through jungle underbrush or butterflies gliding across the sky.

Additional tools let kids add text, create their own sound effects, add original artwork to their scenes, alter the size or shape of stamps or produce crazy effects (like making a bicycle racer turn somersaults down the road). More ambitious techniques let kids link scenes together with transitions and wipes, add their own voice-over narration and produce interactive presentations.

The title's strength: the way it simplifies a tremendously sophisticated process and lets kids discover and manipulate all the essential elements. Its weakness:

JUST THE FACTS

BEST FOR AGES 5–12

★★★ **for Learning**
Best intro to basic animation techniques

★★★ **for Looks**
Good-looking, easy-to-use tools

★ **for Longevity**
Not enough backgrounds and stamps

Macintosh CD-ROM or floppy
About $45
Claris
(800) 325-2747

a limited number of backgrounds and stamps means that kids may exhaust the program's possibilities too quickly.

The bottom line: Young kids will enjoy the click-and-drag ease of creating animated artwork, but older kids may prefer programs with a greater selection of backgrounds and stamps.

Don't underestimate the educational value of the programs in this section. Creating animations or slide shows is a complex and instructive process for children (not unlike writing an essay, preparing a presentation, putting on a skit or staging a puppet show). They'll be challenged to outline their thoughts; select the most effective combination of images, words and sounds; sequence the action and more.

You can do a lot to help your children master those skills. First, take their efforts seriously. Be an attentive and appreciative audience. Talk about what works, and invite discussion about what doesn't. Demonstrate how a script or storyboard, simply sketched on paper, can help with envisioning and planning an animation, step by step. And teach kids to save their work frequently, so no masterpiece is inadvertently lost.

Magic Theatre

★ ★

Wonderfully simple and immediately satisfying. It literally takes five clicks (and one drag) to create an animated scene with *Magic Theatre*. But for some kids, frustration may outweigh the fun after a while.

Kids simply select a background (two clicks). Then choose a stamp (two clicks) and drag it across the scene. Click the "Play" button and a barking dog runs across a meadow at the foot of snow-capped mountains. Or an astronaut hovers above a crater on an alien planet. With a little more clicking, kids can add a host of other objects and characters to their scenes. And they can experiment with visual effects, background music, titling, freehand art and recorded narration. A nice touch, velvety theater curtains are drawn back before each "showing" of a child's movie.

Magic Theatre comes with a microphone so children can narrate their animations (about 30 seconds per scene). But watch out: Saving narrated animations eats up lots of hard disk space. And children may be surprised and upset to discover that voice-overs automatically wipe out the

---

JUST THE FACTS

BEST FOR AGES 6–12

★★ **for Learning**
Create art with animated effects

★★ **for Looks**
Good selection of stamps and backgrounds

★ **for Longevity**
Kids may get discouraged by technical limitations

Worth Noting
Any kid who can click-and-drag can use *Magic Theatre*. Very young children may need some prompting about what button to click when. But with a little help, even 3-year-olds can make an animation.

Windows CD-ROM or floppy; Macintosh CD-ROM
About $30
Knowledge Adventure
(800) 542-4240

wonderful sound effects associated with animated objects.

Other drawbacks: kids can't flip, rotate or scale the objects in their animation (which can be very frustrating since children often want their animations to look *exactly* the way they envision them). Kids can't edit their creations, either. And while kids can make movies with lots of scenes, they can't reorder the scenes.

The bottom line: Good for creative play but for complex productions kids may be happier with *Amazing Animation* **or** *Kid Pix Studio***.**

We prefer to encourage children to draw on their imagination for their artwork and stories. But for kids who live and breathe action figures and superheroes, *Spider-Man Cartoon Maker* (Windows CD-ROM, about $30) is an easy-to-master animation product. It looks and works just like *Magic Theatre* except that its supply of characters, backgrounds and sound effects is based on the Spider-Man TV cartoon series. The CD-ROM provides narrated help, using the voice of the TV Spider-Man, plus three original Spider-Man cartoons.

Kids World

★ ★

An easy-to-use movie-maker with a delightful result: your child's very own animated screen saver for the family computer.

In case you don't have one yet, a screen saver puts a picture on your display whenever your computer sits idle for a few minutes. This extends the life of your screen and protects your work from prying eyes.

In this construction set, kids select a background (Wild West, dinosaur world, haunted house, among others) and choose some stamps (each background has 24) to build a picture. Every stamp has its own sound effect and motion. Kids simply click a selection, drag it into place and push the "Go" button.

A set of paint tools lets kids modify backgrounds or design an original. With a microphone, they can also add personal sound effects. (Don't worry, you can turn off the sound.)

The bottom line: Less ambitious than titles like *Amazing Animation* or *Magic Theatre*, but remarkably simple and fun. And kids can create something really useful.

JUST THE FACTS

BEST FOR AGES 5–10

★★ **for Learning**
Easy intro to basic animation techniques

★★★ **for Looks**
Simple and satisfying stamps

★★ **for Longevity**
Beyond creating screen-savers, not much else to do

Macintosh floppy; Windows floppy
About $30
Bit Jugglers
(415) 968-3908

Fine Artist

★

Despite a wealth of good artistic tools in *Fine Artist*, kids spend too much time clicking when they could be creating.

Fine Artist, like *Creative Writer* (pages 64-65), presents kids with an on-screen world called Imaginopolis. It's dominated by an art building where kids can take a lesson in perspective drawing, design buttons or create comic strips. But to move from one activity to another, kids have to click their way out of one room, onto an elevator and into another location.

Despite all that clicking, there are several things kids can do more readily with *Fine Artist* than with other programs. It's especially useful for creating pin-back or magnet-back buttons that are great for party favors, name tags or crafts-fair activity tables. It also provides easy-to-work-with templates for comic strip panels. But its collection of stickers and sounds is limited compared to other titles.

Fine Artist's other standout feature is its "shape" tool, which lets kids bend words into hearts, arrows, zigzags and other shapes and then add colors and patterns and shadows.

The bottom line: Good for special projects like buttons, comic strips and signs.

JUST THE FACTS

BEST FOR AGES 8-12

★★ **for Learning**
Product design gets in the way of experimentation

★★ **for Looks**
Art tools are inconsistent in quality

★ **for Longevity**
Kids get frustrated with product's design

Macintosh CD-ROM or floppy; Windows CD-ROM or floppy
About $50
Microsoft
(800) 228-6270

The Crayola Art Series
Crayola Amazing Art Adventure
Crayola Art Studio

★

Two *Kid Pix* copycats without the spunk. Lots of opportunities to color but not much room for creativity. And for art programs, the graphics are ho-hum.

Both programs provide the usual tools: crayons, magic markers, water-color brushes, patterns, shapes and stamps. One of the best options is mixing your own rainbow effects. But we were surprised to find a limited choice of those wonderful Crayola colors, only 24 in *Art Studio*, 16 in *Amazing Art Adventure*. On the other hand, colors are represented by good-size crayons, and they're easier for little fingers to click than the tiny color palette in *Kid Pix*.

Beyond painting, *Amazing Art Adventure* (ages 3–6) users can choose among eight activity books with color-in-the-pictures, mazes or hidden pictures. There's also a Placemat Maker with designs for the kids to color and print or, if you don't have a color printer, to print and color. *Art Studio* (ages 6–9) provides predrawn badges, certificates or stationery and eight coloring books filled with familiar games like dot-to-dot and hidden pictures.

JUST THE FACTS

BEST FOR AGES 3–9

★ **for Learning**
Doesn't encourage creativity as well as similar programs

★ **for Looks**
Me-too art tools without personality

★ **for Longevity**
Other programs have more to offer

Macintosh floppy; Windows floppy or CD-ROM
About $40
Micrografx
(800) 676-3110

There's nothing wrong with these activities, *per se*. But why pay $40 when your kids could get the same pleasures from a dime-store coloring book?

The bottom line: Large crayon icons make picking colors easier for little kids, but activities lack the imaginative flair of other titles.

WORDPLAY & STORYTELLING

Creative Writing, Poems, Plays,
Journals, Cards, Storybooks

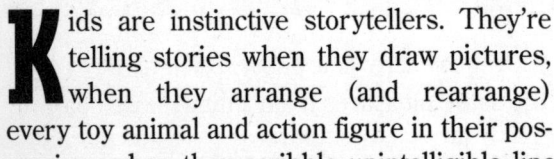

Kids are instinctive storytellers. They're telling stories when they draw pictures, when they arrange (and rearrange) every toy animal and action figure in their possession, when they scribble unintelligible lines across a page, when they play make-believe and, of course, when they actually begin to write. And the titles in this section are a new and creative way of nurturing that knack for storytelling and creative writing.

Recognizing that children tell their stories with pictures as much as text, these programs give youngsters an abundance of backgrounds, stamps and art tools for their homemade books. But unlike Arts & Animation software, these titles also provide an equally compelling showcase for words. The result: It's inviting and relatively easy for kids to start writing. And the more they write, the more they'll read—and the better they'll get at both.

When your kids finish writing, don't forget to print their work. Not only is the printed output from many of these titles quite remarkable, but remember that kids take tremendous pride in their homemade books. They'll read them (even if they can't really read yet), decorate them, mail them to grandparents, take them to school, and otherwise savor the sense of ownership and the power of words.

RATINGS	TITLES	AGES
★★★★	The Amazing Writing Machine (Pages 52-53)	7–12
★★★★	Imagination Express (Pages 54-55)	5–12
★★★★	Star Act (Pages 56-57)	8–12
★★★	Storybook Weaver Deluxe (Pages 58-59)	5–9
★★★	Bailey's Book House (Pages 60-61)	2–5
★★★	Davidson's Kid Works Deluxe (Pages 62-63)	2–5
★★	Creative Writer (Pages 64-65)	7–12

The Amazing Writing Machine

★ ★ ★ ★

The best all-around program for writing essays, poems, stories, letters and journal entries. This aptly named product has a truly amazing wealth of features to delight, encourage and instruct young writers.

What *Kid Pix* did for painting, *The Amazing Writing Machine* does for writing. It puts a refreshing new spin on five, familiar genres. It lets kids have as much fun with words—and sentences and paragraphs—as they do with wacky brushes. (Remember Mad Libs? That's the kind of zany wordplay kids encounter in *Amazing Writing Machine*.) As they play, it allows them to make discoveries about language—about parts of speech, synonyms, alliteration, sentence structure, vocabulary, dialog and more. And it motivates them to apply their new-found knowledge as they write.

Kids start by choosing a genre. Then they can simply start writing. Or, they can click the Spin option for sample compositions (some serious, some silly) that can be altered in part or in their entirety. There's ample opportunity for artistry, too. *Kid Pix* aficionados will be right at home with the stamps, layouts, borders and brushes in *Amazing Writing Machine*.

We love the playful, thought-provoking tools in *Amazing Writ-*

JUST THE FACTS

BEST FOR AGES 7–12

★★★★ **for Learning**
Encourages many types of writing

★★★★ **for Looks**
Exceptional variety of inventive tools

★★★★ **for Longevity**
Always something more to discover

Worth Noting
CD-ROM version lets kids import their own photographic images.

Macintosh CD-ROM or floppy; Windows CD-ROM
About $35–$40
Broderbund
(800) 521-6263

ing Machine. It has an excellent rebus tool for turning text into pictures. A code tool turns text into pig Latin or seven other, less-easily deciphered, codes. When kids are writing poetry, clicking the Return key automatically displays six rhyming words. But the Bright Ideas tool is best of all. By clicking Who, What, Where, When and Why buttons, kids can pick up an understanding of sentence structure while creating story starters like "Sabrina the sentimental serpent turned somersaults beneath a slimy toadstool shortly before midnight." More clicking produces quotes, jokes, random facts (a cockroach can live 10 days without a head), the names of animals, vegetables, minerals and more.

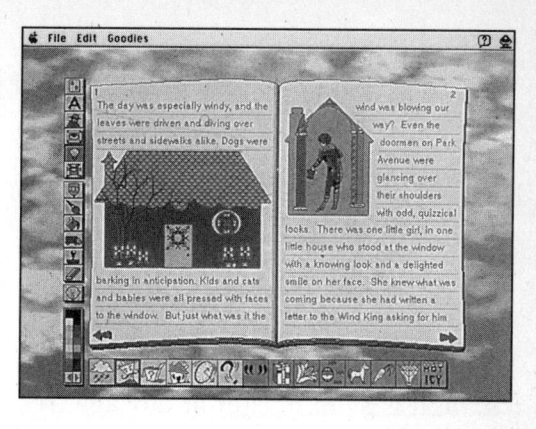

Like Broderbund's art products, *The Amazing Writing Machine* makes kids use pull-down menus to get from one part of the program to another. While the menus are simple enough, navigating would be quicker and easier if there were one or two icons always visible that would instantly take kids back to key parts of the program.

The bottom line: Its imaginative approach to wordplay and writing makes *The Amazing Writing Machine* **a wonderful program for young wordsmiths.**

The opportunities for wordplay in *Amazing Writing Machine* are best shared. Start a book of family Mad Libs and leave blanks not only for the usual words like subjects, predicates and adjectives but also for quotes, jokes or proverbs, then complete the blanks using the Bright Ideas options. Or see what happens when you post unpleasant reminders—clean up your room, take out the garbage—in pig Latin.

Imagination Express

★ ★ ★ ★

The best storymaking program we've seen. Exceptionally beautiful, and easy to master at any age. It's got the uncanny ability to scale stickers to just the right size—*while your child is moving them into the scene*. Best of all is its effect on kids. Just minutes into this product and they're bursting to tell a tale.

Take 5-year-old Sam's first encounter. Five clicks into the program, he discovered a unicorn and was immediately captivated. Next came a wishing well, followed by a peasant with a mysterious sack slung over his shoulder. By then he was "writing" (in pictures) fast and furious. To make his pages look like a proper book, he insisted his mother type (onto a beautiful parchment scroll) while he dictated. When they finished, it was way past bedtime. But he insisted on printing and "binding" his book so she could "read" it to his stuffed animals.

For older children, *Imagination Express* has an equally powerful attraction. They'll find tools to tell their story not only with pictures and words but also with animation, background music and sounds (or voice-overs) that they record themselves. Better still, *Imagination Express* lets kids add to their fund of knowledge as they construct a tale. (FYI, it's the only storytelling product that does

JUST THE FACTS

BEST FOR AGES 5–12

★★★★ **for Learning**
Glorious pictures spark great stories

★★★★ **for Looks**
Most advanced graphics around, but no freehand art

★★★★ **for Longevity**
Kids keep coming back to write more

Worth Noting
Video clips of real kids explain how to start stories; parents also get advice on the value and process of story writing.

Macintosh CD-ROM; Windows CD-ROM
About $35
Edmark
(800) 691-2985

this.) Kids can consult an intriguing Fact Book before they begin a story, or simply click an icon to learn more about any sticker they're using.

The basic *Imagination Express* CD-ROM includes the program itself plus backgrounds, stickers, sounds and animations associated with a real-life neighborhood. Other CD-ROMs in the series focus on different destinations, including a medieval castle and environs (*Imagination Express Destination: Castle*), rainforest flora and fauna (*Imagination Express Destination: Rainforest*), and more. Watch out, the costs can add up.

The bottom line: A terrific combination of unique art elements, space for writing and tips on storytelling. The result: the best-looking books we've ever seen from a computer.

Good as it is, *Imagination Express* is not for every child. Take Juliet, a 9-year-old with a passion for creating her own artwork. "Everything's already done for you in *Imagination Express*," she said. "You just move all these pieces around. The program does too much for you."

If, like Juliet, your child needs to have *total* creative control, you may want to consider a writing program with freehand art capabilities. For little kids, *Davidson's Kid Works Deluxe* is a good bet. For older children, consider *The Amazing Writing Machine* or *Creative Writer*.

Star Act

★ ★ ★ ★

A unique, inventive program for introducing kids to the fun of play-acting. In *Star Act*, kids play both cast *and* backstage crew, rehearsing and performing their roles—both on and off the computer—as well as producing sound effects, props, playbills, tickets and posters. They can even write their own original productions.

The program starts in a funky-looking theater district, complete with glittering marquees. Kids can create original plays in The New Revue or enter one of four different theaters to take a role in Frankenstein, Captain Hook's Treasure, Alice in Wonderland or Arcade of Peril (a mystery styled on the Nancy Drew series).

Inside each theater, kids can head for the Stage to begin rehearsals or the Studio to work on props, tickets and the like. At the heart of each play is a wonderfully interactive script. Before choosing a role, kids can hear the characters describe themselves. They can listen as real actors read any or all roles. They can print a script with their lines highlighted. Or they can read their part aloud while the computer plays the other roles!

For added fun, kids can incor-

JUST THE FACTS

BEST FOR AGES 8–12

★★★★ **for Learning**
Introduction to four dramatic genres—horror, adventure, fantasy, mystery—plus tips on acting and stagecraft

★★★★ **for Looks**
Beautifully illustrated settings; inspired use of sounds and real-life recordings

★★★★ **for Longevity**
Lots of roles to play and great opportunities for creativity

Worth Noting
Great for group or solo practice; good mix of on- and off-computer activities.

Macintosh CD-ROM; Windows CD-ROM
About $40
Maxis
(800) 526-2947

porate sound effects and background music simply by dragging icons right into the script. The program features more than 200 sounds—from the crackle of a walky-talky to a beating heart, a howling dog to a thunder clap. Kids can also record up to 15 original sound effects, each five seconds long. (You'll need 1.6 MB of hard disk space to store all 15.) Once the sounds have been added, the computer will play them at the right moment as kids rehearse the play.

Upstairs in each theater is a suitably messy, paint-spattered Studio where kids can print scripts, tickets, posters, props, masks and playbills, all tailored to their particular play. Clicking the Drama Club magazine produces interactive advice for putting on plays.

Star Act also encourages kids to take on the role of playwright. Using Story-starter templates included in the software, they can make changes or additions to the existing scripts. Or they can try an original play of their own.

The bottom line: Fun and instructive software for kids who love to play-act. Of course, kids don't need a computer to put on a show. But *Star Act's* clever enhancements—actor's voices, realistic sound effects, personalized scripts, professional-looking playbills—add an appealing new twist to traditional fun.

Storybook Weaver Deluxe

★ ★ ★

An updated and expanded old favorite. Despite its graphic facelift, *Storybook Weaver Deluxe* doesn't have the visual flair of some newer titles. But its large stock of stamps and backgrounds plus "storypacks" of thematic clip art will inspire many hours of storytelling.

Storybook Weaver Deluxe is a kind of automatic story illustrator with an uncanny ability to encourage writing. The program's forte is a well-stocked supply of graphics: foregrounds and backgrounds (which can be displayed with different degrees of brightness to simulate dawn, daylight, dusk, nighttime), plants, animals, people and things, plus sound effects and background music. Kids get so jazzed about the pictures they assemble that they just start writing and keep on writing.

Though not as good-looking as *Imagination Express*, *Storybook Weaver Deluxe* has a greater variety of backgrounds and stamps on a single CD-ROM. And its floppy-based story packs, which work with *Storybook Weaver Deluxe* 1.1 or later, each add more than 100 additional graphics, borders and backgrounds, sounds and musical

JUST THE FACTS

BEST FOR AGES 5–9

★★★ **for Learning**
Large variety of art elements encourages storytelling

★★ **for Looks**
Lacks visual flair of newer titles; no freehand art

★★★ **for Longevity**
Kids find lots of stories to tell

Worth Noting
Deluxe version, available only as CD-ROM, has best graphics.

Macintosh CD-ROM or floppy; Windows CD-ROM or floppy
About $40
MECC
(800) 685-6322

> The astronauts floated in space. They worked all day to repair the satellite. Then, they saw two spaceships coming. "Maybe they can help us!" one of the astronauts yelled.

selections to a child's stock of art elements. *The Dinkytown Daycare Kids* story pack features a group of culturally diverse kids; the *Hollywood Hounds* pack presents their pets.

The bottom line: An incredible selection of graphics makes *Storybook Weaver Deluxe* **more open-ended than many programs in this section. Your child's imagination will never be constrained by limited choices.**

Bailey's Book House

★ ★ ★

A wonderful introduction to the world of letters and sounds, words and sentences.

Bailey's Book House helps kids get ready to read by encouraging their natural inclination to play with language. With *Bailey's* even toddlers can have the fun of creating silly stories and rhymes and cards (although they can't actually read or write yet).

While all five activities in *Bailey's* are good, our favorites give children something to take away from the computer. In Make-A-Story, kids can compose and print a simple story by clicking on a series of pictures. For example, Millie the cow (or Sammy the snake, among other choices) can ride a bathtub (or a flying saucer) to the city (or a desert island) and have a birthday party (or play the piano).

As each sentence is completed, it's read aloud, word by word. And when children make all their selections, Bailey reads the whole thing and kids see the tale come to life. The story selections are limited (one of four choices on each of four pages), but kids don't seem to mind.

JUST THE FACTS

BEST FOR AGES 2–5

★★★ **for Learning**
Playful introduction to letters, words, and stories; skills include letter recognition, rhyming

★★★★ **for Looks**
Imaginative, age-appropriate graphics

★★★ **for Longevity**
Activities have unequal staying power

Worth Noting
Other preschool titles from **Edmark** include *Millie's Math House*, *Sammy's Science House*, *Trudy's Time and Place House* and *Thinkin' Things Collection 1*.

Macintosh CD-ROM or floppy; Win/DOS CD-ROM or floppy
About $35
Edmark
(800) 691-2985

In Make-A-Card, little kids can create invitations, valentines and an assortment of other greeting cards. The mechanics are simple, and the sentiments are right on target for little kids.

The bottom line: *Bailey's* **is a wonderful way for kids to pick up prereading skills in the context of play.**

Davidson's Kid Works Deluxe

★ ★ ★

A combination writing and painting program that talks back, *Davidson's Kid Works Deluxe* is a creative introduction to the pleasures—and power—of the written word.

Little kids feel right at home with the program's large letters and ruled paper (rather than the small print and blank screen of a word processing program). We usually type as our kids dictate—such as a note to grandparents, the story of the day, a letter to Santa. And then the kids clamor to hear the computer read back their words, an amusing—and memorable—way to experience the connection between writing and reading.

The program's rebus feature does even more to underscore that relationship. (A rebus is a picture that represents a word.) With the click of a button, words automatically change into pictures. The result: Even prereaders can "read" their stories.

Davidson's Kid Works Deluxe offers lots of ways for kids to embellish their writing: painting and art tools, plenty of stamps, animated stickers, sound effects and more. Kids can record their own voices reading their stories or narrating their pictures. Or they can send their creations via

JUST THE FACTS

BEST FOR AGES 2–7

★★★★ **for Learning**
Large variety of art elements encourages storytelling; skills include letter and word recognition, spelling, and composition

★★★ **for Looks**
Improved looks; charming icons

★★★ **for Longevity**
Kids find lots of stories to tell and inventive ways to share them

Worth Noting
Good value because of its freehand art and painting section; *Deluxe* version only on CD-ROM, *Kid Works 2* on floppy.

Windows CD-ROM
About $50
Davidson
(800) 545-7677

e-mail to Dad's office, distant cousins or to Santa's Internet address through a link to popular on-line services.

For kids who need a little help getting started, *Davidson's Kid Works Deluxe* provides 125 story starters and more than 100 pictures to decorate with paint or stamps.

If you don't have a CD-ROM drive, look for *Kid Works 2* for Macintosh or Windows systems. This floppy based version of the program is a bit klunky to use but offers many of the same great features as the newer *Davidson's Kid Works Deluxe*.

The bottom line: A wonderful program for inspiring little kids to make the leap to writing and reading, packed with inventive features that will see your child through the early school years.

Because of the visual connection it forges between words and meaning, *Davidson's Kid Works Deluxe* is especially good for kindergartners. To find picture-words for their stories, kids can browse a "dictionary" of pictures and readily gain an understanding of initial letter sounds. By grouping pictures into object, action and descriptive categories, *Davidson's Kid Works Deluxe* also helps children understand the elements of storytelling.

Creative Writer

★ ★

Fun to explore, but *Creative Writer*'s over-abundant bells and whistles ultimately get in the way of simple utility.

This program is big on colorful icons, sound effects and comic-style graphics. There's a bee (which represents the spell-checker), a piggy-bank (the "save" command), scissors-and-glue (for cutting and pasting), a horn (for sound effects selection) and a guy named McZee who helps kids along. And anytime, anywhere kids click, there's a sound effect: a barking dog, a cracking egg, a toilet flushing, the noise of a whoopee cushion.

Creative Writer gives kids lots of ways to embellish their words—backgrounds and borders, fonts and formats, colors and type styles and stamps. Our favorite is the "shape" tool, which contours words into zany shapes (heart, arrow, zigzag and more) and adds colors and patterns and shadows.

Trouble is, the title's flamboyant looks and gee-whiz effects make it difficult to get down to work. Finding a blank piece of paper, for example, entails clicking through a city, into a building and up to the Writing Studio (or into the Project Studio for creating cards, newsletters or banners, or the Idea Workshop for story-starting ideas). Actual writing

JUST THE FACTS

BEST FOR AGES 7–12

★ **for Learning**
Doesn't encourage writing as well as other programs

★★ **for Looks**
More inspiration for art than for words

★ **for Longevity**
Gee-whiz features interfere with writing

Macintosh CD-ROM or floppy; Windows CD-ROM or floppy
About $50
Microsoft
(800) 228-6270

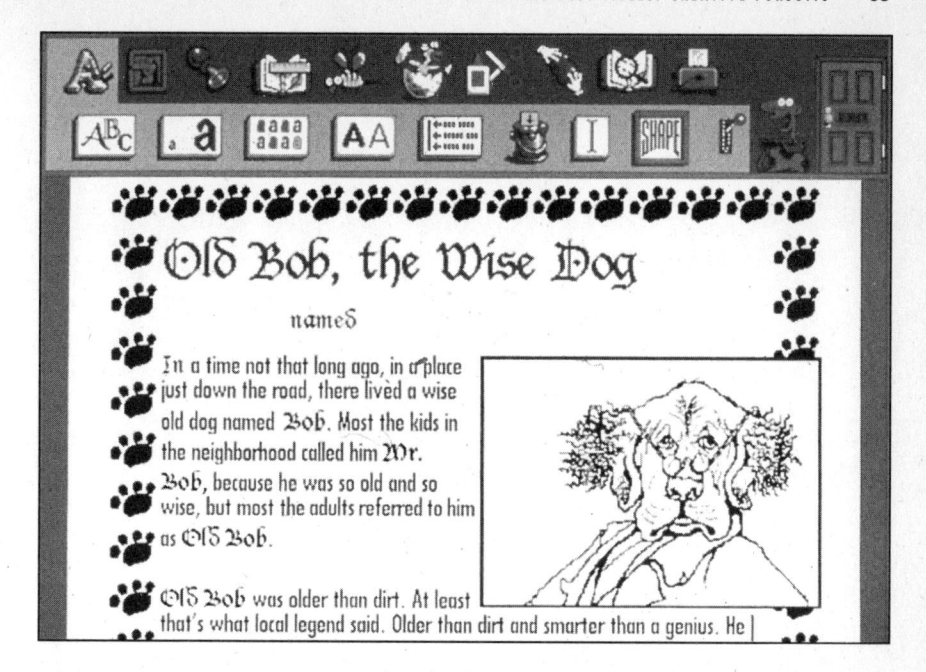

often takes a back seat to decorative effects, all of which require a tedious, multi-click process. And unless kids turn off the "help" feature, they'll be confronted at every click with pop-up balloons full of instructions.

Creative Writer is OK for quickie projects—name tags and to-do lists, greeting cards and household chore charts, flyers and thank-you notes—where the emphasis is on graphics, not on writing. But for school work or anything longer, the product's gimmickry makes it impractical to use.

The bottom line: Plenty of features for creating stories, newsletters, banners and cards, but bells and whistles tend to sidetrack kids rather than encourage them to write.

·THREE·
THE BEST TITLES: READING

In our view, learning to read is 99-percent inspiration and 1-percent perspiration (to turn Edison's famous saying on its head).

That's an exaggeration, of course. But we do believe the inspiration to read should come first (in the form of captivating stories filled with appealing characters, pretty pictures, fine writing), with perspiration second (in the form of phonics practice). And that's how we've organized this chapter on reading software.

There's still nothing better than lots of real books—plus family encouragement and example—to inspire a love of reading. (Maybe we're old-fashioned, but we don't think computers alone will transform your child into a successful reader.) Happily, in "Stories on Screen" you'll find real books served up in a refreshing way.

Once your children seem interested in decoding words for themselves, the software in the "Reading Basics" chapter can help. Historically, skill-and-drill titles have dominated children's software. And they still have a role to play in spicing up the practice-makes-perfect exercises used to teach phonics. But don't rush your children into these titles. Kids acquire literacy skills at their own pace. And don't expect miracles from them—practicing phonics is no shortcut to literacy if your children have no interest in reading.

STORIES ON SCREEN

Interactive books & poetry

Remember your child's pleasure when you read a "lift-the-flap" book for the first time? That kind of delight is what "Stories on Screen" is all about.

But instead of a few flaps to flip, there are dozens of hidden surprises. Children can make characters talk (usually in English, but sometimes Spanish and Japanese, too). They can watch their (mis)adventures unfold, explore the scenery, or simply listen to a familiar tale. With some titles, kids get an even bigger piece of the action. They can play narrator, recording themselves reading the text, or even director, telling the characters where to go and what to do.

For 2–8-year-olds, these interactive storybooks—available *only* on CD-ROM, by the way—can be a powerful way to connect with reading. And kids who love Stories on Screen don't love real books any less.

But a word of caution: Not all electronic books are worthy alternatives to their printed counterparts. Some don't add anything special enough to justify their hefty price. Others are so TV-like that children become passive viewers, not involved readers. So, as with all software, try each Stories on Screen title before you buy it.

RATINGS	TITLES	AGES
★★★★	Just Grandma and Me (Page 71)	2–5
★★★★	Dr. Seuss' ABCs (Page 71)	3–7
★★★★	Arthur's Teacher Trouble (Page 71)	3–8
★★★★	Arthur's Birthday (Page 72)	3–8
★★★★	The New Kid on the Block (Page 72)	3–8
★★★★	The Tortoise and the Hare (Page 72)	3–8
★★★★	Little Monster At School (Page 72)	2–5
★★★★	Harry and the Haunted House (Page 73)	4–6
★★★★	The Berenstain Bears Get in a Fight (Page 73)	3–6
★★	P.B. Bear's Birthday Party (Pages 74-75)	2–4
★★	The Discis Kids Can Read Series (Pages 76-77)	2–8

The Living Book Series

Just Grandma and Me Dr. Seuss' ABCs
Arthur's Teacher Trouble Arthur's Birthday
The New Kid on the Block The Tortoise and the Hare
Little Monster at School The Berenstain Bears Get in a Fight
Harry and the Haunted House

★ ★ ★ ★

The *Living Books* created a whole new genre when they first debuted in 1992. They're an imaginative new breed, alive with sound effects, spoken text, unique voices for each character, added dialog, better-than-TV animation and musical surprises—all sparked by kids at the keyboard.

In each *Living Book*, the original artwork and story are faithfully reproduced, and then magically extended. In every illustration, something wonderful happens wherever kids click. The animations that fill *Living Books* are unmatched for their imagination, wit and fun.

Better still, *Living Books* don't replace the joy of reading real books—they strengthen it. Kids who like *Living Books* characters on-screen invariably want more of them on the printed page. And the

---

JUST THE FACTS

BEST FOR AGES 3–8

★★★★ **for Learning**
Fosters an imaginative new relationship with books

★★★★ **for Looks**
True to the original artwork and spirit of the books

★★★ **for Longevity**
Kids return time and again

Worth Noting
Text can be read in English or Spanish, *Grandma* in Japanese, too; good for students of English as a second language.

Macintosh CD-ROM; Windows CD-ROM
About $40
Broderbund
(800) 521-6263

read-aloud text helps pre-readers get ready for the next step without pushing them too fast.

We suggest choosing among these programs the way you choose books: let the appeal of the story and the artwork be your guide.

Just Grandma and Me (ages 2–5) is a perfect blend of kid-pleasing ingredients, old and new. There's a well-loved Mercer Mayer story, centered on twin childhood delights: a day with grandma *and* a trip to the beach. The words have a satisfying cadence for young children: "We went to the beach, just Grandma and me." The pictures are familiar and colorful, and the hot spot animations continue to delight kids long after they've discovered them all.

A big A (little a) for *Dr. Seuss' ABCs* (ages 3–6)! Preserving all the alliterative alphabet fun of the original book—Aunt Annie's *a*lligator, *D*avid *D*onald *D*oo, *l*ittle *L*ola *L*opp and *w*et *W*aldo *W*oo—this interactive version expands each page with layers of new words, animations and silly humor. On the "C" page, for example, the *c*amel still *c*avorts upside-down across the *c*eiling. But with a click he'll also dance a *c*ool *c*onga. An unremarkable door opens to reveal a costume closet filled with "C" characters–a *c*owboy, a *c*lown, a *c*ook, even the *C*at in the Hat. Dr. Seuss fans, young and old, will enjoy this lively language lesson where every mouse click and animation reinforces a child's connections among sounds, symbols and words.

In *Arthur's Teacher Trouble* (ages 3–8), Arthur (an aardvark) and his friends Buster (a rabbit) and Francine (a monkey) must adjust to third grade with the "Rat," the strictest teacher in the school. Arthur also has to cope with the pressures of competition when he is chosen to compete in the all-school spellathon.

Katie and Sarah first encountered Arthur (on the computer, not in print) when they were 3 and 2, and they couldn't get enough of him. We borrowed Arthur books from the library. We gave them as birthday gifts. We even went to meet Arthur's creator, author/illustrator Marc Brown, when he visited a local bookstore. What's the attraction? Kids love the Arthur adventures because of the real-kid personalities (the know-it-all Prunella, the bratty D.W., the daunting Mr. Ratburn) masquerading beneath Brown's furry characters. And, of course, because Arthur's problems turn out alright in the end.

Arthur's Birthday (ages 3–8) is about the dreaded party predicament: two friends are having their birthday parties on the same day, and they can't change their plans. So the boys decide to go to Arthur's party, while the girls opt for Muffy's. But no one's happy—until Arthur hatches a plan. Like all Marc Brown's *Arthur* stories, this one deftly captures the kid perspective on pint-size dilemmas that loom large—conflicting parties, spelling tests, bratty sisters, new babies, and the like—and provides a satisfying solution.

The New Kid on the Block (ages 3–8) is our favorite program for beginning readers, as superior to other reading software as *Cat in the Hat* was to *Dick and Jane*. It's got the engrossing rhythm, the fiendish rhymes and the puckish humor of Jack Prelutsky's poems. (Can any kid resist absurdities like "My brother's head should be replaced"?) It's got the wry drawings of James Stevenson. And it's got playful animations and zany sound effects that add zing to the poems and drawings.

Unlike other *Living Books*, where animations lurk in the illustrations, *New Kid* puts most of its 100+ hot spots in the text. So, as if to underscore the power and magic of words, clicking words and phrases triggers animations. The animated poems are so irresistible that children instinctively begin to memorize them. And "reading" by heart is just a heartbeat away from the real thing.

The Tortoise and the Hare (ages 3–8) is a contemporary, tongue-in-cheek interpretation of an age-old fable. This hare is a glib, fast-track character ("Gotta go"), aquiver with impatience and conceit. The tortoise is a genial, laid-back type ("I'm listening to the birds sing"), in touch with his inner self and at one with nature. The program plays the inevitable clash of temperaments for all its worth, cartoon-style.

Little Monster At School (ages 2–5) is an engrossing program for giving little kids a taste of school before they actually get there. The basic story is short and simple: kids spend a day with Little Monster as he wakes up, eats breakfast with his family, and goes to school. He and his (strange but sweet) classmates practice letters, go to science, art and music classes, eat lunch and play outside at recess.

The Berenstain Bears have shown up in lots of software and video games. But no product has ever done justice to the sweet characters, moralistic lessons, and appealing artwork until *Living Books* tackled them.

The Berenstain Bears Get in a Fight (ages 3–6) may be about a Bear family—Brother, Sister, Mama and Papa—but kids instantly recognize the adventures and conflicts as a slice from their own lives. In this tale, kids see a perfectly decent day turn rotten when the cubs get quarrelsome. And the story's message about resolving problems comes through loud and clear.

Harry and the Haunted House (ages 4–6) is an engaging program for kids who are at that age when they love to be scared just to see how much spookiness they can take. It starts when Harry pops a fly ball into a creepy old house; he and his friends Earl, Amy, Stinky and his dog Spot screw up their courage and go off in pursuit. With each step over creaking floor boards and past rustling curtains, up rickety stairs and down dark corridors—all packed with hidden animations—the going gets scarier (too scary, in fact, for very young children). But, by the end, they discover that sometimes what you imagine is scarier than what's really there.

The bottom line: *Living Books* **are the best programs for giving prereaders a taste for books and inspiring older kids to read more.**

As kids become more accomplished readers, the *Living Books* lose some of their attraction. But try reintroducing programs that your kids have outgrown when they begin to learn a second language. All *Living Books* can be played in Spanish, and *Just Grandma and Me* can be played in Japanese, too. These programs are also helpful for children learning English as a second language.

P.B. Bear's Birthday Party

★ ★

A beautiful read-along storybook, especially charming for the littlest kids. Different from every other program in this section because of the lively rebus pictures in the text.

The story about P.B. Bear—P for pajamas and B for bed—is read aloud until there's a rebus (a picture that stands for a word). Then the picture jiggles and wiggles, as if to say, "Click me next." When kids click, there are some animated antics and sound effects. Parcels rustle and come unwrapped. Doors creak open. And then the word itself appears and is read aloud.

Besides making kids giggle, this approach has a genuine educational plus: it helps kids learn to "track" the text. You do this when you move your finger along a line of words as you read. P.B. Bear does it by combining highlighted words and jiggling rebuses, making it easy for prereaders not only to follow along but also to anticipate what's coming next.

Kids won't find as many hot spots in *P.B. Bear* as in other Stories on Screen. However, they can click their way to simple but engaging games (something most other Stories on Screen don't offer) on each of the story's 18 pages. These activities—Big Card, Small Card; Match the Paja-

JUST THE FACTS

BEST FOR AGES 2-4

★★★ **for Learning**
A novel, playful approach to reading readiness

★★★★ **for Looks**
Photorealistic pictures and clear text; distinctive DK Multimedia Design

★ **for Longevity**
Kids will outgrow *P.B. Bear* fast

Macintosh CD-ROM; Windows CD-ROM
About $30
DK Multimedia
(800) 225-3362

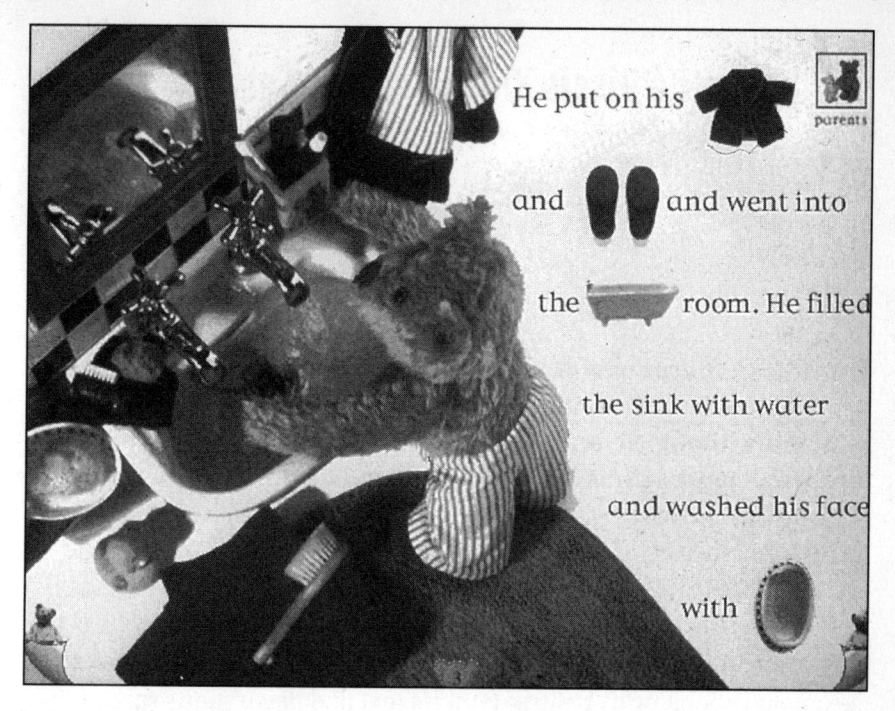

mas; What's in the Box?—invite kids to make discoveries about size, shapes, patterns and the like.

The bottom line: Though it's delightful for 2- and 3-year-olds, don't expect *P.B. Bear* **to be a long-playing hit.**

The Discis Kids Can Read Series

★ ★

The *Kids Can Read* series presents more than a dozen children's stories, classic and contemporary, as electronic books. Unhurried and without the animated detours of other interactive books, the Discis approach is designed to help beginning readers concentrate on words.

With a Discis program, what you see is virtually everything you get. On the computer screen, *The Tale of Peter Rabbit*, for example, looks like an open book, with Beatrix Potter's text and illustrations spread over two pages. As the story is read out loud, sections of the text are highlighted, helping children "track" the words as they hear them.

Clicking on an illustration reveals a corresponding word, like "Mr. MacGregor" or "garden." A child can also click to hear a word's pronunciation (in English or Spanish) or its definition. What you won't find in any Discis program are the multimedia embellishments (like a chorus line of animated starfish tap dancing their way across the page) that enliven other electronic books.

If this approach seems likely to help your child, here are some other *Kids Can Read* titles to con-

---

JUST THE FACTS

BEST FOR AGES 2–6

★★ for Learning
Books on-screen, with no frills; skills include tracking, sight words, vocabulary

★★★ for Looks
True to the original artwork

★ for Longevity
Don't expect frequent use without parental encouragement

Worth Noting
Discis offers family packs that feature 4-5 CD-ROMs at a discount.

Macintosh CD-ROM; Windows CD-ROM
About $30
Discis
(800) 567-4321

sider: *Somebody Catch My Homework, Northern Lights: The Soccer Trails, A Promise is a Promise, The Tale of Benjamin Bunny, Cinderella, The Paper Bag Princess, Thomas' Snowsuit, Mud Puddle, Scary Poems for Rotten Kids, Heather Hits Her First Home Run, Moving Gives Me a Stomach Ache, A Long Hard Day on the Ranch, Aesop's Fables, The Night Before Christmas, Anansi: Three Tales, Johnny Appleseed, Pecos Bill* and *Paul Bunyan.*

"My kids loved the Discis books," one mother reported. "Compared to *Living Books*, I find the sound effects more imaginative and the focus on the printed word better for teaching kids how to read."

The bottom line: The simplicity of the Discis programs makes it easy for beginning readers to concentrate on words. These titles can also be especially helpful for kids learning English as a second language, for kids learning Spanish, or for kids with reading difficulties.

Which storybook software is best for your child? The answer depends on what you're looking for. It could be a program that turns a book into an on-screen adventure, a program expressly designed to help children master reading, or some combination.

The *Living Books* and *Kids Can Read* series represent two ends of the storybook spectrum. Both let young children experience the joy of "reading" on their own: the software reads the story aloud, highlights words as they're read, and pronounces individual words when kids click them. Beyond that, the two series diverge.

Living Books are designed as places for kids to play, not just to hear or read words. They let children as young as two participate in a story by discovering what's hidden in the illustrations—sound effects, music, animations, added dialog. They encourage beginning readers, but don't teach them *per se*.

Kids Can Read titles are designed to be instructive. Kids click to hear words spoken more slowly, to hear them broken into syllables, to learn their meaning or their part of speech. This simple presentation makes it easier for some children to focus and concentrate on reading.

Consider both kinds of programs at different stages of your child's development—*Kids Can Read* titles for helping a fledging reader build skills and confidence, *Living Books* for inspiring enthusiasm for books and providing hours of fun.

READING BASICS

Exercises in Phonics, Spelling and Reading Comprehension

The titles in this chapter focus on the mechanics of reading—phonics, spelling, comprehension and vocabulary. Once your children are ready and eager to read, these products can help make them stronger readers.

But before you buy, we suggest that you find out how (and when) your child's school teaches word skills. Talk with the teacher about your child's learning style and capabilities. Then look at the titles in this chapter with an eye to *complementing* what goes on in the classroom (by reinforcing word skills as your children learn them in school), or *supplementing* the classroom agenda with software that takes a different approach.

For kids who get a steady diet of worksheets in school, interactive books or software that inspire them to write without worrying about spelling can be a welcome relief. On the other hand, for kids who get phonics in dribs and drabs, one of the drills in this chapter may prove helpful.

RATINGS	TITLES	AGES
★★★	Alien Tales (Pages 80-81)	8–12
★★★	Davidson's Kid Phonics (Pages 82-83)	4–6
★★	Reader Rabbit 1 (Pages 84-85)	4–6
★★	Reader Rabbit 2 (Pages 84-85)	6–8
★★	Reader Rabbit's Interactive Reading Journey (Pages 86-87)	4–6
★	Reader Rabbit 3 (Pages 84-85)	6–8
★	Reader Rabbit's Ready for Letters (Pages 84-85)	3–4
★	Reading Blaster (Page 88)	7–10
★	Alphabet Blocks (Page 89)	3–4
★	Beginning Reading (Page 90)	5–7
★	Super Solvers Spellbound! (Page 91)	7–12
★	Super Solvers Midnight Rescue! (Page 91)	7–10
★	WiggleWorks Volume 1 (Page 92)	3–5
★	Word Munchers (Page 117)	6–12
★	The Sound It Out Land Series (Page 93)	4–6

Which drills will best help your children depends on their learning style. *Muncher* and *Blaster* titles may be the way to go for kids who enjoy fast video game-like action. *Beginning Reading*, in contrast, has an appealing simplicity, an unhurried pace, excellent audio and big, clear lettering. The *Reader Rabbit* series falls somewhere in between: there are games to play but they're all self-paced. There's less visual clutter than the *Muncher* and *Blaster* titles, but more than *Beginning Reading*.

You should also take your own tastes into account. You'll be able to take more of an interest in your child's computing activities if you choose titles you can both live with.

Alien Tales

★ ★ ★

A novel approach for honing reading-comprehension skills and inspiring kids' interest in children's literature.

Thoroughly different from every other product in this section, *Alien Tales* couples substantial passages from real books with a good-looking, game-show format. Kids match wits with alien contestants who claim authorship of books by Roald Dahl, E.B. White, L. Frank Baum, Judy Blume, and other award-winning writers. Their mission: To prove that each book was written on Earth by correctly answering questions about the characters, plot, setting, author and other details. A slick game-show host poses the questions and interjects inanities just the way his real-life counterparts do on TV. And each round features a different kind of challenge: true-or-false questions, crossword puzzles, captions to complete, mismatched facts to sort out.

Kids start by selecting an opponent who claims to have written 1 of 30 books. They can read selections from the book first. Or they can plunge right into the game and refer back to the passages whenever they're stumped for an answer.

Either way, kids can opt to read the text themselves or have it read aloud. We've found the read-

JUST THE FACTS

BEST FOR AGES 8–12

★★★ **for Learning**
Appealing game promotes reading comprehension

★★★ **for Looks**
Quirky characters help kids stay involved

★★★ **for Longevity**
Lots of book excerpts for kids to explore over time

Macintosh CD-ROM; Windows CD-ROM
About $45
Broderbund
(800) 521-6263

aloud option is a good way to make the acquaintance of a story that's new. But when they're in the throes of a game, kids quickly discover that they can find answers more quickly if they read the text themselves. In their eagerness to find answers, kids can also teach themselves (for better or for worse) to skim text.

For a text-heavy product, *Alien Tales* is surprisingly easy on the eyes. The game-show elements add color, sound and animated excitement. But happily, they don't distract kids when they're trying to read.

The bottom line: Far more engaging than the out-of-context paragraphs kids usually encounter in reading-comprehension exercises.

By their very nature, game shows are group activities. They're most fun when people collaborate and call out answers. And that's true for *Alien Tales*, too. We've also found that kids may need some adult encouragement to take on an opponent who represents a book they've never read before.

Davidson's Kid Phonics

★ ★ ★

A clever and effective program that uses the computer's audio capabilities to help beginning readers fine-tune their awareness of letter sounds. Filled with sounds, songs and rhymes, *Davidson's Kid Phonics* provides a wealth of appealing opportunities to discover how sounds and letters knit themselves into words and sentences.

In the Sound Buster game, kids hear sound clues and click on different critters called Busters to find a matching sound. Challenges include identifying sounds, songs, rhyming words, words that will end a nursery rhyme and more. (Try a couple yourself; they're not as easy as you may think!)

Every right answer reveals a bit of a hidden scene. When the whole scene appears, kids can choose a picture and build the word it represents, again by clicking different Busters to hear various phonetic possibilities and dragging the right pieces together. Once the word is correctly spelled, kids can easily build sentences around it (some silly, some sensible) by clicking on different verbs, objects and adjectives. Finally, they can color the picture and print the page for their personal word dictionary.

In the Word Builder, kids pick

JUST THE FACTS

BEST FOR AGES 4–6

★★★ **for Learning**
Hands-on exploration of prereading concepts including letter, sound and word recognition; spelling; rhyming; sentence structure

★★★ **for Looks**
Sound and visuals enhance learning experience

★★★ **for Longevity**
Lots to do so kids keep coming back

Macintosh CD-ROM; Windows CD-ROM
About $40
Davidson
(800) 545-7677

one of 200 pictures and again build the word it represents by finding and assembling the right sounds. Its "Show Me" button is a terrific, animated tutor that steps kids through the process of putting letters where they belong and then sounding them out, individually and in combination.

Davidson's Kid Phonics also offers excellent tips for reading activities your kids can do without the computer.

The bottom line: Excellent use of multimedia to enliven the mechanics of reading. A good follow-up to *Bailey's Book House***, and a nice balance to the "Stories on Screen" titles.**

The Reader Rabbit Series

Reader Rabbit 1
Reader Rabbit 2

★ ★

Reader Rabbit 3
Reader Rabbit's Ready for Letters

★

JUST THE FACTS

BEST FOR AGES 3–8

★★ **for Learning**
Short games let kids practice basic phonics/reading skills that span kindergarten through third grade

★ **for Looks**
Improved in CD-ROM but still ordinary

★ **for Longevity**
Highly focused on basic skills. Kids play until they master the games; no open-ended activities.

Macintosh CD-ROM or floppy; Windows CD-ROM or floppy; DOS floppy
About $35–$50
The Learning Company
(800) 852-2255

An early mainstay in the world of educational software, *Reader Rabbit* has been teaching phonics and reading skills for more than a decade. The key to its staying power: a succession of skill-building activities that seem like play to kids and practice to their parents. In truth, *Reader Rabbit*'s games are little more than animated worksheets. But there's no doubt that many youngsters find the repetition (and the little animated rewards) satisfying.

If you want drill software for your child, you can get *Reader Rabbit 1, 2* and *3* on floppy disks or CD-ROMs. Either way, the games are basically the same. But the CD-ROM versions offer substantially improved graphics, a kid-friendlier interface, narrated help and the addition of lifelike voices that read the words out loud.

In *Reader Rabbit 1* (ages 4–6), the energetic bunny leads kids through four, no-pressure games that practice memory skills, initial letter sounds, ending sounds and sight words. Each game offers multiple levels, and the software automatically advances your child to the next level when he or she is ready.

Reader Rabbit 2 (ages 6–8) offers another four games, each with four levels. Beginning readers practice first- and second-grade phonics skills. These include letter blends; word building; short and long vowels; alphabetizing; and matching opposites, homonyms and rhyming words.

Somewhat different from its predecessors, *Reader Rabbit 3* (ages 6–8) has a bit of a plot. Reader Rabbit joins a newspaper and helps kids learn to identify and write sentence parts (who, what, where, when and how). As kids play each of four games, they create a story for the latest issue of the Daily Skywriter. Unfortunately, the stories are trite, the game play repetitive, and the software slow (even on CD-ROM).

The least commendable of this series, *Reader Rabbit's Ready for Letters* (ages 3–4) is short on spunk and humor and disappoints with its graphics, sound and animations. Even the educational content of this floppy-only product misfires. In an activity that asks kids to correctly identify one of two letters, the graphic appearing as a "reward" for correct answers doesn't begin with either of the letters in the exercise.

The bottom line: *Reader Rabbit* **encourages kids to practice basic reading skills but doesn't integrate skills with the process of reading.**

Reader Rabbit's Interactive Reading Journey

★ ★

This ambitious program is an entire "learn-to-read" curriculum on a CD-ROM. It combines dozens of colorful, tried-and-true phonics games and 40 short books that progressively add new sight words as kids master their lessons and advance through "Letterland". Only one thing is missing: the appeal of a good story to draw kids into the pleasures of reading.

Each of the program's "Letterlands" focuses on a different letter and a set of simple words that kids hear, sound out and read in a series of activities. In H-Land, for example, kids hunt for hot spots in a picture filled with H-words like *house*, *horse* and *heart*. They read two simple storybooks that go something like this: "See. I see. I see. I see Sam. Look, Sam, look! I see. I see me. I see Sam. I see Sam. The End." And they play games that build sound-letter recognition, word recognition and reading comprehension skills.

Our kid-testers preferred the on-screen games to the storybooks although the tiny paperbacks packaged with the software are just right for stuffing into a pocket and reading in the car.

As with other *Reader Rabbit* programs, we've found that many kids who happily play *Reading Journey* games over and over on the computer don't necessarily

JUST THE FACTS

BEST FOR AGES 4–6

★★ **for Learning**
A year-long, learn-to-read curriculum; skills include letter recognition, sight words, phonics

★ **for Looks**
Cute characters but repetitive activities

★★ **for Longevity**
Lots of phonics games keep many—but not all—kids engaged

Macintosh CD-ROM; Windows CD-ROM
About $90
The Learning Company
(800) 852-2255

recall those same letters and words off the computer! Still, other parents claim this program has indeed helped their kids learn to read.

The bottom line: A comprehensive but high-priced approach to the basics of reading.

Reading Blaster

★

Hundreds of word-skill drills grafted onto a blast-the-evil-space-aliens game. Hardly the newest approach to reading, but satisfying for some children.

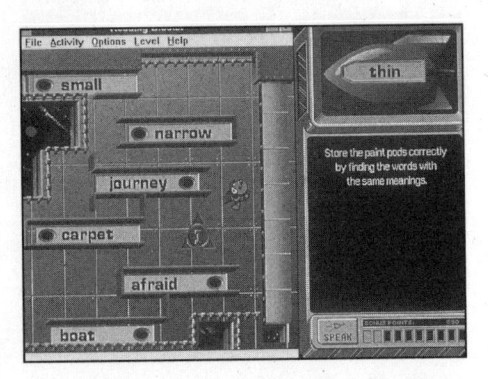

Reading Blaster is based on the characters and the gameplay of the popular *Math Blaster* series (see pages 114–115). In the course of games like Word Zapper, Splatter Pods and Sequence Shocker, kids practice alphabetizing words, spelling, matching synonyms and antonyms, reading and following directions and more. Three levels of play and more than 1,000 words provide a decent workout for second through fifth graders.

The bottom line: If your kids like playing the *Math Blaster* programs at school, they may like mastering word skills through arcade-action games, too.

JUST THE FACTS

BEST FOR AGES 7–10

★ **for Learning**
Reading practice in an arcade-game format; skills include spelling, synonyms, antonyms, alphabetizing

★ **for Looks**
Colorful, but nothing special

★ **for Longevity**
Longer lasting if your kids love blasting aliens

Windows CD-ROM or floppy
About $40
Davidson
(800) 545-7677

Alphabet Blocks

★

A simple, no-frills approach to practicing alphabet skills. Nice to look at, not particularly exciting to use.

The title's four activities encourage kids to use their eyes and ears to match letters and short words with corresponding sounds, while two appealing coaches (a chimp and a jack-in-the-box) shout out instructions and words of encouragement. Parent options let you choose appropriate challenges for your child. For example, you can specify capital or lowercase letters, block writing or cursive.

Choosing the right answers sends tiny surprise animations—a snail, a bicyclist—scuttling across the bottom of the screen. Kids enjoy earning these rewards for a while. But then, because there is nothing else to do, they lose interest.

The bottom line: Lip-synching and exceptionally clear auditory cues are helpful to beginning readers. But other programs (such as *Bailey's Book House, Zurk's Learning Safari, AlphaBonk Farm, Davidson's Kid Phonics*) help kids learn to identify letters while giving them more to do.

JUST THE FACTS

BEST FOR AGES 3-4

★ **for Learning**
Basic letter and sound-recognition skills

★ **for Looks**
Cute characters, large, clear lettering

★ **for Longevity**
Narrow focus, nothing to do but practice

Macintosh CD-ROM or floppy; Windows CD-ROM or floppy
About $35
Sierra
(800) 757-7707

Beginning Reading

★

Picking up where *Alphabet Blocks* leaves off, *Beginning Reading* is the colorful equivalent of a classroom worksheet with a no-nonsense agenda of kindergarten and first-grade phonics.

Coached by an outgoing chimp and a friendly jack-in-the-box, kids practice such skills as identifying two-letter consonant blends and vowel diphthongs, recognizing sight words, matching rhyming words, alphabetizing and combining beginning and ending letters to build words.

As with *Alphabet Blocks*, the auditory cues in this program are excellent. And the lettering is large and exceptionally clear, which can be especially helpful for young children who are just starting to "track" (follow letters and words from left to right) or for beginning readers who focus best with a minimum of visual clutter. But overall, *Beginning Reading* is not particularly exciting or innovative.

The bottom line: Used sparingly, this program is helpful for reinforcing the word skills your children are learning in school.

JUST THE FACTS

BEST FOR AGES 5–7

★ **for Learning**
Basic letter and sound-recognition skills

★ **for Looks**
Cute characters; large, clear lettering

★ **for Longevity**
Narrow focus, nothing to do but practice

Macintosh CD-ROM or floppy; Windows CD-ROM or floppy
About $35
Sierra
(800) 757-7707

Super Solvers Spellbound!
Super Solvers Midnight Rescue!

★

Super Solvers Spellbound! has several things going for it. It can be customized if you type in those weekly lists of spelling words. It uses the tried-and-true activities kids get in school, and it has a spelling-bee game that kids find appealing.

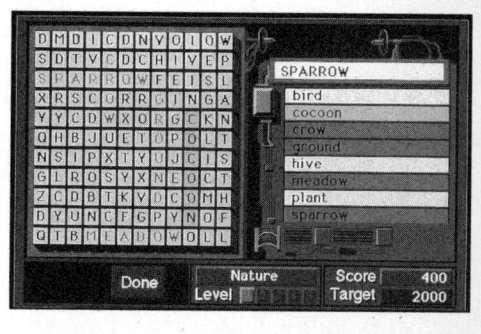

But it's low on inventiveness and good looks. And there are a great many words that the spelling-bee official cannot pronounce out loud.

The chance to confront the evil Morty Maxwell in the Shady Glen spelling bee, however, is appealing to many kids (ages 7–12) and eclipses the title's shortcomings.

Morty shows up again in *Midnight Rescue!* (ages 7–10) where he's trying to erase Shady Glen School with invisible paint. Players have until midnight to stop him by reading short passages, answering questions that test their comprehension and analyzing clues as to his whereabouts.

The bottom line: Sugar-coated versions of the worksheets kids get for homework. But many kids love Morty, and the ability to customize word lists and reading levels in these two programs is a plus.

JUST THE FACTS

BEST FOR AGES 7–12

★ **for Learning**
Worksheet-style spelling and reading activities for grades 2–5

★ **for Looks**
Mediocre

★ **for Longevity**
It's a nice touch that kids can enter their weekly spelling words

Macintosh CD-ROM or floppy; Windows CD-ROM or floppy; DOS floppy
About $45–$50
The Learning Company
(800) 852-2255

WiggleWorks Volume 1

★

An excellent classroom product that won't make the grade at home—unless you take on the role of teacher.

WiggleWorks encourages children to practice literacy skills by working—and playing—with three simple but appealing storybooks. In each story kids can see the text on screen, hear it read, read it aloud, record themselves reading it, write or record their thoughts about it, copy words onto a notepad, play with phonics on a magnet board or even rewrite the text or change the pictures.

There's no question this approach works; it just works better with a teacher's support and lesson plans. Unless you're actively involved, the *WiggleWorks* stories and activities aren't lively and unique enough to bring kids back again and again.

But it can succeed, with your encouragement. "Jocelyn loves reading the stories into the microphone and hearing them played back," the 7-year-old's mother reported.

The bottom line: A good-looking program based on respected teaching methods, but you'll have to be closely involved to help your child stick with it.

JUST THE FACTS

BEST FOR AGES 3–5

★ **for Learning**
It takes your involvement to get the most out of this read-and-write program; skills include spelling, syllables, rhyming, word recognition

★★ **for Looks**
Attractive workspace with storybook illustrations

★ **for Longevity**
Kids don't stick with it on their own

Macintosh CD-ROM; Windows CD-ROM
About $50
Apple Computer
(800) 776-2333 x5924

The Sound It Out Land Series

★

A musical approach to teaching letter sounds and phonics rules. There's a lot of time—perhaps too much time—spent just listening in the *Sound It Out* titles. But for kids who like the songs, it's an alternative to classroom teaching methods.

Sound It Out Land uses original songs to teach a series of lessons about sounding out letters and words. Each song is followed by a short game that lets kids practice the skills they just heard about.

The good news: These three programs actually instruct kids in the process of sounding out words. *Sound It Out Land 1* clearly explains letter sounds and how to sound out three-letter words. *Sound It Out Land 2* introduces vowel sounds and consonant blends and teaches kids to read four- and five-letter words and short sentences. *Sound It Out Land 3* focuses on longer words and that tricky silent "e."

The bad news: Kids are more of a captive audience than interactive explorers. Using *Sound It Out Land* is a lot like watching TV—during the long stretches of songs, kids can only watch and listen.

The bottom line: This series covers much of the same ground as the *Reader Rabbit* titles. While *Reader Rabbit* emphasizes gameplay, *Sound It Out Land* offers more focused instruction.

JUST THE FACTS

BEST FOR AGES 4–6

★★ **for Learning**
Sound-it-out skills, from individual letters to five-letter words

★ **for Looks**
Use of songs is distinctive but overdone; graphics and animation are nothing special

★ **for Longevity**
Best in small doses to avoid musical overkill

Windows CD-ROM
About $35
Conexus
(800) 545-7677

·FOUR·
THE BEST TITLES: MATH

Like the titles in the "Reading" chapters of the *Guide*, the Math programs we recommend fall into two distinct camps. We've dubbed them "Math Explorations" and "Skills & Drills."

If, as a child, you hated chanting multiplication tables or adding up columns of numbers in your head on demand, take a look at "Math Explorations." These titles are challenging and instructive, but they don't "feel" like old-fashioned math at all. (They don't "look" like old-fashioned math, either. They look and sound as good as any of the best new multimedia software out there.) Based on the new standards of the National Council of Teachers of Mathematics, they focus on real-world problem-solving as a way of motivating kids and giving their computational skills an interesting workout.

But if you worry that your kids just don't seem to know their math facts the way you did, "Skills & Drills" may be more up your alley. You'll see all the old familiar skills in these titles and plenty of computational drills . . . with one difference: They're dressed up in Nintendo-like games of high-speed, shoot-'em-up pursuits and escapes.

There's a place for titles of both sorts. Which kind you choose depends on how your child likes to learn and play. We suggest starting with the "Math Explorations" titles. They appeal to kids' instinct to learn by exploring. They're a good fit with today's teaching strategies. And because they're appealing to parents too, they make math into a source of family fun. (Really!)

Because you can tailor them very precisely, Skills & Drills are helpful if your child needs highly targeted math practice. And because they play like games, they're a good choice for fast-action aficionados. But they do foster an image of the computer as a tool for drills, and that's not how we want kids to see technology. Computers should be creative thinking tools. And they can be . . . with the right software.

MATH EXPLORATIONS

Discovering Concepts and Developing
Strategies for Solving Mathematical Problems

If you've got kids in school, you probably know that math is new—again. In today's classrooms, there's a lot more going on than just gaining proficiency with basic math facts. Instead, the focus is on discovering concepts and developing strategies for solving mathematical problems.

The programs in this section reflect this contemporary approach. (They're contemporary in looks, too. In fact, they're among the most visually innovative in the *Guide*.) These titles create mathematical playgrounds and experiences. And then they encourage kids to gain insights on their own, as they explore and experiment and play. Whether they're building bugs or assembling intricate puzzles or manipulating "magic" squares, kids are exercising their mathematical intuition and honing their problem-solving skills. They're developing basic skills like understanding quantity, recognizing numerals, counting, identifying geometric shapes and recognizing patterns, and more advanced ones like classification, comparison, attribute recognition, spatial visualization, estimation, equivalence, logic and strategy. As a result, concepts really seem to "click" when kids play with this kind of software.

The good news: These innovative titles have tremendous appeal—even for kids who say they hate math. And they're a great source of family fun.

RATINGS	TITLES	AGES
★★★★	Math Workshop (Pages 98-99)	5–12
★★★★	Millie's Math House (Pages 100-101)	2–5
★★★	Countdown (Pages 102-103)	5–12
★★	Adventures in Flight (Pages 104-105)	8–12
★★	Counting on Frank (Pages 106-107)	8–12

Math Workshop

★ ★ ★ ★

One of a new breed of titles, *Math Workshop* **puts the fun back into mathematics and reflects the sweeping changes that new standards from the National Council of Teachers of Mathematics are bringing to the nation's classrooms.**

Math Workshop's puzzle-solving and pattern-recognition activities are both visual delights as well as tantalizing brain teasers. The estimation, logic and strategy games are addictive to play solo, with a friend or two, or with Poly Gonzales, the spunky equivalent of on-line help. There's never any rush. But when kids do complete a challenge, a wacky, Monty Python-like animation fills the screen. *Math Workshop* makes the best use of video clips, sound effects and animation that you'll find in a "skill" product, especially during these funny bits. But we're convinced kids don't play *Math Workshop* for the "reward"; they play it because the activities are intrinsically fascinating and somehow deeply satisfying.

Math Workshop does offer a "math facts" workout, but with a contemporary twist. Besides addition, subtraction, multiplication and division problems (displayed with multiple-choice answers),

---

JUST THE FACTS

BEST FOR AGES 5–12

★★★★ **for Learning**
A great new twist on classroom math concepts; skills include estimation, pattern recognition, fractions, equivalency, logic

★★★★ **for Looks**
Clever use of photos, animation, sound

★★★ **for Longevity**
Innovative games keep kids challenged

Worth Noting
Part of the Active Mind series covering reading, math, and science.

Macintosh CD-ROM; Windows CD-ROM
About $40
Broderbund
(800) 521-6263

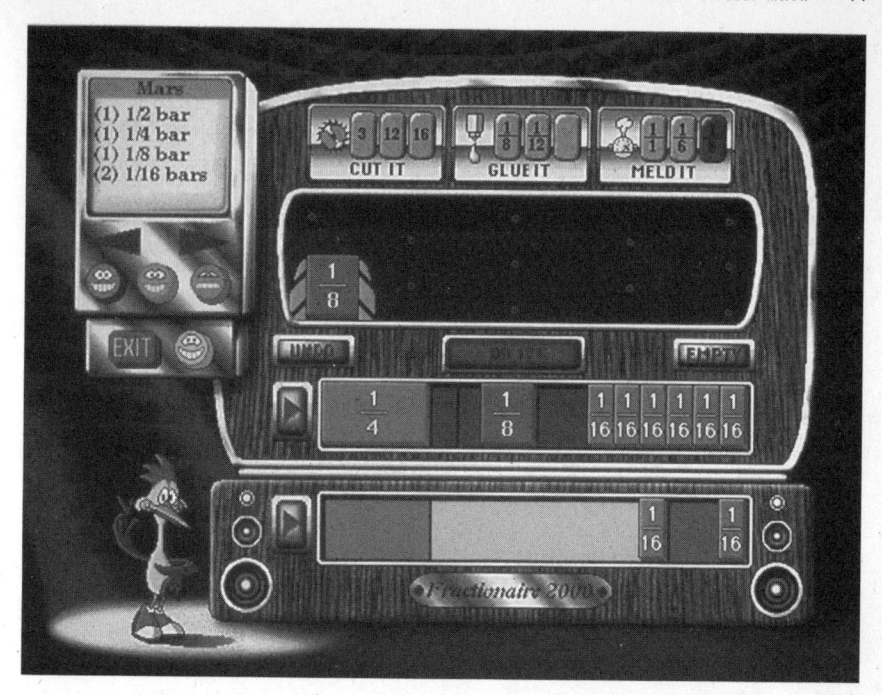

kids can practice their skill at estimation challenges like these: "About how many grapefruits wide is a toilet seat?" or "About how many eggs does an empty lunch box weigh?" These certainly aren't *facts* kids need to know. But they do need to know *how* to make logical guesses, and this activity helps.

We're usually skeptical of products that claim to appeal to so broad an age range, but *Math Workshop*'s multiple levels of play do extend its challenges. Five-year-olds (and even some 4-year-olds) get pleasure from the easier puzzles while 9-year-olds explore fractions and 12-year-olds tackle tough logic games.

The bottom line: The best use of multimedia to present intriguing mathematical challenges.

Millie's Math House

★ ★ ★ ★

With its spunky characters, lively music, silly humor and kid-size challenges, *Millie's Math House* is a great first software program for little kids.

Millie's six activities provide whimsical opportunities to explore beginning math concepts like quantity, number recognition, counting, shapes, patterns, sizes and comparison. In Build-A-Bug kids see (and hear) a zany metamorphosis when they click body parts and numbers: 5 tails, 3 eyes and 10 antennae, or 10 eyes, 6 ears and 2 spots—you get the idea. Printing these creations extends the fun (and learning).

Our favorite, Little, Middle and Big, enlists kids' help to find the right size shoes for the world's most engaging peanut figures. Like every activity in *Millie's*, this one stimulates multiple senses. Kids can *see* that the big cowboy boots practically engulf Little and they can *hear* its squeaky protest: "Oh, no! Too big."

Most activities in *Millie's* offer two modes of play (as do all Edmark titles). There's explore

JUST THE FACTS

BEST FOR AGES 2-5

★★★★ for Learning
Hands-on exploration of beginning math concepts; skills include number, shape and pattern recognition; counting; and comparison

★★★★ for Looks
Imaginative, age-appropriate graphics

★★★★ for Longevity
Even kids who outgrow it come back for more

Worth Noting
Other preschool titles from Edmark include *Sammy's Science House*, *Bailey's Book House*, *Trudy's Time and Place House*, **and** *Thinkin' Things Collection 1*.

Macintosh CD-ROM or floppy; Windows, DOS CD-ROM or floppy
About $35
Edmark
(800) 691-2985

and discover, where kids can experiment at their own pace; and there's question and answer, where kids are challenged to find the best answer (with lots of hints along the way).

Because of these options, *Millie's Math House* can grow with your kids, engaging them in different ways as they become ready for new challenges. Two-year-olds play happily in the Cookie Factory, unconcerned that their jelly-bean selections may be "wrong" (the frog eats them). Older children play the same games in a different way, counting out exactly the number of jelly beans Harley the horse needs for his cookie.

The bottom line: A software classic. We've never met a child under 5 who didn't love Millie and her pals.

Countdown

★ ★ ★

Countdown **pointed the way for the new generation of software that invites kids to explore math through hands-on manipulation.**

In this CD-ROM, kids are inspired to hone their estimation skills and problem-solving strategies by playing with food! (And what kids don't play with their food?) They start by choosing an object from a series of bright, realistic photographs: a bowl of noodles, a carton of eggs, a red delicious apple, as well as nonedibles like a pyramid of marbles or crumpled paper heaped in a wastebasket. Then kids choose one of three games: Guesstimation, Nimbles or Leftovers.

Our favorite is Nimbles. Based on the ancient game of Nim, Nimbles is a two-player game in which kids have to take away one, two or three objects at a time from the group. The player who takes the last object wins. At first your kids may just remove objects willy-nilly. But eventually they'll start thinking about what their opponent is up to and how to develop a strategy of their own. (Where's the math? We're talking number sense, estimation skills, logical reasoning, mental computation and more.)

Countdown games are fast, spirited and loads of fun, and the software makes brilliant use of video.

JUST THE FACTS

BEST FOR AGES 5–12

★★★ **for Learning**
A fun approach to problem-solving; concepts include estimation, probability, logic

★★★ **for Looks**
Visually exciting and innovative

★★ **for Longevity**
Try reintroducing this title as your child encounters new challenges in school

Macintosh CD-ROM; Windows CD-ROM
About $30
Voyager
(800) 337-4989

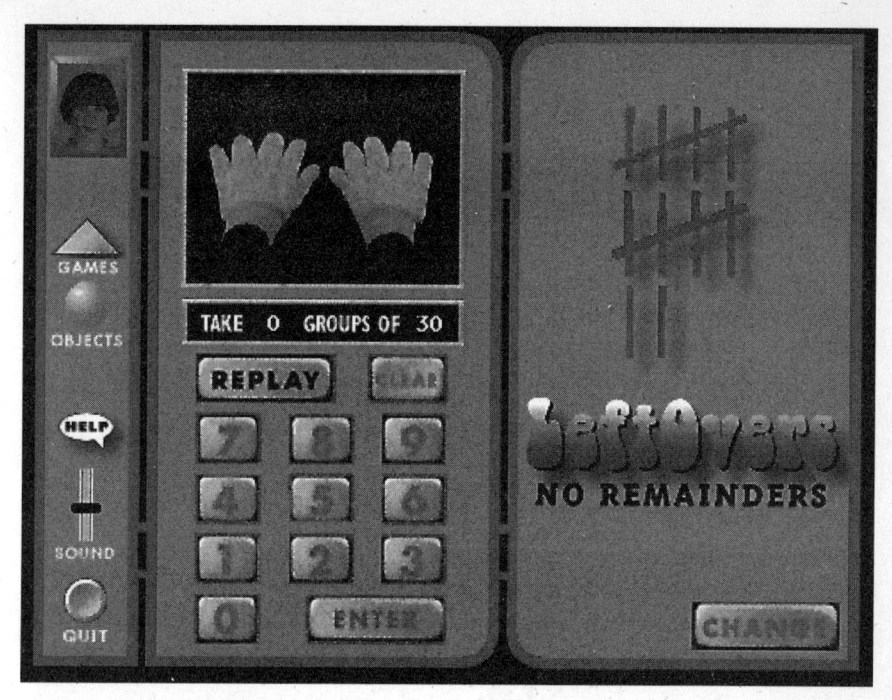

The bottom line: An innovative program that can grow with your kids, especially if you put it aside from time to time and reintroduce it as your child encounters new challenges in school.

The beauty of Nimbles and the other *Countdown* games is that you can play them not only on the computer but just about anywhere, anytime. Try it with a pile of peas at the dinner table or with popcorn while you're waiting for the movie to start or with pennies in the back seat of the car.

Adventures in Flight

★ ★

If your kids have ever whined that math just doesn't matter in "real life," try *Adventures in Flight*. This challenging program convincingly shows how math *does* matter for real-life people who work at an airport.

As kids explore a passenger cabin, cockpit, control tower, repair hangar and service area, they encounter realistic (and reasonably intriguing) scenarios that entail using math. Kids discover, for example, how flight attendants interpret the numbers and letters of a seating chart to seat passengers; how baggage handlers use codes to route luggage; how pilots calculate flight time; or how passengers figure out which gifts they can afford from an in-flight shopping catalog.

Underlying these and other "data demos" are such topics as estimation, pattern recognition, place value, calculation, geometry, graph interpretation and measurement. Once kids understand a "data demo," they can apply what they've learned in a "data quiz." Correct answers earn them points toward "certification" as pilots of different aircraft.

The title's exploratory, try-it-then-apply-it approach is very much in line with today's class-

JUST THE FACTS

BEST FOR AGES 8–12

★★★ **for Learning**
Excellent try-it-then-apply-it approach, plus a real-life setting; skills include place value, geometry, graphing, measurement

★★ **for Looks**
Nicely illustrated but too tame

★★ **for Longevity**
When the math gets tough, gameplay isn't incentive enough

Macintosh CD-ROM; Windows CD-ROM
About $40
Sanctuary Woods
(800) 872-3518

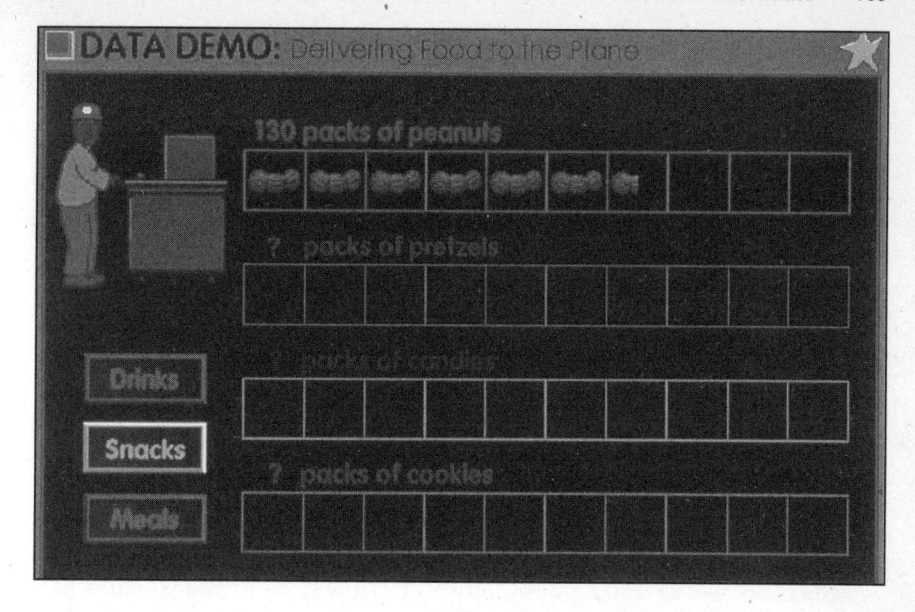

> **DATA DEMO:** Delivering Food to the Plane
>
> 130 packs of peanuts
> ? packs of pretzels
> ? packs of candies
> ? packs of cookies

room methods and also makes it a good product for kids who have outgrown *Math Workshop*. But, reflecting its origins as an Addison-Wesley textbook, *Adventures in Flight* doesn't use enough sound effects, photos, animation or video. The airport scenes are nicely illustrated but rather static. Unless your kids are really hooked on the title's "air time" game, you may not get your money's worth.

The bottom line: Inventive, challenging problems, but without your interest and encouragement, kids may find it too tame for long-term home use.

Counting on Frank

★ ★

A program with a real-life motivation for applying math skills. The premise of *Counting on Frank* has instant kid-appeal: Guess how many jellybeans are in the jar at Mrs. Sherman's store and win a trip to Hawaii.

Kids can't just hazard a guess, however. They have to collect clues to make an educated guess. To collect clues they have to solve word problems. And to find the word problems they have to poke around with a kid named Henry and his dog, Frank.

Whenever the cursor turns into a jellybean, Henry whips out a calculator and a note pad with a problem. All the problems have a contemporary twist and relate to Henry's life in some way: If I rake two bags of leaves and Dad pays me 50 cents a bag, how much will I make? If our TV gets 24 channels and we watch each channel for two hours, how much time would we spend watching TV?

In keeping with the standards of the National Council of Teachers of Mathematics, the emphasis is on complex reasoning and understanding how to apply basic computational skills. In fact, kids can't simply type in an answer; they have to type in the equation they're using to get the answer. Excellent explanations are just a click away.

JUST THE FACTS

BEST FOR AGES 8-12

★★ **for Learning**
Word problems with plenty of real-life kid appeal; skills include addition, subtraction, multiplication, division

★★ **for Looks**
Bold, colorful graphics and a funky hero

★★ **for Longevity**
Low-key adventure won't work for fast-action kids

Macintosh CD-ROM; DOS CD-ROM
About $50
Creative Wonders
(800) 543-9778

It only takes one game to find all the title's hot spots and to discover that word problems always pop up in the same places. But the problems differ in every game, and they differ at each of the title's three levels, so there's always a math challenge.

The bottom line: A contemporary program that's especially good for practicing word problems.

MORE MATH FUN

You'll find some intriguing math adventures in "nonmath"' programs, too. Here are a few of our favorites:

Thinkin' Things Collection I
Ages 3–8
Feathered Friends and the Fripple Shop let kids explore attributes and play with Boolean logic (and, or, not).

Sammy's Science House
Ages 2–5
Make-A-Movie encourages children to practice sequencing. In the Sorting Station kids find similarities and differences in pictures of plants and animals.

Zurk's Rainforest Lab
Ages 5–9
Seek & Sort challenges older kids to group animals by their characteristics, developing the analytic skills of classifying and sorting. Puzzle Patterns provides a colorful opportunity for kids to visualize geometric and spatial relationships.

What's the Secret?
Ages 7–12
The "How many pieces can a pizza produce?" activity is a concrete example of fractions in everyday life; it lets kids build their understanding by manipulating numerators and denominators. It also convincingly demonstrates the connection between fractions, decimals and percentages.

Recess in Greece
Ages 7–12
Magic Squares is a classic game that helps kids develop analytic and computational skills.

Travelrama USA
Ages 8–12
Because calculating mileage is an important part of this geography game, kids have an opportunity to strengthen their mental computational abilities.

Widget Workshop
Ages 10–12
Science experiments and widget construction encourage conceptual thinking and number-crunching. Kids encounter equations, scientific notation, probability and logic. They can even build their own calculator.

SKILLS & DRILLS

Exercises in Addition, Subtraction, Multiplication, Division & Other Math Basics

These practice-makes-perfect titles are a much-respected source of progressive drills in computation. They feature thousands (actually, tens of thousands) of problems in addition, subtraction, multiplication and division. Not to mention exercises in estimation, prime numbers, algebra, factors, multiples and other math basics. All sugar-coated with video-game action.

Why are there no 3- or 4-star titles in this product section? Most of these products have been around for years. Although many have had a facelift, their looks don't compare to newer titles. Their games, modeled on 1980s fight-the-bad-guys arcade action, are dated. And although lots of kids enjoy them in school, most kids prefer to do something more creative than math drills at home.

Still, if you feel your kids need a computational workout, these titles offer a solid set of graduated skills. Choose a title that covers the particular skills you want your child to practice. Then put yourself in your kids' shoes: look at the premise of the titles, and ask yourself if they'd be hooked. And be sure to ask your offspring. Since these titles are popular in schools, kids may already have a preference. But if they inform you that what they really need is practice with tangrams, consider one of the alternative math programs in the "Math Explorations" section.

THE BEST TITLES: MATH • 111

RATINGS	TITLES	AGES
★★	Troggle Trouble (Pages 112-113)	6–12
★	Math Blaster: Episode 1—In Search of Spot (Page 114)	6–12
★	Math Blaster: Episode 2—Secret of the Lost City (Page 115)	8–12
★	Math Blaster Mystery: The Great Brain Robbery (Page 115)	10–12
★	Alge-Blaster 3 (Page 115)	12 & Up
★	Math Munchers Deluxe (Page 116)	8–12
★	Number Munchers (Page 117)	8–12
★	Word Munchers (Page 117)	6–12
★	Super Munchers (Page 117)	8–12
★	Treasure Mountain! (Page 118)	5–9
★	Treasure MathStorm! (Page 118)	5–9
★	Treasure Cove! (Page 118)	5–9
★	Treasure Galaxy! (Page 118)	5–9
★	Super Solvers OutNumbered! (Page 120)	5–9

Troggle Trouble

★ ★

A vast improvement—in looks and philosophy—over the old *Muncher* titles. The bare-bones graphics are gone, the characters speak (or bark, in the case of Sparky, the title's hero), and computation at break-neck speed has been replaced by thoughtful problem-solving with a Troggulator.

JUST THE FACTS

BEST FOR AGES 6–12

★★ **for Learning**
Kids create equations *Jeopardy*-style to practice basic math; skills span addition, subtraction, multiplication, division for grades 1–5

★★ **for Looks**
Colorful, cartoonlike characters and settings

★★ **for Longevity**
If kids like the game, they'll stick with the math

Worth Noting
The CD-ROM version adds realistic speech—and barking—for the title's main characters.

Macintosh CD-ROM or floppy; Windows CD-ROM or floppy
About $40–$46
MECC
(800) 685-6322

There's still an addictive game in *Troggle Trouble* for kids who prefer their math with bad guys, good guys and the thrill of pursuit. But there's also a new kind of math, more contemporary and thought-provoking than right-or-wrong arithmetic.

Here's how the game works: After an evil Trog captures the Muncher, players guide Sparky through a colorful, funky-looking town in a search for clues to Muncher's whereabouts. But Sparky's in danger, too; gangs of Troggles are after his dog treats. And when they appear, kids must quickly protect Sparky with a force field.

Here's how the math works: Once Sparky's temporarily protected, kids have to get rid of the Troggles. They do that by creating an equation equivalent to the number of Troggles surrounding Sparky.

Depending on the difficulty level you've selected, equations can use addition, subtraction, multiplication, division or a combination. The computation takes place on an on-screen Troggulator, which kids must recharge periodically by solving a series of equations (rather than creating them).

The bottom line: Much more attuned to the math activities kids do in school, *Troggle Trouble* **is a great improvement over old-fashioned drill titles.**

The Math Blaster Series
Math Blaster: Episode 1—In Search of Spot
Math Blaster: Episode 2—Secret of the Lost City
Math Blaster Mystery: The Great Brain Robbery
Alge-Blaster 3

★

One of the oldest series of math drills around (since 1982!), and still going strong. Almost every computing family we know owns at least one *Math Blaster* title. But kids can get "blastered out," and it usually takes a parent's insistence for them to stick to computer math practice.

The *Math Blaster* series is based on a simple formula: package math drills in a video game. Kids do the math so they can play the game.

We find that even the latest *Blaster* adventures look and feel dated next to the contemporary pizzazz of many newly created titles. But their appeal lives on for younger kids, especially those who love fast action video games . . . kids who love defeat-the-evil-aliens adventures.

In *Episode 1—In Search of Spot* (ages 6–12), kids take on Trash Aliens who have littered the solar

---

JUST THE FACTS

BEST FOR AGES 6-12

★ **for Learning**
Math drill in a blast-the-aliens game

★ **for Looks**
Video game-style graphics

★ **for Longevity**
Game may persuade some kids to stick with math practice

Formats vary according to title; see review for details
About $40
Davidson
(800) 545-7677

system and kidnapped Blasternaut's buddy Spot. Players accomplish their mission by tackling four games, each with thousands of math problems targeted at first- through seventh-graders. (Available as Macintosh and Windows CD-ROM or floppy, DOS floppy; $40.)

Episode 2—Secret of the Lost City (ages 8–12) is aimed at slightly older kids. After a crash landing masterminded by the evil Dr. Minus, kids must help Blasternaut, Spot and their Galactic Commander "activate" deserted buildings by completing four math activities. But *Episode 2* is not all math drills; one of its four games, for example, exercises logic skills as kids create space creatures with varying attributes. And, like newer math titles, an on-screen calculator is a click away. (Available as Windows CD-ROM or floppy; $40.)

In *Math Blaster Mystery: The Great Brain Robbery* (ages 10 & Up) kids get practice with prealgebra and word problems. This program plays much like the others, but this time the bad guy is Dr. Dabble, and the setting is a creepy mansion. (Available as Windows CD-ROM; $40.)

Alge-Blaster 3 (ages 12 & Up) takes a more tutorial approach than the other *Blasters*. But gamers still have plenty of evil aliens to defeat (the Red Nasties this time) while mastering algebra. (Available as Macintosh and Windows CD-ROM or floppy; $40.)

The bottom line: A fine choice for fast-action fanatics who need practice in math facts. But kids who don't like the *Blaster* pace and plot will never make it to the math.

The Muncher Series
Math Munchers Deluxe Number Munchers
Word Munchers Super Munchers

★

Like the goofy cast of characters in the *Math Blaster*, *Treasure*, and *Super Solvers* titles, the quirky green Munchers (and their enemies the Troggles) have developed quite a following over the years. And like all these drill products, they can be effective for children who like their "get-the-right-answer-quick-so-you-can-escape-(or vanquish)-the-enemy" approach.

Remember Pac-Man? That's what playing *Munchers* is like. And if you think an adrenaline rush may entice your child to practice, you may want to take a closer look at these products.

The best title in the series, *Math Munchers Deluxe*, sports a great new 3-D look, lots of color and animation, more Troggles, a new section of geometry problems, plus a parent video guide right on the CD-ROM. In the other Muncher titles, however, visual appeal is virtually nil. The game play is the same in all four titles. The action takes place on a grid of 30 squares. Each contains

---

JUST THE FACTS

BEST FOR AGES 6–12

★★ **for Learning**
Math drill in a Pac Man-like game; skills cover addition, subtraction, multiplication, division, prime numbers, factors and multiples for grades 1–6

★ **for Looks**
Math Munchers Deluxe has lively graphics and sound; other titles are primitive looking

★ **for Longevity**
Appealing to fast-action kids

Worth Noting
Check out *Troggle Trouble* for math practice with the same characters but in a much more contemporary game.

Win/Mac CD-ROM only for *Math Munchers Deluxe*; Macintosh floppy; Windows floppy
$20–$40
MECC
(800) 685-6322

an answer: A number, or an equation, or a word. Kids have to figure out which answers correctly match a target rule at the top of the grid that has rules like "multiples of 10" or "animals with scales" or "words with 'u' as in use." Then they maneuver their Muncher to gobble up right answers—and outmaneuver the Troggles that can pop up anywhere, anytime.

Number Munchers and *Math Munchers Deluxe* focus on arithmetic skills for children ages 8–12. The products are intended for kids who already know about prime numbers, factors, whole numbers, fractions, decimals, percents, multiples, and adding, subtracting, multiplying and dividing numbers up to 20. (It doesn't explain, it just provides an opportunity for practice.) And kids have to work things out in their head; there's no time for pencil and paper, or even a calculator, with Troggles around!

Word Munchers (ages 6–12) is intended for kids who are just getting beyond the beginning stages of reading. It focuses on recognizing phonetic rules fast. If your kids are still shaky at sounding out words or need lots of time to decode the words on the grid, they'll be frustrated by the pace of this game.

Super Munchers (ages 8–12) takes the "move and munch" approach beyond basic skills to a general knowledge of geography, science, social studies and popular culture. It also adds a new twist to the basic game: after 20 right answers, a Muncher will (very briefly) change into a Super Muncher with the power to destroy Troggles.

The bottom line: Good for video-game aficionados who need practice in math facts. But not for kids who don't like the relentless, chomp-chomp-chomp pace.

The Treasure Series

Treasure MathStorm! Treasure Mountain!
Treasure Cove! Treasure Galaxy!

★

The *Treasure* titles have moved to CD-ROM with some fairly substantial improvements: a graphic make-over, spoken introductions and hints, plus new character voices. They're still rather dated-looking, but they've been kid-pleasers for years, and the math problems are well matched to the first- through third-grade curriculum.

Like the *Blaster* programs, the *Treasure* series makes math exercises part of Nintendo-like games. The titles even look like video games; their fantasy worlds have a flat, fuzzy appearance. Characters move across the screen, jerk by jerk. But if the prospect of defeating yet another diabolical plot by the Master of Mischief is a surefire way to get your kids near math or reading practice, they'll get some educational benefit from these games.

All four titles have a similar premise, with slight variations. In *Treasure Mountain!*—the first program in the series and the most improved—players have to vanquish the Master of Mischief by restoring stolen treasures to a castle atop a mountain. In *Trea-*

JUST THE FACTS

BEST FOR AGES 5–9

★★ **for Learning**
To thwart bad guys, kids apply reading and math skills including basic facts, telling time, fractions, place value, measurement

★ **for Looks**
Video game-like graphics

★ **for Longevity**
If they like the game, they'll do the math

Macintosh CD-ROM or floppy; Windows CD-ROM or floppy; DOS floppy
About $45–$50
The Learning Company
(800) 852-2255

sure MathStorm! (which is still stuck with its old-style graphics), this same fiend has put the mountain into a deep freeze, and kids have to recover snowbound treasures to melt his evil magic. *Treasure Cove!* has the worst looks and the silliest plot: kids have to stop gooey creatures called goobies from polluting a cove, collect hidden gems and rebuild a bridge destroyed by you-know-who. The Master of Mischief moves into outer space in *Treasure Galaxy!* and players must search for Queen Astral's missing crystals to break his hold on Crystal City.

Success hinges on brain power: figuring out what's going on, what the rules are, where to find clues, where to get tools and what each one is good for, and then solving lots of math, reading, or thinking problems.

The bottom line: Video game-like adventures popular with both girls and boys. But more contemporary titles like *Troggle Trouble* **or** *Math Workshop* **offer better graphics and a closer connection to the math kids encounter in school.**

Parents of *Treasure* aficionados tell us that the math their kids practice during a game doesn't always stick with them.

Five-year-old Alexandra, for example, played *Treasure Mountain!* daily for weeks until she "unfroze" the mountain. Her goal accomplished, she rarely played again. And her mother reported that Alex didn't remember the math facts she seemed to have mastered during the game.

Super Solvers OutNumbered!

★

Word problems like the ones your kids get for homework, except these are sugar-coated in an elaborate track-the-villain game. In looks and gameplay *Super Solvers OutNumbered!* is dated. But it's still popular. And it gives kids a workout in math, reading, and reasoning that can be tailored to their grade level.

In *OutNumbered!* players have to prevent Morty Maxwell and his gang of robots from taking over the Shady Glen TV station. Kids collect clues to his whereabouts by searching the studio, zapping robots, solving word problems and answering math drills.

Typical questions show a chart, table, graph or a map. Kids must interpret the data and answer questions like this one: "Cleo the Clown has ordered 16 more boxes of red balloons. When they are added to the boxes already on hand, how many boxes will there be altogether?"

Thanks to dozens of skill levels, the *Super Solvers* titles can be used by second through fifth graders. But, compared to newer titles, we're dubious about their staying power for 9- or 10-year-olds.

The bottom line: Hundreds of math word problems for kids in grades 2–5, surrounded by video game action.

JUST THE FACTS

BEST FOR AGES 7–10

★★ **for Learning**
Kids thwart bad guys by applying reading and math skills

★ **for Looks**
Video game-like graphics

★ **for Longevity**
If they like facing off against Morty, they'll do the math

Macintosh floppy; DOS, Windows floppy
About $35–$45
The Learning Company
(800) 852-2255

•FIVE•
THE BEST TITLES: EXPLORATIONS FOR CURIOUS KIDS

Kids are natural explorers, and the programs in this section have a wonderful knack for taking them to places they can't ordinarily go. Like the hold of a 16th century galleon. A snowbound trail in the turn-of-the-century Klondike. Olympus Mons, the highest mountain in the solar system. A minuscule capillary. The canopy of a rainforest. Or the feeding ground of a whale pod.

Good exploration software (thanks to photographic imagery, full-motion video clips, stereo sound, realistic computer-generated graphics and animation) makes kids feel as if they've entered the "world" of a particular program. And the best programs go even further, offering children a hands-on opportunity to experiment with their on-screen surroundings.

Be warned: A great many exploration titles are little more than click-and-watch databases. They let kids dip into a topic, or time period, any way they want—by reading definitions and descriptions, listening to narration, flipping through pictures, or watching movie clips—but they don't necessarily encourage kids to ponder what they're encountering.

Titles that present kids with a challenge, a quest, an adventure or a story do a better job of engaging them and getting them to think about the things they see on the computer screen. And, to keep kids even more involved, encourage them to explore these programs with a friend, sibling or parent.

...AROUND THE WORLD

Geography, Map Reading and Reasoning

Of all the software in the "Exploration" section, "Around the World" titles have the best games to play. They're good-looking, challenging, sometimes addictive, OK to play solo, but even better with friends or family. And they're just as much fun whether kids choose to collaborate or compete.

Whether kids retain the geographical information they encounter in these titles is another matter, however. In a classroom setting—where there's a report to be written or a quiz to be aced—kids probably pay closer attention. At home you may want to conjure up some incentives and activities such as planning a vacation or visiting a museum that will help children put the fun facts from these games to good use.

RATINGS	TITLES	AGES
★★★★	Where in the World Is Carmen Sandiego? (Pages 124-125)	8–12
★★★★	Where in the USA Is Carmen Sandiego? (Pages 126-127)	8–12
★★★	Where in the World Is Carmen Sandiego? Junior Detective Edition (Pages 128-129)	5–8
★★★	Travelrama USA (Pages 130-131)	8–12

Programs that let children create or print maps make a nice complement to these titles. And they can serve as homework helpers, too. CD-ROM encyclopedias, like *Encarta* (Page 194), include a broad selection of maps. For kids 10 and up, *PC Globe Maps 'N Facts* from Broderbund is a compendium of nearly 500 maps, plus information on more than 4,000 cities. Kids can print the program's maps and charts, incorporate them into reports, or customize maps of their own. (Available as Macintosh or Windows CD-ROM, $35.)

For more creative mapmaking, try the *Map Art Pack* that works with *Flying Colors* from Davidson (Page 36). Using tools from both programs, kids as young as seven can embellish topographical and road maps for all 50 states, dotting them with symbols for parks, forests, beaches, bridges, oil rigs, farms, lakes and much more. Even younger children can stamp simple maps of their neighborhood or create treasure maps.

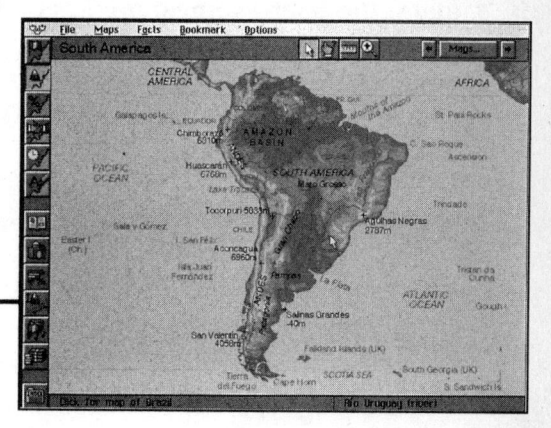

Where in the World Is Carmen Sandiego?
Deluxe CD-ROM

★ ★ ★ ★

Chances are, your kids already know Carmen Sandiego—from the PBS game show, the cartoon series, the card games, the calendars, the board games, the jigsaw puzzles, the sweatshirts, the backpacks, the books, etc., etc. But she's first and foremost a software superstar. That's where she got her start (10 years ago!). And that's still where Carmen's at her best.

JUST THE FACTS

BEST FOR AGES 8-12

★★★★ **for Learning**
Plenty of geography facts in a track-the-villains game; skills include reading, logic, memory, research practice

★★★ **for Looks**
Real photos of real places

★★★★ **for Longevity**
Challenge to rise through the ranks keeps kids coming back

Worth Noting
CD-ROM has multimedia extras that floppy version lacks.

Macintosh CD-ROM or floppy; Windows CD-ROM; DOS floppy
About $40–$50
Broderbund
(800) 521-6263

Here's what happens in *Where in the World Is Carmen Sandiego?*: kids play gumshoes following a trail of geographical clues in order to recover artifacts stolen by Carmen and her gang and nab the villains. Success brings a promotion (sometimes) and a more complex set of clues for the next case.

Sparked by this challenge, kids really throw themselves into the pursuit of information with amazing enthusiasm. Kids who have never cracked an atlas will scrutinize maps in search of the Volga. Beginning readers will painstakingly sound out three-syllable words to figure out their next destination. And competitive kids (and even siblings) find themselves collaborating to catch a common enemy—Carmen.

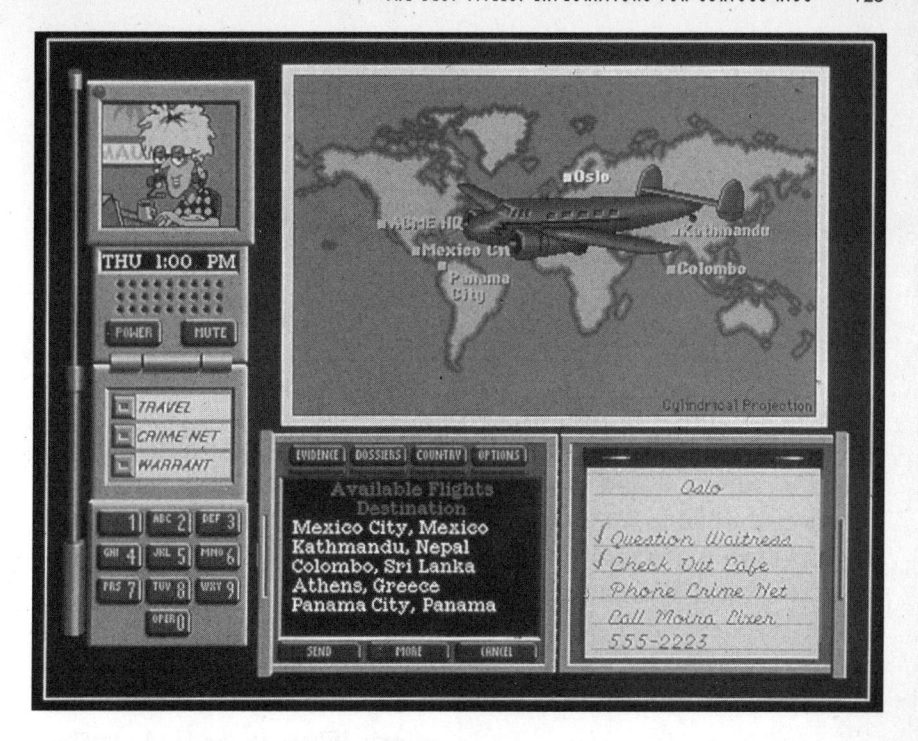

For parents and teachers, *Carmen* pushes all the right buttons. It provides a fun way for kids to pick up factual information (though whether they retain it is another matter). It fosters research skills. It cultivates a spirit of cooperation. It connects kids with books (some sort of reference work comes with every *Carmen* program). And it breeds respect for knowledge—because the lesson implicit in this and the other eight *Carmen* titles is that it's fun to get smart, and smart kids win.

The bottom line: A classic mix of adventure and fun facts makes *Where in the World Is Carmen Sandiego?* **a great program.**

Where in the USA Is Carmen Sandiego?
Deluxe CD-ROM

★ ★ ★ ★

Another exciting pursuit, this time across the United States. Filled with postcard-perfect photos, detailed topographical maps for every state, sound effects, music, and nearly 3,000 clues. Cartoon-style animations (usually featuring 1 of 16 bad guys on the lam) are particularly zany against photographic backdrops like the Grand Tetons or a Wisconsin dairy farm.

Because it's about familiar territory, *Where in the USA* may be a better first Carmen program than the wider-ranging *Where in the World*. Which program you start with depends on your child's enthusiasms, what's going on in school, and the family's interests.

Just for fun, shelve the book that comes with the CD-ROM. *You* be the reference, instead. When you puzzle out a clue, your kids will be impressed. But be prepared for heckling when you're in the dark and the crook gets away. (You can always console yourself with the thought that you're showing them how to make educated guesses or how to look up things you don't know.)

JUST THE FACTS

BEST FOR AGES 8–12

★★★★ **for Learning**
Plenty of geography facts in a track-the-villains game; skills include reading, logic, memory, look-it-up practice

★★★ **for Looks**
Real photos of real places

★★★★ **for Longevity**
Challenge to rise through the ranks keeps kids coming back

Worth Noting
CD-ROM has multimedia extras that floppy version lacks.

Macintosh CD-ROM or floppy; Windows CD-ROM; DOS floppy
About $40–$50
Broderbund
(800) 521-6263

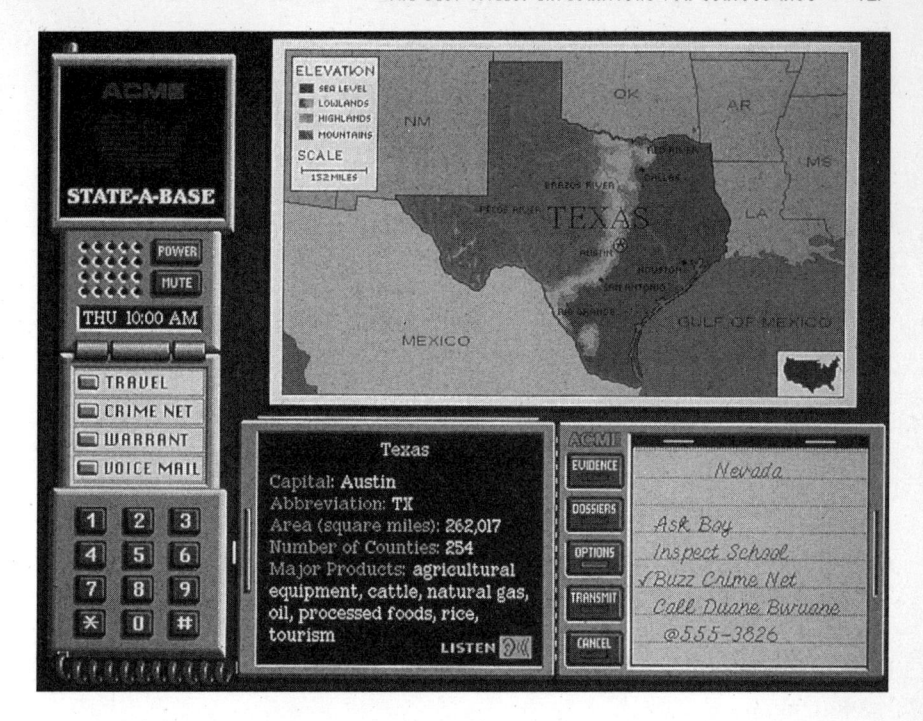

Other Carmen titles include *Where in Time Is Carmen Sandiego?*, *Where in America's Past Is Carmen Sandiego?*, *Where in Europe Is Carmen Sandiego?*, and *Where in Space Is Carmen Sandiego?* The gameplay in these titles is much the same as *Where in the USA* and *Where in the World*. But because they are floppy-based products, rather than CD-ROMs, they have considerably less visual flair. If your kids first encounter Carmen on a CD-ROM, they may be disappointed by the floppy versions.

The bottom line: Kids never seem to get enough of Carmen, so you won't go wrong with more than one title.

Where in the World Is Carmen Sandiego? Junior Detective Edition

★ ★ ★

Looks great, sounds great, plays great. Packed with thinking challenges and geographical tidbits.

But don't expect the *Junior Detective Edition* of this wildly popular program to turn players into geography whiz kids. Unlike the other *Carmen* programs, this title is less about exposing kids to world geography than it is about exercising visual and auditory memory and developing reasoning skills.

Masterfully redesigned for a younger audience, the game provides a trail of visual and spoken (versus text-based) clues for tracking down the villainous Carmen and her cohorts. Hidden in stunning photographs, the clues to a thief's whereabouts include pictures of national flags, local crops, native wildlife and the like. Junior detectives have to remember what each clue looks like —and listen carefully to comments from fellow agents and the Chief—to correctly choose their next destination. Comical cartoon interludes show glimpses of the suspect followed by inept photographers who snap incomplete photos that kids must piece together into a wanted poster.

Our one quibble with *Carmen Junior* is that kids can master the game without retaining much information about different cul-

---

JUST THE FACTS

BEST FOR AGES 5–8

★★★★ **for Learning**
Lots of visual memory practice and reasoning, plus some geography

★★★★ **for Looks**
Real photos of real places, plus cartoon antics

★★★ **for Longevity**
Lasts until kids graduate to other *Carmens*

Macintosh CD-ROM; Windows CD-ROM
About $40
Broderbund
(800) 521-6263

tures and regions of the world. Once they catch a thief, do they remember that Zaire is known for its copper mines? That both ostriches and giraffes are native to Ethiopia? Broderbund could have done more to help facts stick simply by ending each episode with a "what you learned" postcard, picturing the places gumshoes visited and the clues they collected.

The bottom line: Wonderful use of multimedia to exercise kids' visual memory and reasoning skills. But geography concepts and facts will stick better if you get involved.

You can easily help your kids get more benefit from playing *Carmen Junior*. Make a project of creating *Junior Detective* postcards or passports. Kids probably don't want you hovering around, but, once in a while, note down the countries your gumshoes visit and the clues they collect. Then using an art program, have your kids draw a postcard or passport shape and stamp on icons to represent the clues. The *Junior Detective Edition* handbook also suggests some good off-the-computer activities for extending the title's fun.

Travelrama USA

★ ★ ★

Best geography game to come along since *Carmen Sandiego*.

Travelrama is quick to hook kids with its good looks, lively music and an appealing challenge: hit the road to collect five postcards—before your opponents get their postcards—and before your mileage meter runs out.

Besides sheer fun, this cross-country adventure for one to four players gives kids a fairly rigorous workout not only in U.S. geography but also in problem-solving, map-reading, math and strategic thinking. If kids don't know which states are represented by the postcards on their list, they have to figure it out. (Players who opt for the Learner's Permit playing level get a few hints; players who select the Driver's License level have to use their wits, the resources of the *Travelrama* album, or outside references to pick the right destinations.) Kids also have to pick an advantageous starting point (a good choice may

JUST THE FACTS

BEST FOR AGES 8-12

★★★★ **for Learning**
Learn U.S. landmarks and geography on a novel road trip; skills include computation, map reading, memory

★★★★ **for Looks**
Best combination of photos, maps, gameplay

★★★ **for Longevity**
Families can enjoy this for years

Macintosh CD-ROM; Windows CD-ROM
About $30
Zenda Studios
(800) 872-3518

net two, or even three, postcards right off the bat). They have to map out the shortest route to other states. And they have to outthink their opponents, too.

Younger players might want to play solo at first to become familiar with the game and to hone their geographical know-how before taking on opponents. Or, they might team up with an older sibling, friend or parent. The game is most fun when lots of people play.

The bottom line: A great family game since each player can compete at a different skill level. Unlike *Carmen,* *Travelrama* **has good multimedia resources** *within* **the program for kids to learn things they don't know.**

... BACK IN TIME

History, Mythology and Simulations

"Back in Time" titles offer involving and informative encounters with history. The best ones—historical simulations—let kids experience the past by trying someone else's life on for size. Our other recommendations include history-based games and historical click-and-watch titles.

All three play well with friends or family. In fact, your kids will play longer, and get more from the experience, with a companion at the computer.

RATINGS	TITLES	AGES
★★★★	The Oregon Trail II (Pages 134-135)	10–16
★★★★	The Yukon Trail (Pages 136-137)	10–16
★★★★	The Amazon Trail (Pages 138-139)	10–16
★★	Ancient Lands (Pages 140-141)	8 & Up
★★	Wrath of the Gods (Pages 142-143)	9 & Up
★★	Leonardo The Inventor (Pages 144-145)	8 & Up
★	Stowaway! (Pages 146-147)	8–12
★	Recess in Greece (Page 148)	7–12

WHAT ARE HISTORICAL SIMULATIONS?

Simulation programs are imaginative explorations of "what-if" questions. What if I were a pioneer? A big-city mayor? A fish? An inventor? A video game designer? Their forté is putting kids right in the thick of things, giving them a role to play, letting their decisions make a difference in the outcome. Because they let kids take such an active hand, simulations are great for self-directed learning.

You'll find simulations in the *Guide*'s science section (*Widget Workshop, Odell Down Under*), among the "Fun & Games" titles (*SimCity 2000, Klik & Play*), and here in the history section.

Oregon Trail, which just celebrated its 20th anniversary, pioneered the historical simulation genre. These are programs in which kids step into someone else's shoes and, using their wits and the wealth of information within the software, figure out how to think, act, struggle and survive (or more likely, die) just as that character might have.

But no one tells players the rules, how to play, what to do, or where to go. So the perennial attraction of titles like *Oregon Trail* is their double challenge: kids have to master both *skills* required to play the game and *knowledge* about the era and environment into which they've been transported.

The Oregon Trail II

★ ★ ★ ★

An extraordinary new version of an educational classic. Kids step into the shoes of 19th century pioneers heading West and experience the harrowing choices and life-or-death decisions of life on the trail.

In *Oregon Trail*, kids adopt a historical *persona*, join a wagon train, outfit their party for the journey and then hit the trail. Along the way, they face hundreds of decisions and challenges (and absorb historical facts as if by osmosis). Should they ford Red Vermilion River or pay for a ferry? What should they use to treat cholera? Should they trade five pounds of bacon for a 30-foot length of chain? Should they press on in subzero temperatures or make camp?

This new version completely changes the look and feel of the game with added realism and historical complexity. Kids can now choose among 25 occupations, from baker to wainwright. They can choose one of three trails: Oregon, California, or Mormon. They can choose different kinds of wagons and draft animals, how

JUST THE FACTS

BEST FOR AGES 10-16

★★★★ **for Learning**
Best historical simulation ever

★★★★ **for Looks**
Compelling mix of photorealism and 3-D graphics

★★★★ **for Longevity**
With three trails, the possibilities are endless

Worth Noting

Wonderful to play in teams or a small group. And with your help, kids younger than 10 can handle many of the *Trails*' challenges. (Older versions are also available on floppy disks.)

Macintosh CD-ROM; Windows CD-ROM
About $58
MECC
(800) 685-6322

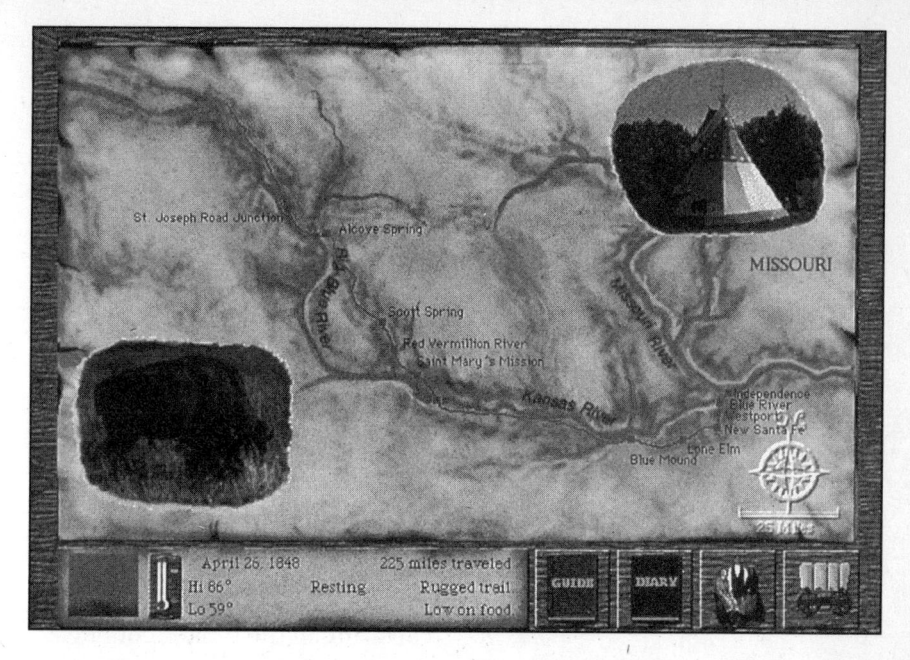

many other wagons and emigrants to travel with, what month and year (from 1840 to 1860) to depart. The endless combination of choices—plus luck and savvy decision-making on the trail—makes every game different and challenging.

What's more, thanks to its realistic sights and sounds, *Oregon Trail II* does a better job than ever of encouraging children to exercise their historical imagination. Kids feel as if they're actually shooting the rapids; walking into camps, forts, or towns; exploring the streets and entering the buildings; conversing with tradespeople, historical figures and other pioneers. The places are a convincing combination of photographic images and 3-D graphics. And the people are a clever blend of real speech, actual video and computer-generated animation.

Players would be well advised to consult the intriguing and detailed guidebook that's filled with advice and information on their itinerary. Otherwise, how will kids know the right quantity of breadstuffs to buy or how heavy a load a team of oxen can pull? Keeping notes in the on-screen diary can also prove useful.

The bottom line: An exceptional program because of its historical challenges and its gameplay strategy.

The Yukon Trail

★ ★ ★ ★

The makers of *The Oregon Trail* have done it again.

This time the year is 1897 and the Klondike gold rush is on. Kids take on the role of stampeders, bound from Seattle for Dawson City. The odds are pretty grim. But *The Yukon Trail* is so riveting that kids are willing to risk all—getting hit by an iceberg, fleeced by cardsharps, capsizing in the rapids, coming down with scurvy or starving when cutthroats make off with their food—in the hope of striking it rich.

As with all the *Trail* titles, the journey itself is fascinating and thought-provoking. Exceptional graphics, original photographs and topographical maps convincingly re-create the feel of turn-of-the-century Alaskan ports, the dreaded White Pass trail (littered with the carcasses of pack animals), a bleak encampment along the shores of Lake Bennett and other landmarks.

Along the way players glean information and advice by "conversing" with more than 50 people, including historical figures like Jack London and Skookum Jim (you'll find out if you make it

---

JUST THE FACTS

BEST FOR AGES 10–16

★★★★ **for Learning**
Kids get a workout in history and game strategy

★★★★ **for Looks**
Compelling mix of photorealism and 3-D graphics; CD-ROM looks best

★★★★ **for Longevity**
Lots of choices make for long-lasting play

Worth Noting
Kids younger than 10 can play with adult help because much of the info needed to succeed is narrated.

Macintosh CD-ROM or floppy; Windows CD-ROM or floppy
About $40–$46
MECC
(800) 685-6322

to Dawson City!) and archetypes like ticket agents, outfitters and saloon keepers.

For added realism, *The Yukon Trail* lets kids "walk" around towns or camps, and enter more than a dozen buildings in their search for information and supplies.

Because of the title's commitment to historical accuracy, kids encounter several gambling games along the trail. You can turn off these games, but we don't recommend it. After all, gambling was a reality in the Klondike and kids will learn a lot by losing!

The bottom line: Kids never seem to get enough of MECC's *Trail* **adventures, so you won't go wrong with more than one title.**

The Amazon Trail

★ ★ ★ ★

Another great *Trail* product, with special appeal for mystery buffs and kids enamored of the rainforest.

For three centuries the Amazon has exerted an irresistible pull on adventurers, and *Amazon Trail* has the same allure for young cyber-explorers. The mission is deceptively simple: find some cinchona (you figure it out!) and take it to the Incan king at the headwaters of the river. Paddling upriver—and going back in time—seem easy enough at first. But kids soon encounter a host of perils: capsizing and being bitten by a pirhana, being cheated by dishonest traders, running out of supplies, fishing for food only to discover the catch is inedible, getting lost in one of the Amazon's many tributaries.

With its skillful combination of photographic backdrops, rainforest illustrations, South American music, maps and more, *Amazon Trail* is as appealing to look at (and listen to) as it is absorbing to play. The best visual touch is the player's perspective: kids navigate through their adventure as if they were seated in a canoe.

Amazon Trail supplies lots of sound and narration to help kids along. But to succeed, players need reading skills (to learn history, biography, zoology, ecology, plant biology and more), strategic thinking and luck!

JUST THE FACTS

BEST FOR AGES 10–16

★★★★ **for Learning**
Kids absorb history and ecology while playing

★★★★ **for Looks**
Compelling mix of photorealism and 3-D graphics; CD-ROM looks best

★★★★ **for Longevity**
Mystery element adds replay value

Macintosh CD-ROM or floppy; Windows CD-ROM or floppy
About $40–$46
MECC
(800) 685-6322

THE BEST TITLES: EXPLORATIONS FOR CURIOUS KIDS • 139

The bottom line: Kids never seem to get enough of MECC's *Trail* **adventures, so you won't go wrong with more than one title.**

Ancient Lands

★ ★

An attractively designed program, more suitable for research than recreation.

Eleven-year-old Andrew hit the nail on the head: "It's good if you want facts. But you can't play with it for an hour and have a tremendous amount of fun."

Like *Dangerous Creatures* (Page 160), *Ancient Lands* is an upscale database combining well-written text, excellent illustrations, video clips and animations. This CD-ROM gives kids lots of ways to plunge into the annals of ancient Egypt, Greece and Rome. They can zero in on a topic by using the index. Better still, they can choose one of three thematic approaches: Work & Play, Monuments & Mysteries or People & Politics. But for children the best route back in time is to step into someone else's shoes by choosing a slave, a soldier or another character as a guide.

Because this story-telling approach "personalizes" and extends what might otherwise be a casual dip into a vast database, *Ancient Lands* has more staying power than some interactive reference titles.

JUST THE FACTS

BEST FOR AGES 8 & UP

★★ **for Learning**
Facts about life in ancient Egypt, Greece, Rome

★★★ **for Looks**
Good multimedia mix

★ **for Longevity**
No challenges, but nice for occasional browsing or school reports

Macintosh CD-ROM; Windows CD-ROM
About $60
Microsoft
(800) 228-6270

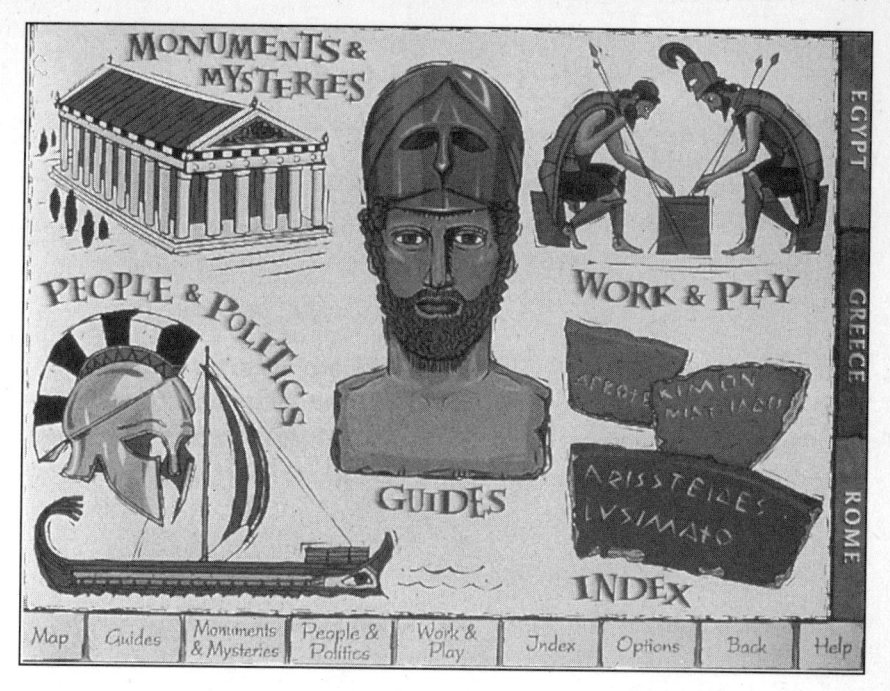

The bottom line: Appealing to history buffs, but don't expect kids to return to *Ancient Lands* the way they do to a *Trail* program or a *Carmen* title.

Informational programs like *Ancient Lands* may take on new interest for your kids when you take an interest. "The kids don't want me to 'do' the software with them," explained Andrew's mother. "But I find I can serve as a catalyst, by using it on my own and calling them over when I get excited about something."

Wrath of the Gods

★ ★

More fun than *Bullfinch's Mythology*, this adventure game immerses kids in the strange world of immortals and mortals, oracles and minotaurs. *Wrath of the Gods* **doesn't teach anything, *per se*, but kids absorb information about ancient Greece as they play.**

Players take on the role of the abandoned grandson of King Minos. The goal: find the lad's true parents and claim the throne. At every step kids encounter challenges and puzzles borrowed from the classic adventures of Greek heroes. Success depends on ingenuity, a knowledge of Greek myths and persistence.

For younger players who may be in the dark about Hades or other things mythological, trips to the Oracle of Delphi and forays into an information section are essential for garnering useful facts and clues. Playing with friends or family is also helpful—and more fun.

Visually, this program plays neat tricks with multimedia technology. Animated actors stroll across photorealistic backdrops of the Greek countryside. While their bodies move with the angular stiffness of video-game characters, they have the faces of real actors captured in video! Strange-looking, but with an odd, otherworldly appeal for kids.

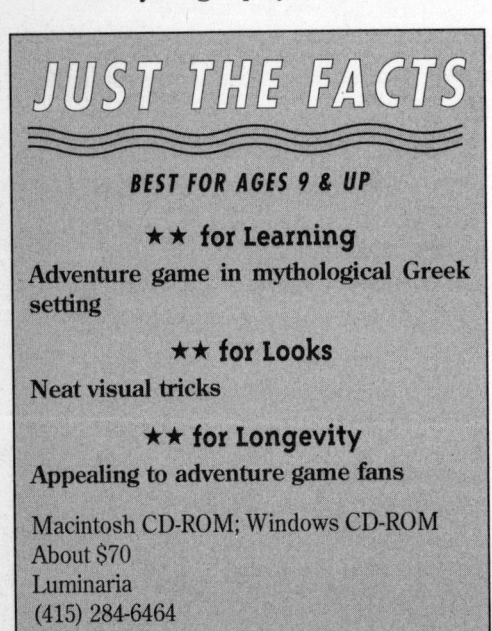

JUST THE FACTS

BEST FOR AGES 9 & UP

★★ **for Learning**
Adventure game in mythological Greek setting

★★ **for Looks**
Neat visual tricks

★★ **for Longevity**
Appealing to adventure game fans

Macintosh CD-ROM; Windows CD-ROM
About $70
Luminaria
(415) 284-6464

The bottom line: The role-playing adventure will appeal to kids, the mythology to their parents!

Good software can have a far-reaching effect on kids—sparking new interests and prompting them to learn more—as one family's experience with *Wrath of the Gods* shows.

This program was a real hit with 10-year-old Brian. He loved playing the role of the hero, doing "the stuff that Jason and the heroes do," and seeing how his decisions and strategy shaped the game and his fate.

He even bought and read an entire book about Greek mythology (to his mother's surprise and pleasure). As Brian explained: "You should know a lot about Greek myths. Or else you have to ask the oracle way too much."

Leonardo the Inventor

★ ★

If the only Leonardo your kids know is a Ninja turtle, consider this CD-ROM. *Leonardo the Inventor* is beautiful to look at and intriguing to explore. In fact, it's one of the most striking reference products we've seen.

From the moment we heard the strains of Renaissance music and saw the graceful illustrations against a parchment-paper backdrop, we were hooked. And as soon as the children saw the Mona Lisa roll her eyes (among other short, zany animations), they were hooked, too.

The real beauty of this product is that it plays on things kids already know to lure them back in time. Starting with familiar objects like snorkels and parachutes and helicopters and life preservers, this program draws kids into discovering how Leonardo's sketches and notes foreshadowed those inventions (and others) hundreds of years before they were successfully built.

For every invention, the program provides a short, informative narration and reproduces a notebook page and sketch, often animated. Then kids can choose to hear a pertinent quote from Leonardo and a narrated video clip describing the similarities or differences between Leonardo's sketch and its counterpart today. The product also offers a look at Leonardo's paintings, a timeline that charts not only Leonardo's activities but also other important developments in the world, and a

JUST THE FACTS

BEST FOR AGES 8 & UP

★★ **for Learning**
Insight into Leonardo's inventions and modern counterparts

★★★ **for Looks**
Beautiful to look at, intriguing to explore

★ **for Longevity**
Great for occasional browsing

Macintosh CD-ROM; Windows CD-ROM
About $50
Future Vision Multimedia
(800) 472-8777

short biography. A bibliography suggesting further reading is a nice touch because *Leonardo the Inventor* is sure to pique your child's curiosity.

But as 8-year-old Jason told us: "It's interesting but I don't use it a lot; it's not a 'playing' program."

The bottom line: An innovative and striking multimedia reference work. But its click-watch-and-read format is not as compelling over time as programs with a game, adventure or quest.

Stowaway!
Stephen Biesty's Incredible Cross-Sections

★

Stowaway! **does a nice job of transforming Stephen Biesty's** *Man-Of-War* **book of into a full-scale, inside-out exploration of a 16th century galleon.**

Kids can roam around the 550-ton ship, clicking their way into all the decks and everything they contain. Or they can explore the galleon from the vantage point of one of 12 crewmen, from the captain to the cook, surgeon to midshipman. Their stories are presented as slender books and narrated—complete with British accent and a touch of drama—by each character. As kids make their way around the ship, fun facts abound: why shipboard toilets are called heads, how to get maggots out of biscuits, how crewmen cleaned their clothes without soap, why British sailors were nicknamed "limeys."

A *Where's Waldo?*-like type of game also helps engage youngsters: there's a stowaway on board and kids must find the 10 places where he's hiding.

In general, the additions in the CD-ROM are worthwhile. The illustrations are fascinating and beautifully drawn. The sound effects heighten the sense of being there. The glossary is gen-

---

JUST THE FACTS

BEST FOR AGES 8-12

★ **for Learning**
Facts aplenty for kids intrigued by the subject

★★★ **for Looks**
True to the book; distinctive DK Multimedia design

★ **for Longevity**
OK for occasional browsing

Macintosh CD-ROM; Windows CD-ROM
About $60
DK Multimedia
(800) 225-3362

uinely useful since shipboard vocabulary (whipstaff, jardines and such) can be pretty obscure. Some of the animations, however, are sophomoric—the captain skewering a rat as it scuttles across the dining table, an ailing seaman vomiting in sick bay.

The bottom line: Once they click their way into every deck and find every hiding place, will kids come back to this program? Maybe not—unless you weave related activities and projects around this program like visiting museums, watching documentaries, reading *Treasure Island***, and the like.**

Recess in Greece

★

A cartoon romp through ancient Greece that's interrupted by too many quizzes.

The story: An impertinent, don't-know-much-about-history monkey named Morgan is sucked through the classroom blackboard into ancient Greece. Suddenly, everyone thinks he's Odysseus. And to get back to the 20th century, he has to help the Greeks win the Trojan War.

By clicking around the title's 17 screens, kids can pick up a smattering of Greek mythology, history and geography, plus insights into the Greek influence on word origins, mathematics and music. At intervals kids encounter quizzes: Word Builder, for example, tests kids on the Greek roots in English words. Magic Squares challenges kids to make three rows, columns, and diagonals each add up to 15.

Kids must successfully complete two multiple choice quizzes or the adventure grinds to a halt. The problem is there's no way to adjust the difficulty level of the quizzes (although kids can consult the know-it-all Athena for help). So, some kids may get bogged down in the quizzes and never finish the adventure.

The bottom line: An irreverent journey through Greek mythology. The interactive cartoon and smart-alecky Morgan have kid appeal, but the quizzes don't.

JUST THE FACTS

BEST FOR AGES 7–12

★ **for Learning**
Plenty of facts wrapped in a cartoon adventure through ancient Greece

★★ **for Looks**
Colorful, bold graphics

★ **for Longevity**
Games can derail the adventure

Macintosh CD-ROM; Windows CD-ROM
About $35
Morgan Interactive
(415) 693-9596

... INTO SCIENCE, NATURE & BEYOND

Life Sciences, Outer Space, Wildlife & More

The range of software in this section is dazzling. Your kids will find animals from arachnids to zebras, voyages to the bottom of the sea or the outer reaches of the solar system, anatomical adventures, close encounters with the laws of physics and much more.

Many of these titles provide good-looking ways of browsing through factual information. Others approach learning through simulations and games. The best ones let kids poke around, experiment and experience the "Ah ha!" of scientific discovery for themselves.

RATINGS	TITLES	AGES
★★★★	Sammy's Science House (Pages 150-151)	3–5
★★★★	Planetary Taxi (Pages 152-153)	7–12
★★★★	What's the Secret? (Pages 154-155)	7–12
★★★	Odell Down Under (Page 156)	8–12
★★	Safari (Page 157)	8 & Up
★★	Widget Workshop (Pages 158-159)	10–12
★★	Dangerous Creatures (Pages 160-161)	8 & Up
★★	Scavenger Hunt Adventure Series (Pages 162-163)	7–12
★	The Magic School Bus Series (Pages 164-165)	6–10
★	The Knowledge Adventure Series (Pages 166-167)	3–12

Sammy's Science House

★ ★ ★ ★

Another great collection of learning games from the *Millie's Math House* and *Bailey's Book House* people. This one provides a charming playspace for little kids who are curious about the world around them.

The five activities in *Sammy's Science House* strike the perfect balance: freedom to poke around just to see what happens plus many playful opportunities to practice skills like observation, classification, comparison and sequencing.

Our favorites are Weather Machine, Acorn Pond and Make-A-Movie. Children tinkering with temperature, wind and precipitation in the Weather Machine can discover what it takes to make a blizzard—and giggle at the animated results. Acorn Pond lets kids explore seasonal changes in habitat, animal growth and behavior. In Make-A-Movie kids figure out the logical sequence for natural phenomena like a sunset or an eclipse. When they drag the stages of an event into the right order, they can play it as a movie—forward or backward.

The adventuring that *Sammy's*

JUST THE FACTS

BEST FOR AGES 3–5

★★★★ **for Learning**
Hands-on experience with scientific thinking; skills include classification, comparison, sequencing

★★★★ **for Looks**
Imaginative, age-appropriate graphics

★★★★ **for Longevity**
Kids come back time and again

Worth Noting
Other preschool titles from Edmark include *Millie's Math House*, *Bailey's Book House*, *Trudy's Time and Place House*, and *Thinkin' Things Collection 1*.

Macintosh CD-ROM or floppy; Windows, DOS CD-ROM or floppy
About $35
Edmark
(800) 691-2985

Science House encourages *away from* the computer is a real plus. The program features a wonderful little field notebook about Acorn Pond, with simple sketches and just the right amount of information for 3–5-year-olds. Kids can print it and take it on excursions into the backyard, the park or beyond. It's just right for kids who are inveterate collectors of "stuff." And what kids aren't?

The bottom line: An all-time favorite for this age group—even if they already have other Edmark programs.

Planetary Taxi

★ ★ ★ ★

Thanks to NASA's planetary probes and space launches, lots of astronomy titles feature still photos and video footage of the solar system. But *Planetary Taxi* is hands down the best one for kids. Designers Margo Nanny and Robert Mohl have an unerring instinct for how kids play and how kids learn—and how to dish up an astronomy adventure that satisfies their knack for both.

Here's the story: Kids drive a taxi cab along a (correctly scaled) highway through the solar system, picking up as many passengers (and tips) as they can, and figuring out their destinations. The passengers are likeably quirky, like the hayseed with a Midwestern twang: "I'm raising my prize pig Wilbur for 4H Club, and I want him to win first place as the heaviest pig ever. He already weighs 100 pounds on Earth. But that's not enough, so I'm thinking, 'Why not get Wilbur weighed on another planet?' Take me to the planet where Wilbur will weigh the most."

As the requests get more challenging, players can easily dip into the title's vast fund of information—some of it written, some narrated, more in the form of photos, video clips, animations,

JUST THE FACTS

BEST FOR AGES 7–12

★★★★ **for Learning**
Hands-on insights into the solar system; skills include interpreting graphs, charts, database information

★★★★ **for Looks**
Inventive graphics and video "transport" kids into space

★★★ **for Longevity**
Wacky characters and a great storyline hook kids

Macintosh CD-ROM; Windows CD-ROM
About $40
Voyager
(800) 337-4989

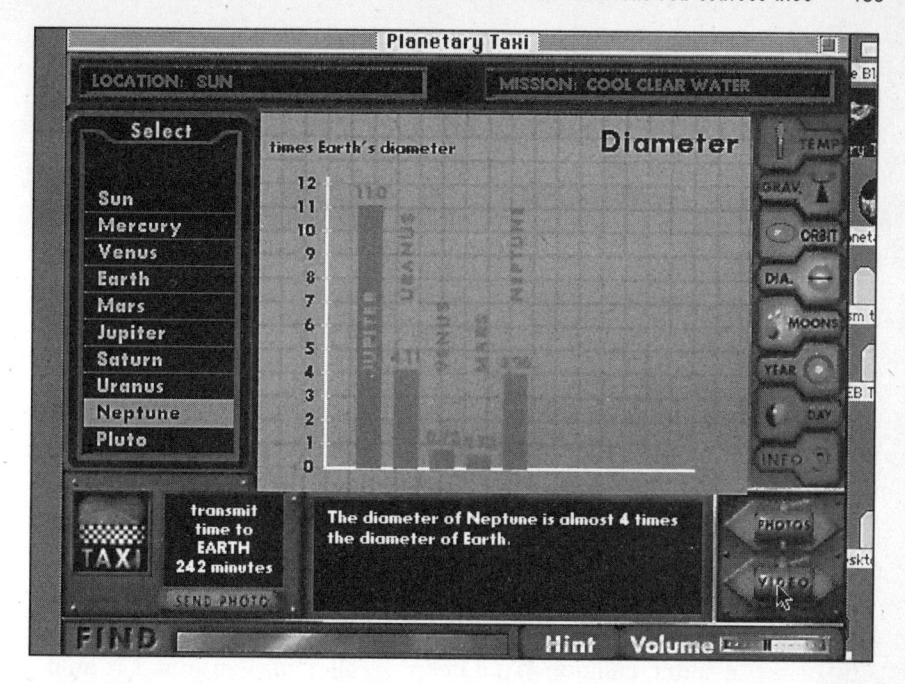

charts and graphs—by clicking buttons on the cab's dashboard. Or they can get a hint from Rita, the wisecracking but kindly dispatcher with a New York accent.

Visually inventive and cleverly designed, even adults will enjoy playing this game. But it's not for everyone: fast-action kids may not like the pace.

The bottom line: Humor and hands-on discovery make *Planetary Taxi* **one of the best of the outer space programs.**

What's the Secret?

★ ★ ★ ★

What's the secret to great kids' software? You'll find the answer by clicking around this CD-ROM. It's the best science discovery program we've seen. *What's the Secret?* **gives kids a real feel for doing . . . and understanding . . . and enjoying . . . science.**

What's the Secret? invites kids to explore the answers to 12 familiar but intriguing questions, plus a host of related ones: When a train passes by, why does the sound change? What keeps a roller coaster going? (Can it fall off? Why do I get queasy?) Why do bears hibernate? What makes my heart beat? (In answering that question, by the way, *What's the Secret?* does a far better job than any of the dozens of anatomy titles available.)

Playing with *What's the Secret?* is a little like taking a field trip. But when kids get interested in something, they can stick around (instead of sticking to the teacher's timetable) and delve as deeply as they want. Each topic holds a little universe of information that kids can explore in several ways. There's simple but accurate text to read. There are real-life scientists to listen to, illustrations to scrutinize, animations to probe, video clips to watch and fun experiments to conduct, both on the computer and off. Along the way, *What's the Secret?* poses

---

JUST THE FACTS

BEST FOR AGES 7–12

★★★★ **for Learning**
Wonderful questions invite science discovery

★★★★ **for Looks**
Dynamic graphics help pique curiosity

★★★★ **for Longevity**
There's always more to explore

Macintosh CD-ROM; Windows CD-ROM
About $60
3M Software
(612) 737-3249

lots of related questions, so kids can take off on as many excursions as they want.

What's the Secret? does a great job of making meaningful connections between science and other disciplines. Take the What Makes My Heart Beat? area, for example. Kids might find themselves experimenting with the systolic and diastolic components of blood pressure. Or, they might find themselves reading about how (and why) the word "heart" pervades the English language.

The bottom line: The best software to get kids really excited about science. Based on the award-winning science TV show *Newton's Apple,* *What's the Secret?* **is part adventure, part live-action lab and 100 percent terrific.**

Odell Down Under

★ ★ ★

Odell Down Under **transforms 9-year-olds into sharks. In this fast-paced simulation, kids become inhabitants of Australia's Great Barrier Reef and learn what it takes to survive.**

Although they can choose from more than 60 sea creatures, kids invariably start out as sharks. (Is this a reflection of our competitive culture? A sophisticated instinct for survival? Or kids showing their true colors as vicious beasts?) Players can also create a fish and experiment with the impact of different attributes (speed, size, coloration, defense strategies like poison or electric shocks) in their quest for survival. Staying alive—and moving up the food chain—is not easy, and kids must learn quickly from experience (or the help of the field guide) in order to live long enough to become Reef Ruler.

This game is especially fun to play with friends, siblings or parents. And, naturally, there's an added attraction when your kid gets to eat you.

The bottom line: A good marine life simulation game from the same folks who brought you the *Trail* titles (*Oregon, Amazon, Yukon*).

JUST THE FACTS

BEST FOR AGES 8–12

★★★ for Learning
Survival game offers hands-on insights into marine biology

★★ for Looks
Colorful animation, no video or photos

★★★ for Longevity
Kids keep on trying to survive

Macintosh floppy; DOS floppy
About $28
MECC
(800) 685-6322

Safari

★ ★

A mesmerizing collection of wildlife photographs, like a glossy coffee-table book. Good when your kids are in the mood just to look. Not so good when they need to look up information.

No other product we've shown to kids has gotten so many "Oohs" and "Aahs" as *Safari*. It's built around 800 or so breathtaking photographs of the Masai Mara National Reserve and Serengeti National Park taken by Jonathan Scott, who also provides narration.

Kids can look at *Safari*'s photos in six different ways. They can go on safari, take 1 of 11 guided tours, peruse an alphabetical field guide and more. Whatever their choice, photos fill the screen. Pictures continue to appear, slide-show fashion, until kids click on a photo. Then successive layers of information pop up. Unfortunately, the look and organization of the text doesn't compare to the quality of the photography. And video clips, while interesting, are disappointingly fuzzy.

The bottom line: A good alternative to TV because it's so beautiful and thoughtfully narrated, but not really convenient as a reference tool.

JUST THE FACTS

BEST FOR AGES 8 & UP

★ for Learning
Kids can learn a lot from the narration, but the text is "unfriendly"

★★★ for Looks
Software is a showcase for stellar wildlife photography

★ for Longevity
Captivating at first, then interest tapers off

Worth Noting
Safari includes a collection of sounds, from baboons foraging to zebras braying.

Windows CD-ROM
About $40
Medio
(800) 788-3866

Widget Workshop

★ ★

An intriguing hands-on science kit, for use on the computer and off. *Widget Workshop* lets kids devise gadgets and puzzles and "what if?" experiments by connecting up widgets and seeing what happens. It pushes them to think harder than most other software. But it's so challenging that many kids will need your help to take advantage of everything it offers.

In *Widget Workshop*, kids build things simply by clicking among a wide array of widget parts—like timers, sounds and switches— dragging them into an on-screen workspace and clicking to connect them all. Click a keypad widget, for example, and click again to connect it to the solar system "superpart." Click and connect a "multiplier." Then, push the green "Go" button and watch the results. Kids jump right into this kind of trial-and-error discovery without hesitation (although our testers recommend working through the software tutorial, too).

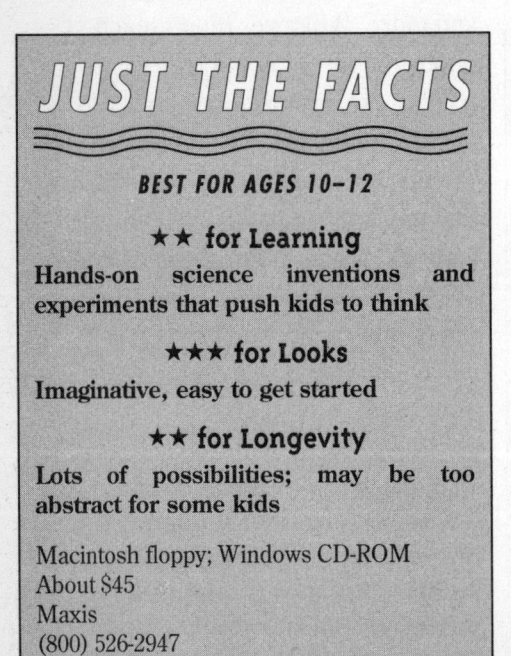

Beside making their own inventions, kids can tackle 1 of 25 challenging puzzle widgets or 30 experiments in the Workshop Activities book. Using both the software and the tools packaged with it—magnifier, thermometer, spinning top and more—kids can explore distance, speed, gravity,

JUST THE FACTS

BEST FOR AGES 10-12

★★ **for Learning**
Hands-on science inventions and experiments that push kids to think

★★★ **for Looks**
Imaginative, easy to get started

★★ **for Longevity**
Lots of possibilities; may be too abstract for some kids

Macintosh floppy; Windows CD-ROM
About $45
Maxis
(800) 526-2947

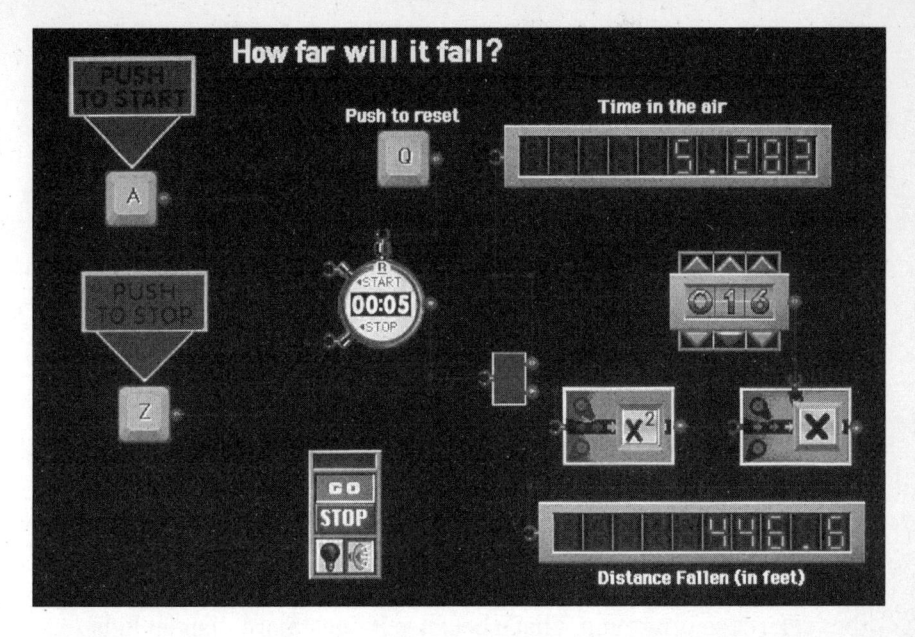

sound, light and weather, computer programming and a lot of math. Starting with simple constructions, *Widget Workshop* takes kids into abstractions like digital data, logic gates, flow charts and mathematical formulas.

The bottom line: A good program for children who love mental challenges and for families that like to explore science together.

Dangerous Creatures

★ ★

Despite considerable visual appeal, this program falls prey to the dangers of click-watch-and-listen databases. *Dangerous Creatures* **shows. It tells. But it doesn't provide much of an opportunity for kids to creatively apply new-found facts in compelling activities.**

Nevertheless, *Dangerous Creatures* has a bit more staying power than other reference programs. That's because it does more than let kids wander around aimlessly. Of course, they can go it alone, encountering animals by clicking on atlas, habitat, weapons or index icons. But they can also follow one of several "guides" who chart different paths through the title's potentially overwhelming amount of information, providing a commentary that puts animal "fun facts" in a more meaningful context.

Better still are the storytelling guides who offer an imaginative perspective on animals in the database by recounting the fables of ancient peoples. Kids can hear legendary explanations for how the platypus came to have the bill of a duck and fur of a rat . . . why rhinos are bad-tempered . . . why owls and cougars can see at night.

The activities in *Dangerous Creatures* are less "test-what-you've-learned" quizzes than "get-up-close-and-personal" games. I See You, for example, lets children "see" in the way various ani-

---

JUST THE FACTS

BEST FOR AGES 8 & UP

★★ **for Learning**
Facts about big cats and other creatures kids love; beginning reference skills

★★★ **for Looks**
Good multimedia mix

★ **for Longevity**
No challenges, but good for occasional browsing

Macintosh CD-ROM; Windows CD-ROM
About $60
Microsoft
(800) 228-6270

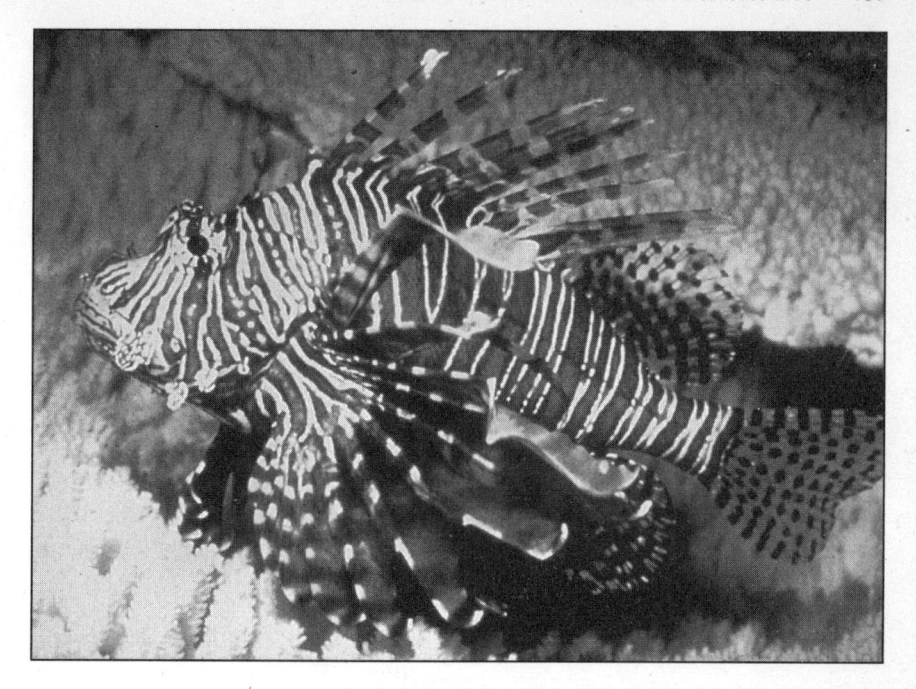

mals experience vision. Nonetheless, there's little reason for kids to revisit these games once they've played them all.

Kids are likely to get more mileage out of *Dangerous Creatures* in school, where thoughtful assignments can encourage them to use the database effectively in problem solving. At home, it's up to you to get your money's worth.

The bottom line: A well-researched, good-looking database, but don't expect kids to use it as much as a program with a challenge, quest or wealth of activities.

The Scavenger Hunt Adventure Series
Scavenger Hunt: Africa
Scavenger Hunt: Oceans

★ ★

An intelligent and challenging game with an innovative look and an offbeat sense of humor. But kids may find it too time-consuming to pursue on their own.

Scavenger Hunt: Africa is the first in this series. *Scavenger Hunt: Oceans* is the second. Also planned are adventures in the rest of the continents and the Arctic. Each game works the same way: kids get a set of clues and then "hunt" animals in a thoroughly modern (and politically correct) way, by photographing them.

As they scroll through a panoramic setting, kids absorb facts about animals and their habitats. Clicking on an animal produces information about life in the wild. The more kids click, the more they can learn. And the animals themselves tell their stories with a variety of accents, songs, raps and rhymes that gives each one a distinct and memorable personality.

This Africa has a vivid, storybook look. (Who says good software has to be photorealistic?)

JUST THE FACTS

BEST FOR AGES 7–12

★★ **for Learning**
Kids hone reasoning skills as they track inventive clues

★★★ **for Looks**
Unique artistic techniques

★★ **for Longevity**
Kids love scavenger hunts

Macintosh CD-ROM; Windows CD-ROM
About $40
Swede
(800) 545-7677

THE BEST TITLES: EXPLORATIONS FOR CURIOUS KIDS • 163

Against watercolor landscapes, animals stand out like torn-paper collage figures by children's illustrator Eric Carle. (The zebra's white stripes look like faded newsprint, for example.) Ambient sound, featuring roaring elephants, gibbering monkeys, distant drums and the like, adds to the "you-are-there" atmosphere.

Scavenger Hunt: Africa works best when kids, friends, or parents play together. On their own, kids can get frustrated. (Sometimes they can play for 30 minutes without finding an animal to match a clue!) When adults join in, we find that kids are more willing to persist. And happily, the animals' antics are sophisticated enough to keep parents amused, too.

The bottom line: This program may have more staying power than database-style programs because of the challenge it presents and its unique art.

The Magic School Bus Series
The Magic School Bus Explores the Human Body
The Magic School Bus Visits the Solar System

★

As long-time fans of Ms. Frizzle, we wanted to love these CD-ROMs. Instead, we were blitzed by technology overkill. After a couple of "Wows," the products' over-abundant, time-consuming special effects simply get in the way of a good adventure.

The Magic School Bus adventures were inspired by the popular books by Joanna Cole and Bruce Degen. Kids join the eccentric Ms. Frizzle as she magically transports her students on field trips into the body, under the sea, into space and to other ordinarily inaccessible places. The books weave science facts into entertaining stories, told from an irreverent kid-perspective and spiced with 8-year-old humor.

The Magic School Bus Explores the Human Body, the first in the series, uses a combination of dazzling 3-D animations, illustrations, dialog and games to tell the story of how a busload of kids winds up inside their classmate Arnold's body. Kids are in the driver's seat—literally—controlling the action through an enormous assortment of buttons and gadgets spread across the dashboard of the magic bus. Players encounter lots of information as the bus tumbles through Arnold,

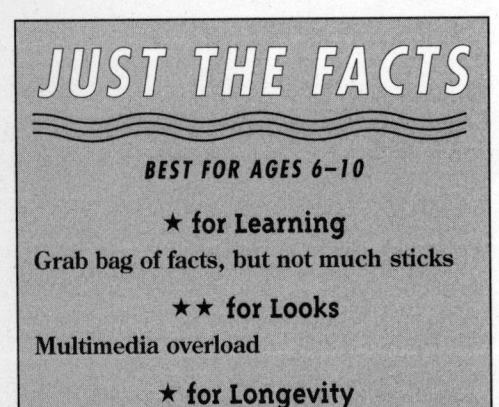

JUST THE FACTS

BEST FOR AGES 6–10

★ **for Learning**
Grab bag of facts, but not much sticks

★★ **for Looks**
Multimedia overload

★ **for Longevity**
Once or twice through, and that's it

Macintosh CD-ROM; Windows CD-ROM
About $50
Microsoft
(800) 228-6270

and lots of mediocre games. But the experience is so disjointed that it's hard to learn much.

The Magic School Bus Visits the Solar System is a bit better. The story: Ms. Frizzle has disappeared into outer space and her students are on their own in their bus-turned-spaceship. Kids have to play games to win tokens to get clues to find her.

Through the windshield of the bus, kids see real fly-by videos from NASA and the Jet Propulsion Laboratory. Student reports have an appealing combination of still photographs, computer-animated drawings, fun facts in kid's handwriting, plus the voices of real kids explaining why they want to visit a particular planet.

The title's best feature is the experimentation players can do on each planet they visit. Kids can get a sense of Jupiter's tremendous size, for example, by filling it up with other planets. (It would hold 1,402 Earths!)

The title's worst feature is the gameplay. There are nine games, practically all the same. And they don't call for any solar-system smarts, just fast action on the space bar and arrow keys.

The bottom line: Once the novelty has worn off, there aren't sufficient challenges to bring kids back.

The Knowledge Adventure Series

3-D Dinosaur Adventure (3–8)   Bug Adventure (3–8)
Undersea Adventure (5–12)   3-D Body Adventure (8–12)
Aviation Adventure (8–12)   Space Adventure II (8–12)
Science Adventure II (8–12)

★

Riding the wave of dinosaur-mania stirred up by *Jurassic Park*, *Dinosaur Adventure* has brought lots of attention to Knowledge Adventure and its programs. All of them serve up information with a blast of multimedia. But after the initial "Wows," they're not as challenging as science titles can be.

The Knowledge Adventure programs offer an entertaining way to explore topics high in kid-appeal like airplanes, insects and outer space. There are buttons to push, videos and photographs to watch, sound effects to hear, special 3-D glasses to wear and games to play. Kids can zoom instantly from one topic to related subjects with a click of the mouse, charting their own path through a visual database of information.

So why only one star? Because once the thrill of the gee-whiz effects like 3-D graphics and full-motion video wears off, these titles are not particularly com-

JUST THE FACTS

BEST FOR AGES 3–12

★ **for Learning**
Fosters random acquisition of facts

★★ **for Looks**
Gee-whiz technical effects, too much fuzzy video

★ **for Longevity**
Too much looking, not enough doing

Macintosh CD-ROM; Windows CD-ROM or floppy
About $45–$55
Knowledge Adventure
(800) 542-4240

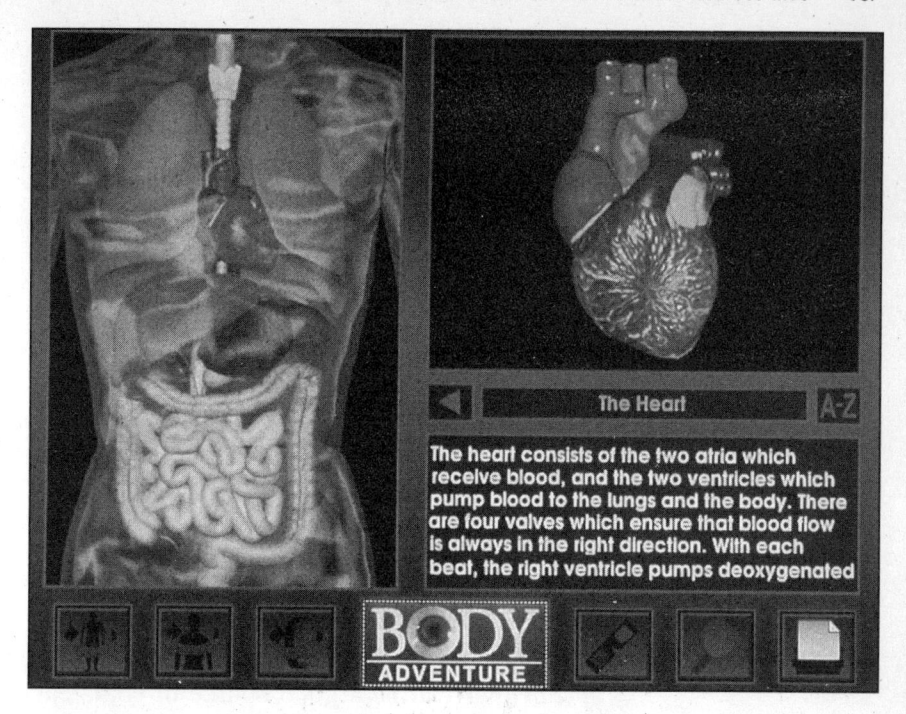

pelling. They don't engross kids like exploration programs that pose adventures (the *Carmen* series, for example), challenges (like the *SimCity* series), or experiments (like the *What's the Secret?* series).

As 12-year-old Laura commented: "It's more like a scientific report than a game. You can't really do anything but look at it."

The bottom line: Good for kids who want more information about their particular passions, from dinosaurs to bugs to planes.

SIX

THE BEST TITLES: FUN & GAMES

Adventures, Quests, Simulations, Strategy & Problem-solving

A child's life is filled with fun and games, and the computer can be a good source of both. The titles in this section are selected with fun as their most important element. But that's not all your kids will find here. There's mystery, intrigue, challenge, adventure. And you'll be pleased to know that many of these game programs are as demanding and thought-provoking as any in the *Guide*.

The universe of computer games is vast. We've narrowed it considerably by avoiding video games, programs that contain violence and titles that make little or no demands on kids' brain power.

And just because these titles are games, don't expect them to be easy. Many of the games we've selected are problem-solving adventures. And problem-solving is hard work.

RATINGS	TITLES	AGES
★★★★	Myst (Pages 170-171)	9 & Up
★★★★	SimCity 2000 (Pages 172-173)	10 & Up
	SimTower (Page 172)	10 & Up
	SimIsle (Page 173)	10 & Up
	SimAnt (Page 173)	10 & Up
	SimEarth (Page 173)	10 & Up
	SimFarm (Page 173)	10 & Up

RATINGS	TITLES	AGES
	SimCity Classic (Page 173)	10 & Up
	SimTown (Page 173)	8–12
★★★★	Freddi Fish and the Case of the Missing Kelp Seeds (Pages 174-175)	3–6
★★★★	Putt-Putt Saves the Zoo (Pages 176-177)	3–5
★★★★	At Bat (Pages 178-179)	7–12
★★★	Klik & Play (Pages 180-181)	10 & Up
★★★	Gahan Wilson's The Ultimate Haunted House (Pages 182-183)	8–12
★★	The Eagle Eye Mysteries Series (Pages 184-185)	7–10
★★	GeoSafari (Pages 186-187)	8–12

Why do kids love simulations? "Because I really count and I can make something different happen every time I play," according to 10-year-old Anita.

A computer simulation creates a place or an experience that models the real thing. In the world of the simulation, kids call the shots. Every choice they make has consequences. Every decision affects what happens. When kids build houses in *SimTown*, for example, they boost the town's population—which in turn increases the need for jobs, schools, roads and food supplies. And that means more decisions to be made by the players. When they simulate life as a fish in *Odell Down Under*, split-second decisions about what to eat and where to swim determine whether they live or die.

We think simulations like these are a great way for kids to learn by doing. As kids experiment, they figure out what works. And on a computer they can immediately test their theories and see the results.

Myst

★ ★ ★ ★

The best adventure kids can have on a computer. *Myst* is a journey through time and space in a strange fantasy world filled with breathtaking 3-D graphics. Or, in the words of one of our 10-year-old reviewers: "A mystery with weird things you have to figure out."

JUST THE FACTS

BEST FOR AGES 9 & UP

★★★★ **for Learning**
Challenging puzzles, strategy and problem-solving

★★★★ **for Looks**
Stunning 3-D vision of an imaginary world

★★★★ **for Longevity**
Lure of solving a mystery, plus a vast world to explore

Worth Noting
Younger kids may enjoy *Cosmic Osmo*, an early click-and-discover program from the creators of *Myst*. Graphics are primitive by comparison but the spirit of adventure is similar.

Macintosh CD-ROM; Windows CD-ROM
About $55
Broderbund
(800) 521-6125

Since its release in 1993, *Myst* has developed an unprecedented following. And with good reason. It's got an intriguing story. There's a mystery to solve. There's a vast, visually detailed world to explore. There are photo-realistic graphics, and hours of great gameplay. Both kids and adults love the sensation of moving first-person through a changing landscape and collecting scattered clues in search of the final answer. Along the way, they encounter logic puzzles (complicated codes or number combinations, detailed sequences of actions) which they must solve to move to other locations or time periods.

According to one young aficionado, the trick to playing *Myst* is this: "You have to be willing to keep trying new things." Kids use other strategies to make progress through the game as well. Some play with a parent, many share clues among a network of *Myst*-playing peers, and others dip into a book called *The Official Strategy Guide*.

The opposite of a video action game, *Myst* is sophisticated and unhurried. It demands patience and endurance and problem-solving. And until they uncover the mystery, older kids revisit the world of *Myst* again and again.

The bottom line: A unique computer experience for kids who enjoy mysteries and adventure games.

SimCity 2000

★ ★ ★ ★

Intensely involving and thought-provoking, *SimCity 2000* **lets kids play masters of the universe as they design, build, manage and destroy cities. If they play wisely, the city thrives and grows; if not, it falls into a spiral of decline.**

As urban planners, kids use *SimCity*'s tools to build roads, railroads, homes, businesses, factories, stores, schools, airports, parks and more. Acting as mayor, they set zoning regulations, levy taxes and cope with disasters like fires, earthquakes or floods. In the process they learn firsthand about the complex interdependencies of urban life. "If people don't move to your city, you don't get enough taxes. If you run out of money, you need to issue bonds," explained Edward, who at age 11 has already mastered a strategy of lower taxes, improved services, and expanding debt. (Available as Macintosh, Windows, DOS floppy; $50.)

SimCity aficionados should also check out *SimTower* (Macintosh floppy; $40). The principle of the game is the same, but this time the challenge is to create a vertical city. High-rise twists include leasing space for offices, shops, con-

JUST THE FACTS

BEST FOR AGES 10 & UP

★★★★ **for Learning**
Hands-on insights into real-world trade-offs

★★★ **for Looks**
Fascinating detail and realistic audio

★★★★ **for Longevity**
Endless possibilities, new challenges as your child grows

Worth Noting

For *SimCity* junkies, there are lots of strategy books available, plus tips and support from Maxis via its bulletin board and its forums on on-line services.

Formats vary for different titles; see review for details
About $25–$55
Maxis
(800) 526-2947

dos, and hotels while managing elevators, garbage collection, parking, and other services. Much to their delight, kids can also follow the daily lives of the residents—called Sims—who populate their Tower.

Since these are sophisticated simulations, kids may need some help getting started.

The bottom line: The *Sim* titles are the best there are for hands-on learning and thought-provoking challenge.

If your kids (or you or your spouse) crave the stimulation of another simulation, there are plenty of options.

SimIsle (DOS CD-ROM; $45) lets kids balance economic exploitation and ecological protection in a cluster of rainforest islands. This program has a great new feature: kids can send agents, each with a different field of expertise, to carry out their orders around the islands.

In *SimFarm* (Macintosh, Windows, DOS floppy; $30), players plant crops and wrestle with financing, harvesting, climate, natural disasters and more. In *SimEarth* (Macintosh, DOS floppy; $30), they get to create a planet. Families who occasionally have a real-life ant farm on the kitchen table should try *SimAnt* (Macintosh, Windows, DOS floppy; $25). *SimCity Classic*, the original version of *SimCity*, is still available (Macintosh, Windows, or DOS floppy for about $25). *SimTown* adapts the *SimCity* concept for 8–12-year-olds. Kids create a town by laying roads, building parks and schools, positioning the hardware store and movie theater, and constructing neighborhoods. The goal: Keep resident Sims happy by balancing homes and businesses, providing services, and maintaining adequate resources like water, food and crops. The graphics are larger and more whimsical; homes range from pagodas to castles, and the Chinese restaurant looks like a giant take-out carton. (Windows and Macintosh CD-ROMs, about $40.)

Freddi Fish and the Case of the Missing Kelp Seeds

★ ★ ★ ★

One of the best little-kid adventures we've seen. The graphics are great. The characters are sweet yet spunky. And there's just the right mix of challenge and fun.

The story: Grandma Grouper's kelp seeds have disappeared, and without them the whole fish population is doomed. "Don't worry Grandma. I'll find your kelp seeds!" Freddi exclaims. And with that, the brave heroine and her sidekick Luther lead kids on a treasure hunt they will return to again and again.

Even though Freddi and Luther are doing the swimming, kids love this game because they're controlling the action. Kids decide where Freddi and Luther go and what they do. It's up to them to figure out ways around obstacles and out of predicaments—how to rescue Fiddler Crab from the trap, get past Eddie Eel (who fiercely guards the cave's entrance) and find a pearl for old King Crab.

Scattered bottles hold notes that guide Freddi and Luther in the right direction, but the journey is never simple. Kids quickly learn that objects they see along the way may serve some impor-

JUST THE FACTS

BEST FOR AGES 3–6

★★★ **for Learning**
Kids figure what to do and how to do it

★★★★ **for Looks**
Hollywood-quality animation

★★★★ **for Longevity**
Being in control is tremendously satisfying

Worth Noting
Freddi fans may like the *Putt-Putt* adventures, too.

Windows CD-ROM
About $40
Humongous
(206) 485-1212

tant purpose later. Once they've played the game a few times, they know what to do. But the treasure's location changes with every new game, so the journey is never quite the same. Freddi fans may enjoy the heroine's continuing adventures in *Freddi Fish and the Haunted House*.

Nothing bad happens in *Freddi*. But little kids may take fright. Sarah, at 3, scrambled away from the computer saying the growling Junkyard Dogfish was "too scary."

The bottom line: One of the best games for little kids.

Putt-Putt Saves the Zoo

★ ★ ★ ★

Putt-Putt Joins the Parade
Putt-Putt Goes to the Moon

★ ★

We've never met a child who didn't adore playing this pint-sized, problem-solving adventure. Perhaps it's the appeal of Putt-Putt, a cute little purple car. Perhaps it's the involvement kids feel as they direct the story. Whatever the reasons, the challenge of getting Putt-Putt to the zoo or the parade or back to Earth is somehow deeply satisfying for little kids.

Putt-Putt Saves the Zoo is the newest and best-looking title in this series. (If you're buying your first *Putt-Putt*, start with this one.) In this story, kids help Putt-Putt find missing animals and return them safely to the zoo. To rescue the animals—like a lion cub perched on a ledge midway down a roaring waterfall—kids really have to think and explore and experiment.

The object of *Putt-Putt Joins the*

JUST THE FACTS

BEST FOR AGES 3-5

★★★★ **for Learning**
Kids figure out what to do and how to do it

★★★★ **for Looks**
Putt-Putt Saves the Zoo has great graphics; other titles look jaggy

★★★★ **for Longevity**
Kids love the little car and the gameplay

Worth Noting
Putt-Putt fans will enjoy *Freddi Fish*, a little kid problem-solving game from the same publisher.

Windows or Macintosh CD-ROM
About $40
Humongous
(206) 485-1212

Parade is to help Putt-Putt find a balloon and a pet and get a car wash so it can participate in the first annual Cartown Pet Parade. It's up to the kids to locate the things they need, earn money for a car wash, and tackle occasional predicaments like getting a cow out of the road.

Kids will find the same sweet purple car but a new challenge in *Putt-Putt Goes to the Moon*. An accident at the fireworks factory has landed Putt-Putt on the moon, and kids need to figure out how to get Putt-Putt and a lost lunar vehicle back to Earth.

You won't find any educational agenda in the *Putt-Putt* titles, but there is educational value. Kids often stick with the challenge for 45 minutes at a stretch(!), following directions and thinking their way through Putt-Putt's little problems.

The programs' staying power depends on your child's personality. Some kids, once they figure out how to get Putt-Putt to the parade or back to Earth, never come back for more. But others return again and again, much as they reread a well-thumbed picture book you thought they'd outgrown.

The bottom line: Tremendously satisfying and absorbing for many youngsters.

At Bat

★ ★ ★ ★

A terrific interactive comic strip that's not just for baseball fanatics, not just for boys, and not just for kids, either.

This program scores a home run with its absorbing story, believable characters, spunky dialog, clever games and wealth of facts (some fun, some serious). Best of all, *At Bat* drafts your child as an active player whose choices determine different routes through the story . . . and the ending itself.

At Bat is the story of the Hawks' star batter Rudy, her kid brother Joey (who knows everything about baseball except how to play), her efforts to teach him the basics, how the team made it to the finals, and what happens when Joey (much to his teammates' horror) has the final at-bat.

Told comic-strip style, the action jumps from panel to panel as your child clicks speech balloons and narrative boxes. And every panel has something with genuine kid-appeal.

There's escalating abuse between siblings: "What's a paramecium? You're a paramecium. Am not. Are too. Am not. Are too." There's plenty of jokes: "What did the Martian say when he landed in the garden? Take me to your weeder." There's a gross songfest aboard the bus to the semi-finals, including "Great

JUST THE FACTS

BEST FOR AGES 7–12

★★★★ **for Learning**
A great story, and kids make it unfold

★★★★ **for Looks**
Animated comic strip

★★★★ **for Longevity**
Lots of games, lively characters keep kids coming back

Macintosh CD-ROM; Windows CD-ROM
About $35
JAmbone Comics
(604) 739-7281

green gobs of greasy grimy gopher guts . . . ." (For some more gross stuff check out Hurlman, a zany variation on hangman, in the games section.) And, of course, there's fun facts for aficionados: Who hit more home runs than either Babe Ruth or Hank Aaron? Which team scored the most runs in a single inning?

While *At Bat* doesn't "teach" reading or anything else, it does make kids *want* to read. (They'll find out what happens next more quickly by reading the text themselves rather than having it read aloud). It also lets team members share their interests—about African-Americans, Hispanics, and women in baseball history—in a way that kids will accept and absorb.

The bottom line: Innovative software with a good story, convincing characters and genuine interactivity.

Klik & Play

★ ★ ★

An innovative construction kit that lets kids (and parents) create their own computer games. *Klik & Play* provides the parts and tools; kids supply the imagination and brain power.

Before getting started, kids need to think about the kind of game they want to build (action, adventure, strategy, logic or learning), where the action will take place, which characters or objects will be in the game and what will happen. Then with a rough game plan in place, the software guides kids through the process of building the game.

The first step: Select backgrounds, characters and game objects from *Klik & Play*'s huge collection of backdrops, sound effects and stamps. These pre-drawn elements include such things as people, animals, monsters, sports figures, jewels, bathtubs, doors, windows and more. The second step: Follow the software's step-by-step guidance to define the game's actions and reactions. What happens, for example, when the asteroid collides with the spaceship? What sound effect should players hear when the bouncing ball hits the big ape?

At any time in the process, kids

JUST THE FACTS

BEST FOR AGES 10 & UP

★★★★ **for Learning**
Building games provides good practice in planning, organization, logic and reasoning; teachers could use this title as an intro to object-oriented programming

★★ **for Looks**
Functional; heavy use of pop-up menus

★★★★ **for Longevity**
Open-ended tools for creating different types of computer games

Worth Noting
Not for kids only; more challenging than most kids' software.

Windows CD-ROM or floppy
About $55
Maxis
(800) 526-2947

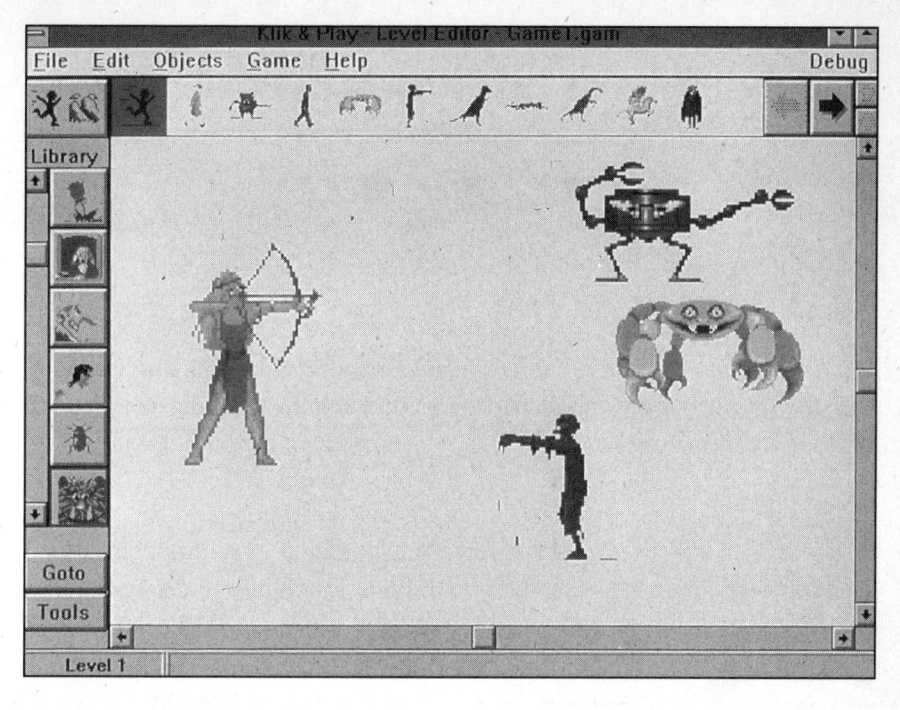

can test—and change—their game design. And when a game is completed, kids can easily share it with their friends. (Since games are saved as stand-alone files, other players don't need to have *Klik & Play* installed to play.)

As kids get more adept, *Klik and Play* offers increasing levels of complexity. The program comes with a useful manual, tutorials that step kids through the process and the use of tools and sample games to take apart, redesign or simply play. We suggest that initially parents help kids work through the tutorials to make sure they understand what's going on.

Kids may be surprised—and challenged—by the level of detail and decision-making the game-building process entails. The designer must define each cause and effect, the timing of each event, the speed of each movement and the way the game is scored. The manual rightly warns beginners that their first few creations may disappoint them. But if they stick with it, budding game designers will find their games improve with experience.

The bottom line: A fascinating challenge and mental workout for kids who love video and computer games.

Gahan Wilson's The Ultimate Haunted House

★ ★ ★

Playing *Gahan Wilson's The Ultimate Haunted House* **is like striking out on your own in an amusement-park spook house—after hours and up close.**

The goal: Collect 13 keys that have vanished in a 13-room, three-story house before the clock strikes the 13th hour. If you fail, you're trapped for life. If you succeed, special treats await.

To get keys, kids have to scavenge objects from around the house and give the "right" thing to the ghosts, vampires, monsters, skeletons and assorted ghouls who inhabit the house. There are more than 50 things kids can collect, from severed hands to mallets to monstrous bird eggs.

It's not easy to win because it's so much fun getting sidetracked. There are monsters to build in the lab, magic spells to read in the library, classic Gahan Wilson cartoons to look at in a magic mirror, a game of hangman in the game room, explosive formulas to concoct in the bathroom. And every time kids play, the ghostly inhabitants and collectibles appear in different places.

JUST THE FACTS

BEST FOR AGES 8–12

★★ **for Learning**
Seek-and-find challenges

★★★ **for Looks**
Great cartoonist gets better with animation

★★★ **for Longevity**
Many, many levels of play

Worth Noting
Younger kids who are competent at using a mouse will be able to play this program without difficulty, but it may be too scary for kids under eight.

Macintosh CD-ROM
About $50
Microsoft
(800) 228-6270

The bottom line: A visual treat, and especially fun to play with friends (or even siblings or parents).

The Eagle Eye Mysteries Series
Eagle Eye Mysteries: The Original   Eagle Eye Mysteries: In London

★   ★

Jennifer and Jake Eagle, teenage detectives, are the Nancy Drew and Hardy Boys of the late '90s. Instead of a yellow roadster, they use public transportation or Rollerblades (more environmentally correct) to race about town, collecting clues in their notebook computer. And in this age of interactivity, kids can jump into the fray, helping the twins solve the mysteries they confront.

Eagle Eye Mysteries: The Original is set in the twin's hometown of Richview, where they run a detective agency from a high-tech treehouse. After taking a drive around town to get the lay of the land, players choose Jennifer or Jake as a partner and select 1 of 25 cases. The mysteries are just right for the 7–12-year-old crowd: "The Case of the Stolen Skateboard," "The Case of the Puzzling Pooch," "The Case of the Creepy Cinema," and the like. Kids have to collect evidence and hunt down clues to zero in on a suspect. If they "prove" their solution (by

---

JUST THE FACTS

BEST FOR AGES 7–10

★★ **for Learning**
Kids hone reasoning skills and reading comprehension as they track clues, but the challenges don't increase from mystery to mystery

★★ **for Looks**
"Real" kids as characters, for a change; CD-ROM versions look better

★★ **for Longevity**
Mystery-loving kids will come back for more

Worth Noting
After they've solved five cases or so, urge your kids to put the program aside for a couple of days (or even weeks) so they don't "overdose" and permanently lose interest.

Macintosh CD-ROM or floppy; DOS CD-ROM or floppy
About $50
Creative Wonders
(800) 543-9778

selecting the five most revealing clues), the case—and your child's name—will make the front page of the Richview newspaper.

Eagle Eye Mysteries: In London finds the duo in London, summering with their aunt and uncle. Thanks to their worldwide reputation (and their relatives' professional connections), the twins are tapped to investigate 25 local mysteries. Each case takes them to well-known landmarks—the British Museum, the Tower of London, Scotland Yard—where they gather information and collect clues.

We like the fact that both of these titles require more reading and reasoning than many software products. To succeed, players must listen, read and think carefully. The twins' observations and notebook entries as well as comments from victims, suspects and bystanders are both spoken aloud and presented as text. (And if you want to put added emphasis on reading, you can turn off the audio.)

The bottom line: If your kids are in their mystery-loving phase, one of the *Eagle Eye Mysteries* CD-ROMs can provide hours of sleuthing (plus some solid but unobtrusive practice in reading, problem-solving and logical thinking). But once your kids have figured out how to crack cases, the intellectual challenge wears thin.

GeoSafari

★ ★

A fast-moving, multimedia version of the popular educational toy of the same name, *GeoSafari* is a well-designed quiz game filled with facts about geography, history and science.

Here's how the game works. Playing solo or in competition with up to four people, kids test their knowledge of 45 different subjects, such as world landmarks, state capitals, first Americans, dinosaurs and space exploration. Once kids choose a category—say presidents—the software poses a question: "Which president was responsible for the passage of NAFTA?" Kids have one minute, or three tries, to choose the answer from a set of illustrated choices. In this case, kids search among black-and-white photographs of presidents' faces and click on Bill Clinton.

The software tracks each player's time and score, and when kids answer all the questions in a section, they win a medal. But there's no penalty for not knowing a right answer. Instead, *GeoSafari* provides the correct information, improving a kid's chance of getting the answer right next time.

If your kids like quiz games, *GeoSafari*'s abundant questions-

---

JUST THE FACTS

BEST FOR AGES 8–12

★★★ **for Learning**
Opportunities to learn geography, history, science facts

★★ **for Looks**
Colorful design supports fast-moving gameplay

★★ **for Longevity**
Lots of questions keep kids challenged

Worth Noting
Kids enter their names from among 3,000 names and nicknames. Because each one has been prerecorded, they hear Richie Haven's voice addressing them "personally" when it's their turn.

Macintosh CD-ROM; Windows CD-ROM
About $45
Educational Insights
(800) 526-2947

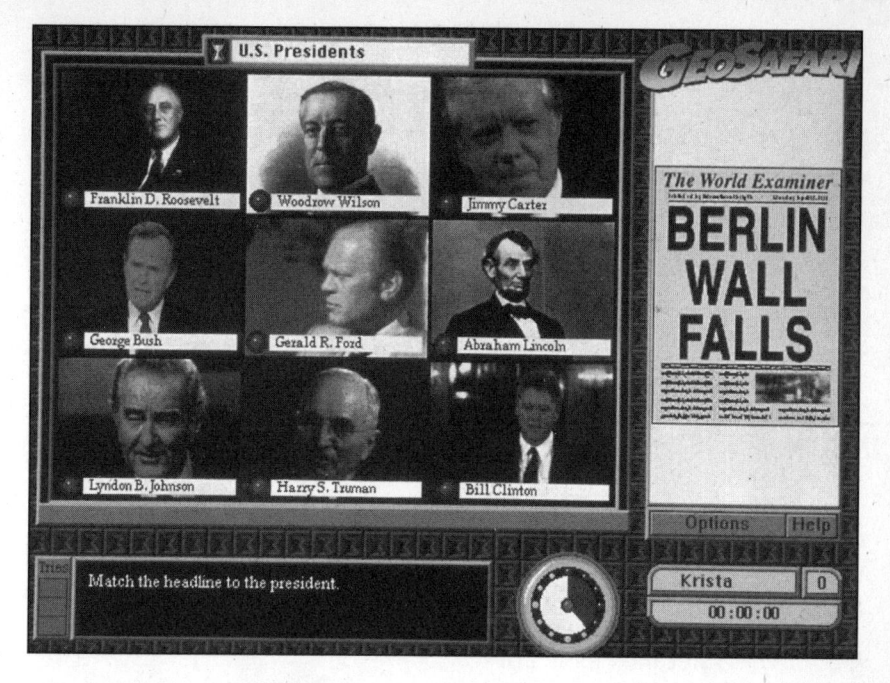

and-answers (900 in all) and plentiful visuals, plus the voice of Richie Havens reading everything out loud, make it a good bet for extended family play. The software offers greater variety than the original toy. But some parents may like the way the toy keeps kids occupied anywhere, anytime (including the back seat of the car!).

The bottom line: A fun way for kids to quiz themselves, play with their friends and challenge their parents.

•SEVEN•
THE BEST TITLES: INFORMATION, PLEASE!

Interactive Reference Tools

CD-ROM reference tools are probably the fastest growing part of the software market. So you may be surprised to find that the *Guide*'s "Information, Please!" section is quite small.

But unless you have an unlimited software budget, we suggest sticking to a few basic references. The reason: CD-ROM encyclopedias don't get daily (or even weekly) use. Few encyclopedias do. Still, it's important to have good resources at the ready when questions come up.

If your child is passionate about the topic, consider additional titles. Or lobby your local library or video store to start lending or renting electronic references so your kids can explore titles without buying them.

You can also use the encyclopedia offered by your on-line service. America OnLine has *Compton's*, CompuServe has a version of *Grolier's Academic American Encyclopedia*, both in text-only form. Most on-line services also carry numerous other resources.

RATINGS	TITLES	AGES
★★★	The Explorapedia Series: The World of Nature, The World of People (Pages 190-191)	6–10
★★★	3D Atlas (Pages 192-193)	8 & Up
★★★	Encarta 1996 (Pages 194-195)	11 & Up
★★★	The Eyewitness Encyclopedia: Series: Science, History, Nature (Pages 196-197)	11 & Up

The Explorapedia Series
Explorapedia: The World of Nature   Explorapedia: The World of People

★ ★ ★

An intelligent and inviting children's encyclopedia, with just the right mix of illustrations and text, photos and narration, animation and video.

The *Explorapedia* programs are easy to navigate. They're good looking. They're pleasant for browsing. They're useful for reports. And, with more than two dozen activities and games, they challenge kids to stick around and explore.

Kids venture into each program from a futuristic ship with a frog named Thaddeus ("Call me Tad") Pole as their guide. Within the ship, assorted buttons let kids listen to songs, see videos, play games or search directly for particular topics. Outside the ship's window lies the best part of the programs: scenes that kids can click and explore.

In *The World of Nature*, the scene is the Earth. Click a spot on the globe and a beautifully illustrated landscape fills the screen. Click the flora and fauna in each picture and a windowful of infor-

JUST THE FACTS

BEST FOR AGES 6–10

★★★ **for Learning**
Intelligently presented, age-appropriate information on many topics; promotes beginning reference skills

★★★ **for Looks**
Attractive multimedia mix

★★★ **for Longevity**
A good resource, but don't expect everyday usage

Worth Noting
Clicking icons in Tad's ship takes kids directly into writing or drawing programs so they can use *Explorapedia* information in a report.

Windows CD-ROM
About $50
Microsoft
(800) 228-6270

mation appears. Several windows-worth of details are available for every topic. And within each window, kids can read text or listen to narration, watch animations, see a video clip, click for definitions, get additional information or jump to related topics. (They can also zero in on information more directly by clicking the Find button.)

Topics in *The World of Nature* center on 16 habitats, including grasslands and deciduous forests, polar regions and coral reefs, deserts and outer space and more. *The World of People* covers art, literature, sports, farming and the sciences, among other topics.

If your kids have clicked around *Explorapedia* a few times and seem at loose ends, urge them to try Wise Crackers. It's a game that poses five questions and sends kids to find the topics containing the answers. A Hint button provides excellent tips for charting a course to the right topic. And a surprise awaits kids who find the right answers.

The bottom line: 6–10-year-olds won't use *Explorapedia* as much as a creativity program, an adventure game or an interactive story. But when they need an answer to a question, *Explorapedia* is a terrific starting place.

3D Atlas

★ ★ ★

A fascinating multimedia exploration of the Earth. What's equally impressive is this title's refreshing approach to presenting an earth-shattering quantity of information.

3D Atlas organizes its vast database of satellite images, statistical information, photographs, video and audio clips, maps and more into three main perspectives: environmental, physical and political. From the title's "physical" viewpoint, for example, you'll see the Earth's topology at any location you choose, from the vantage of space, up close or anywhere in between.

No matter what viewpoint you choose, there's a "location list" to get you to continents or countries, from Afghanistan to Zimbabwe. Double-clicking a country's icon produces "postcards" with photographs and information. You can also choose to display features like cities, mountains, rivers, volcanoes and the like.

For kids, the most inviting aspects of *3D Atlas* are its up-close-and-personal adventures. There are exceptionally realistic 3-D flights through four mountain ranges. (In a nice touch, these

---

JUST THE FACTS

BEST FOR AGES 8 & UP

★★★ **for Learning**
Up-close-and-personal views of geography

★★★ **for Looks**
Clarity, realism, detail

★★ **for Longevity**
Good resource, when kids need it

Worth Noting
3D Atlas also includes a decent-looking trivia challenge called Around the Word. But there's no way to "stop the clock" so kids can look up what they don't know.

Macintosh CD-ROM; Windows CD-ROM
About $80
Creative Wonders
(800) 543-9778

flights provide information far beyond geographic detail. The flight through the Rockies, for example, touches on westward migration, the Gold Rush and the transcontinental railroad.) There's a narrated series of time-lapse photographs showing the impact of various phenomena (like the eruption of Mount Pinatubo) over time. There are expeditions (created from photos, satellite data and graphical simulation) through nine different ecological regions. And much more.

The bottom line: A unique family reference tool, easy and interesting enough for 8-year-olds yet compelling enough for their parents.

Encarta 1996

★ ★ ★

The best family CD-ROM encyclopedia, updated annually.

It's easy enough for kids 8 and up to use (with some guidance), yet extensive enough for adult inquiries. With its let's-get-down-to-business look, *Encarta* is more workmanlike than many reference tools created expressly for kids. But the trade-off is worthwhile: lots more information, plus aptly-chosen photographs, maps, diagrams, animations, video footage and audio clips to shed light on thousands of well-written entries.

Encarta features lots of ways to track down information (and lots of byways to explore when you're not in hot pursuit of facts and figures). It also lets users segue smoothly from one quest to another, or from general information to specifics.

Take the afternoon, for example, when a group of third-graders came in with an assignment to write haiku. We clicked the Contents button and found it, right near Hail Mary and Haile Selassie. A double-click took us to the entry itself, including a reading of a famous Basho verse: "Now the swinging bridge/Is quieted with creepers/Like our ten-

JUST THE FACTS

BEST FOR AGES 11 & UP

★★★ **for Learning**
Tremendous breadth and depth; promotes beginning reference skills

★★★ **for Looks**
Excellent use of multimedia, powerful search capability

★★ **for Longevity**
Great resource, when kids need it

Worth Noting

Encarta owners who buy a new edition (released every Fall) can get a rebate of about $45. Follow the rebate instructions in the package.

Macintosh CD-ROM; Windows CD-ROM
About $99
Microsoft
(800) 228-6270

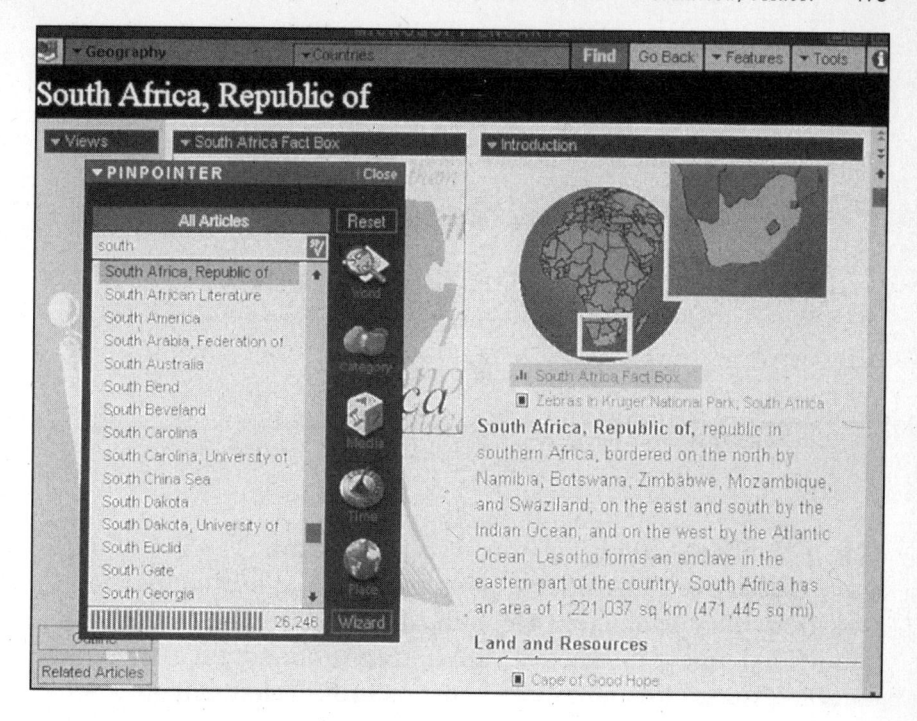

drilled life." In hopes of hearing haiku in Japanese, we checked *Encarta*'s vast collection of foreign-language audio clips. We didn't get exactly what we wanted. But the kids did get to hear more than a dozen words, phrases and a proverb (a rolling stone gathers no moss) in Japanese.

The bottom line: If you're looking for a family reference tool, *Encarta* **is a great choice.**

The Eyewitness Encyclopedia Series
The Eyewitness Encyclopedia of Science
The Eyewitness Encyclopedia of Nature
The Eyewitness Encyclopedia of History

★ ★ ★

One of the best-looking reference series around. You'll find the same distinctive illustrations, photographs, and text as the Dorling Kindersley books (on which these CD-ROMs are based). Plus a judicious mix of interactive extras: narration, sound effects, animations, video clips and instantaneous cross-referencing.

The Eyewitness Encyclopedia of Science features more than 200 entries in four areas: mathematics, physics, chemistry and life sciences. Kids choose a jumping-off point from an intriguing main screen—it looks a bit like an inventor's laboratory, complete with the crackle of electric sparks—and then click their way to more and more details or to related topics.

No science homework this week? Can't decide what to look up? Uncertain how to get around an electronic database? Try using the title's Quiz Master to encourage some purposeful browsing. This machine tosses out random

---

JUST THE FACTS

BEST FOR AGES 11 & UP

★★★ **for Learning**
More depth on selected topics promotes beginning reference skills

★★★ **for Looks**
Design makes it easy for kids to use; distinctive DK Multimedia graphics

★★ **for Longevity**
Great, when kids need it

Macintosh CD-ROM; Windows CD-ROM
About $50
DK Multimedia
(800) 225-3362

questions, and one of them is sure to pique your child's curiosity: When will the Earth be swallowed up by the sun? What kind of carbon molecule looks like a soccer ball? How do penguins keep warm?

By clicking on the Look Up button beneath a question, the program will chart an efficient path through its vast database, demonstrating step-by-step how to reach the answer.

Of the three, *The Eyewitness Encyclopedia of Nature* is most accessible to young children; their love of animals makes them eager to plunge right in. They can browse through "drawers"—akin to specimen drawers in a museum—labeled amphibians, reptiles, birds, insects, invertebrates, and the like. Or they can click "books" about microorganisms and prehistoric life. But the best choice for kids is 1 of 10 habitats. Click the desert, for example, and a beautiful illustrated landscape fills the screen, dotted with plants and animals. (It reminds us a little of museum dioramas with their painted backdrops and taxidermy specimens.) The scene is filled with click points that conduct kids to successive layers of information.

The Eyewitness Encyclopedia of History works much the same way, but the main screen looks a bit like a time machine, with a chronometer that instantly whisks kids to different periods. Alternately, kids can browse through history by geographical regions. Or use the Quiz Master to chart a course through time.

The bottom line: Because these CD-ROMs cover specialized topics, they're not for everyone. But if your child has a particular interest in these subjects, the *Eyewitness* programs are good resources.

• EIGHT •
THE BEST TITLES: PRODUCTIVITY

Typing, E-mail, Word Processing, Organizers, Utilities

Productivity is an adult compulsion; kids shouldn't be organized for maximum efficiency like their harried parents. They're supposed to be enjoying the freedom of childhood, after all. But there are a few titles that can help youngsters get more fun and enrichment from their other computer software titles.

Typing titles are a good example. While the hunt-and-peck method is fine for little kids, older children can make quicker work of homework assignments and tackle creative writing projects more readily with a little touch-typing instruction.

Desktop organizers are another useful tool. They make it easy for children to get to their software (without grappling with the complexities of the family computer). And they keep everything else safely out of reach.

RATINGS	TITLES	AGES
★★★★	KidDesk (Page 200)	All
★★★★	KidDesk Family Edition (Page 201)	All
★★★★	At Ease (Page 201)	All
★★★★	Launch Pad (Page 201)	All
★★★	Student Writing Center (Pages 202-203)	10 & Up
★★	Keroppi Day Hopper (Pages 204-205)	7–12
★★	KidMail Connection (Pages 206-207)	5–12
★★	Kid's Typing (Pages 208-209)	6–8
★★	Davidson's Kid Keys (Pages 210-211)	3–8

Desktop Utilities
KidDesk KidDesk Family Edition
At Ease Launch Pad

★ ★ ★ ★

An essential tool for kids and parents alike, a desktop utility makes it easy for children as young as 3 to use their software titles independently. And at the same time, it protects your data files and applications from curious kids.

All the utilities reviewed here let you choose which software your child can launch. They hide *everything* else, showing only icons representing the software titles you've authorized your kids to use.

How do you choose among them? Price is one consideration. In some cases, you may get these programs for free! *At Ease*, for example, is bundled with many systems sold by Apple Computer. *KidDesk* and *KidDesk Family Edition* (for Windows systems) often come free with other Edmark programs.

Looks are another consideration; choose the one that takes your fancy. The *KidDesk* products make the computer screen look like a very organized kid's desktop complete with calculator, clock, nameplate, telephone (click it to hear built-in sounds or record your child's voice), and a calendar

---

JUST THE FACTS

The KidDesk Products
Macintosh floppy; Windows floppy
About $30
Edmark
(800) 225-3362

At Ease
Macintosh floppy
About $60
Apple
(800) 769-2775 x5924

Launch Pad
Macintosh CD-ROM or floppy; Windows CD-ROM or floppy
About $30
Berkeley Systems
(510) 540-5535

that kids can customize and then print. As a nice touch, kids can select the desktop style they like: primary colors or pastels, traditional, circus or dinosaur themes. Emily was so enchanted with the look she created for her computer desktop that she rearranged her real desk to look the same.

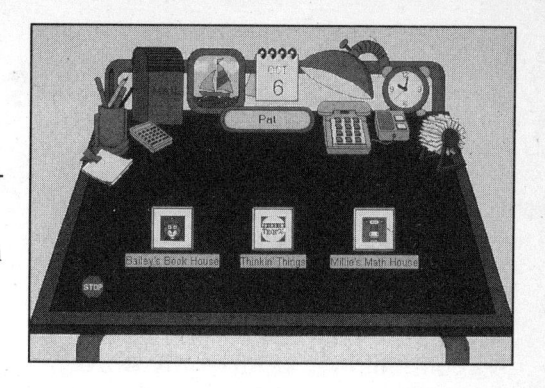

KidDesk Family Edition adds some extra features, including an address book, a notepad that kids can embellish and print, a voice-mail feature that lets kids record a message and send it to a parent's or sibling's desktop and a mailbox for writing or receiving messages from other *KidDesk* users.

Launch Pad has a lot of little-kid appeal. Rather than creating a kid version of a computer desktop, it transforms the screen into one of six fanciful landscapes. These include a dinosaur scene, haunted house, enchanted castle, outer space and more. Like kids' programs, these landscapes have hot spots where kids can click and have fun. Or they can click their way to other applications, which appear as icons on the console of a futuristic car. A unique feature: *Launch Pad* makes it especially easy for kids to save their work in other programs by substituting its own kid-friendly save procedure whenever they click the save button.

The bottom line: all the utilities mentioned here are worthy products. If one is bundled free with your computer system or another software program, so much the better for you. If not, go for a look you can live with—you'll be seeing a lot of it.

Though intended for adults, *Microsoft BOB* also provides a way to launch applications right from the desktop. *BOB* is a utility that looks like the room of a home and lets adults launch built-in productivity programs like a calendar and checkbook. But because it keeps your files private, kids can safely use *BOB* to launch applications that have been installed on the hard drive. Bundled free with many Windows computers, *BOB* is also available on Windows floppy for $99.

Student Writing Center

★ ★ ★

A good-looking, kid-friendly word processor, loaded with advice about book reports, research papers, making outlines and more. But we're not sure your kids need a word processor all to themselves. If you already have one at home, why not just teach your kids to use that?

Still, *Student Writing Center* is a good homework helper. And since it offers all the basics, adults who don't need such special features as indices, tables, annotations and the like could easily use it for their family writing needs as well.

Student Writing Center guides kids through the steps of creating five kinds of documents—reports, newsletters, journals, letters and signs. Pop-up boxes automatically present many of the available options. Open a letter template, for example, and the software offers a choice of layout and letterhead styles. Select newsletter, and it steps kids through design options: Masthead or not? Number of columns? (We particularly like the little black-and-white illustrations that help kids visualize the options.)

The spelling checker and thesaurus are standard fare these days. But this title does offer

JUST THE FACTS

BEST FOR AGES 10 & UP

★★★ **for Learning**
Useful tutorials and step-by-step help with different kinds of documents

★★ **for Looks**
Efficient looking workspace with clip art for enlivening reports; older floppy versions contain fewer images

★★ **for Longevity**
Lasts until kids graduate to the family word processor

Macintosh CD-ROM; Windows CD-ROM
About $60–$70
The Learning Company
(800) 852-2255

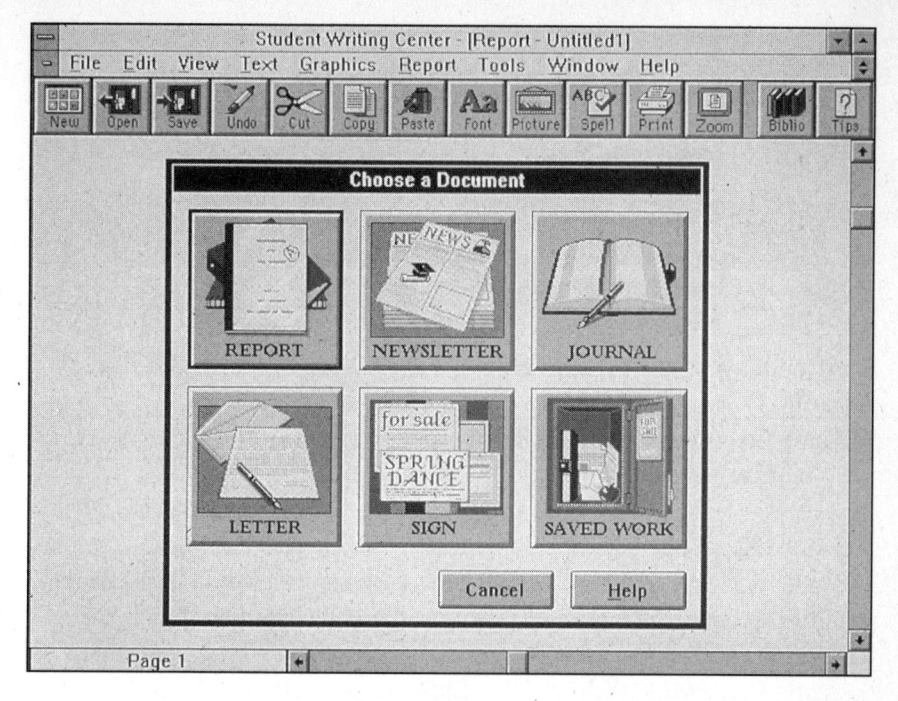

some kid-friendly features not found in "adult" word processors: design tools and clip art (120 items included on the CD-ROM) to create signs, certificates and cards; writing and grammar tips like how to organize an outline or write a business letter; and a bibliography maker that automatically formats different reference sources.

The bottom line: if you want a word processor just for kids, this is a good choice.

Keroppi Day Hopper

★ ★

A nifty tool for getting organized (a skill kids seem to need at an alarmingly young age these days). Plus, it's an interactive journal with surprises that make kids want to write.

As a personal organizer, *Keroppi* features a kid-friendly address book and calendar with monthly, weekly and daily views (all printable). Kids schedule events by dragging icons onto the daily calendar. Icons depict kid-events like last day of school, soccer practice, camping trips, birthdays and sleepovers, with text that kids can personalize.

The journal is our favorite section for two reasons. First, it's linked to events in the calendar, so kids get the feeling that Keroppi (the frog) actually knows what's going on in their lives. Click Keroppi and a personalized comment or suggestion appears: What are you getting for Mom's birthday tomorrow? Did you study for tomorrow's test?

Better still are the unexpected sound effects. As kids write, they'll discover that certain words produce sound effects. Type "cold" and they'll hear "atchoo." "Supper" produces the sound of carrots being crunched. The jingle of bells accompanies "Christmas." There's no way of knowing which words trigger sounds... except to write (and write and write).

The first time kids launch

JUST THE FACTS

BEST FOR AGES 7–12

★★ **for Learning**
Encourages kids to take responsibility

★★★ **for Looks**
Colorful, easy to use

★ **for Longevity**
Not as much staying power as a full-featured writing program; kids can graduate quickly to adult calendar or address book programs

Macintosh CD-ROM or floppy; Windows CD-ROM or floppy
About $55
Big Top Productions
(415) 978-5363

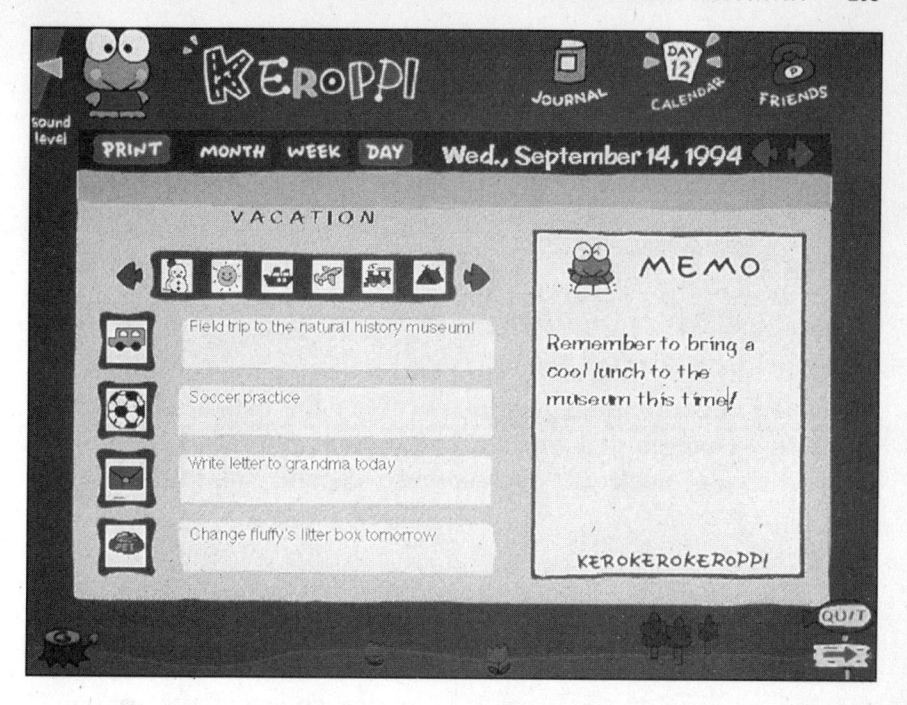

Keroppi, the program supplies some personal fun facts based on each user's birth date: How many days they've been alive, how many days till their next birthday and what day of the week it will be on. The better to start planning the party!

The bottom line: good for organized kids who want to get more organized. And a diary that makes noise will delight many kids.

KidMail Connection

★ ★

A handy way for children to send and receive e-mail—without the confusion of communications protocols or the danger of running up on-line charges. It's so easy, in fact, that you may be tempted to handle your electronic correspondence with *KidMail*, too!

JUST THE FACTS

BEST FOR AGES 5–12

★★ for Learning
Sending mail is a great incentive for kids to write and read

★★★ for Looks
Kooky graphics have lots of kid appeal

★★ for Longevity
Lasts until you feel your kids are ready to use the other features available from on-line services responsibly

Worth Noting
To make the set-up procedure easier, make sure you have details about your modem, your on-line or network service, and your friends' e-mail addresses *before* you begin the process.

Windows CD-ROM or floppy
About $30
ConnectSoft
(800) 234-9497

KidMail Connection lets families with CompuServe, MCI Mail, Prodigy, or America Online service, among others, set up messaging centers for their children. Adults are in charge of the set-up procedure, selecting who can receive mail from each child and how many messages a child may send. Then the kids are on their own.

The software gives kids a choice of three "communication centers" (with dinosaur, outer space or secret agent themes), each with three activities. Kids can check their mail for incoming messages. They can write and send letters. Or they can click the Quick Message option for a choice of 50 greetings that kids can send as is or personalize.

Once their missive is written, kids select a recipient from *Kid-*

Mail's built-in Address Book. Then they affix a stamp in the Dispatch Center and click Send. That's all there is to it. *KidMail* automatically routes the message via your on-line service to the service appropriate for the recipient.

The bottom line: Convenient and fun, the program's simplicity has the happy effect of making kids want to write messages—and read the mail they get in response.

Kid's Typing

★ ★

The look of these touch-typing lessons is great: crisp, colorful graphics, a friendly typing tutor named Spooky the Ghost and rewarding little animations. But nothing can disguise the fact that learning to type is just a matter of practice, practice, practice.

Spooky lives in the attic of a suburban home and haunts the family downstairs. He guides kids through typing lessons with gentle encouragement: "Look at that speed. It's your best yet!" At regular intervals kids get to help him with his tricks. Typing the home keys, for example, levitates a baby above the dining room table.

Each lesson ends with a diagnostic report on the child's progress, noting both accuracy and speed. Useful for a supervising adult, but not particularly relevant for younger kids.

The bottom line: A series of typing lessons with a clean, contemporary look. But kids will need your encouragement to stick with the practice.

JUST THE FACTS

BEST FOR AGES 6-8

★★ **for Learning**
Basic touch-typing skills

★★ **for Looks**
Appealing haunted-attic setting

★ **for Longevity**
Learning to type is still a chore that kids try to avoid

Macintosh CD-ROM or floppy; Windows CD-ROM or floppy
About $35
Sierra
(800) 757-7707

LEARNING TO TYPE

Be honest: Is learning to type high on any kid's list of fun things to do? Adults understand that working at the keyboard is faster and easier if you know how to touch-type. But the process of learning—typing lines of letters and silly words over and over—is intrinsically dull. So even in the guise of "computer fun," kids understandably chafe at the practice.

Computer typing programs for kids do provide a useful structure of lessons and feedback. And, unlike the typing classes you may remember from high school, today's programs emphasize mechanics over speed. But if you want your child to follow the routine to gain the skills, you'll probably need to impose a schedule of practice. Don't expect the software to provide motivation enough.

Davidson's Kid Keys

★ ★

A 2-in-1 program that encourages little kids to learn the alphabet and teaches older kids touch-typing skills.

With young children in mind, *Davidson's Kid Keys* takes a very different approach than most other typing programs. For one thing, it introduces keyboard locations in alphabetical order. For another, it stresses accuracy over speed. The short typing exercises are right for a child's attention span. And bright colors, spunky graphics and bouncy music reinforce the connections between a letter and its location on the keyboard.

Kids practice by playing three simple games, each with three levels. At the basic level, Keystone the dragon asks kids to find a letter on the keyboard. Clicking on the right letter produces both reward, in the form of a silly animation, and reinforcement, when the letter is repeated. In another activity kids type letters and hear the notes from the "ABC" song, "Farmer in the Dell" and other familiar tunes. To practice finger placement kids type three letter words and patterns. As they type, silly creatures that have been locked up in a dungeon find their way out.

Although it seems logical for children to learn keyboarding skills while they're learning to read and write letters, we've found that most kids expect using the computer to be more fun.

JUST THE FACTS

BEST FOR AGES 3-8

★★ **for Learning**
Letter recognition and touch-typing skills

★★ **for Looks**
Graphics create a gamelike setting

★ **for Longevity**
Learning to type is still a chore that kids try to avoid

Macintosh floppy; DOS floppy
About $35
Davidson
(800) 545-7677

The bottom line: A good option if you want young children to learn keyboarding skills as they learn to read and write. But they'll need your encouragement to stick with the practice.

·NINE·
NEW & NOTABLE

This chapter highlights some of the best of the hundreds of new products scheduled for release by year-end 1995 and early 1996. They're diverse, exciting, and available *only* in CD-ROM format.

Our recommendations in this section are listed by subject and, within each subject, by age. But unlike the titles we recommend elsewhere in the *Guide*, these products have no rating. The reason: because of their release dates, they didn't get the same level of hands-on kid and parent testing that our rated titles received.

Still, depending on the ages and interests of your kids, these products are worth your consideration. Our only caveat: call the software publisher to double-check when and where you can find the product and how much it costs *before* you head out to make a purchase.

For more updates on new and noteworthy software not included in this edition of the *Guide*, check The Computer Museum's Worldwide Web page. You'll find us at http://www.tcm.org.

PLAYING TO LEARN

Baby ROM
Ages 6–48 months

Software for babies? We kid you not. *Baby ROM* is lap-ware designed for you and your baby to play together. And as your baby grows, this CD-

ROM offers charming new ways for your child to explore numbers, letters, shapes and colors.

Start your littlest one in BabyTalk, a kind of interactive board-book filled with pictures of other babies. Touching any keyboard key fills the screen with a video of a baby laughing, crying, giggling or eating. As your child gains hand-eye coordination, you'll find activities that introduce numbers (find the key that corresponds to the number on the screen), letters (press the L key and see a picture-book illustration of a lawnmower or a lemon) and body parts (click on a little boy's nose and watch it lengthen like Pinocchio's).

Because *Baby ROM* has three levels of play, children can continue to play it up through the ages of 3 or 4. But even when your child takes over the mouse, parents should stay close. Like reading a book together, what happens between you and your child at the computer is just as important as what they see on the screen.

(Byron Preiss Multimedia, (800) 274-6800, Win/Mac CD-ROM, about $20)

Trudy's Time and Place House
Ages 3–6

More early-learning magic from the *Millie's Math House* people. This time the title character is an alligator who invites kids to explore time and geography through five hands-on activities.

In Calendar Clock, kids enter an animated outdoor environment and see how it changes over the course of a year. But they do more than watch—they can actually manipulate the march of time. Using different clocks, kids can advance time in increments of a second, a minute, an hour, a day or a month. And the software instantly shows them the impact of the change. In addition to experimenting, children can try answering a character's request such as: "It's going to snow in three hours. Can you make it happen?"

Another activity, Earth Scout, casts kids as pilots of a spaceship. They can fly to any location on Earth, take photos, and print their personal atlas. (As with most Edmark products, *Trudy's* gives kids something personal to take away from the computer to extend their fun.) Once kids gain some familiarity with continents, oceans and major geographical landmarks, they can challenge themselves with Question & Answer mode by trying to zoom to specific locations.

(Edmark, (800) 691-2985, Win/Mac CD-ROM, about $40)

The Adventures of Peter Rabbit & Benjamin Bunny
Peter Rabbit's 123
Ages 3-6

Admirers of Beatrix Potter will be happy to know that her original artwork and stories have weathered the move to the computer screen relatively well. These CD-ROMs preserve the gentle, watercolor look of Potter's illustrations while adding music, animations and games to the classic stories.

In *The Adventures of Peter Rabbit & Benjamin Bunny*, little kids can wander through the gardens and forests of Peter Rabbit's world, clicking on hidden animations, playing hide and seek and encountering learning games like scrambled pictures and mazes. *Peter Rabbit's 123* presents four games that let kids practice early math skills—counting the bugs in Mrs. Tittlemouse's house, for example, or helping Jeremy Fisher catch and sort fish.

Truth to tell, the characters themselves are more distinctive than any of the newly added activities. But if your child delights in the antics of Potter's animals, you may want to take a closer look at these CD-ROMs. For Beatrix Potter stories presented with a learn-to-read approach, try the Benjamin Bunny and Peter Rabbit titles in the *Discis Kids Can Read Series* (Page 76).

(Mindscape Inc., (800) 234-3088, Win/Mac CD-ROMs, about $40)

The Junior Encyclopedia Series
Ages 3-6

An attractive set of programs where little kids are free to click around, absorbing the sights and sounds of a farm, an airport and a jungle. Five games in each environment and different levels of challenge help give focus to kids' explorations.

Starting from a bird's-eye view of a farm, *Junior Encyclopedias: The Farm* lets kids take progressively closer looks at an apple orchard, a beaver dam, a chicken coop and more than 30 other places. In every location, there are hidden animations to discover, every click revealing more and more pictorial detail. By clicking the Question Mark button, kids can hear (and/or read) definitions and short encyclopedia entries for scores of topics.

In a similar way, *Junior Encyclopedias: The Airport* and *Junior Encyclopedias: The Jungle* let kids click and explore layers of details at an airport and in a jungle.

The products feature matching games for the youngest players, hangman for beginning readers (using words kids learn during their explorations), and a scavenger hunt with pictorial lists of objects that differ virtually every time kids play. A nice touch: The trivia game lets kids explore before clicking one of the pictorial multiple-choice answers, encouraging them to learn rather than hazard a guess.

(Humongous (206) 485-1212, Win/Mac CD-ROM, about $30)

Pantsylvania
Ages 4–8

The folks at Headbone Interactive are back again with their refreshingly original approach to kids' software. Like its predecessor, *AlphaBonk Farm* (see Page 12), this imaginative CD-ROM is part exploration and part escapade, topped with visual pizzazz and loads of silly fun.

This time the action moves to Pantsylvania, home of the Fancypants and their befuddled leader, Kingamajig. Kids can visit 10 different locations in this wacky world—the factory, Symfunny Hall, Kid U., the House of Beauty, the hub of Pantsportation and more—all with plenty of songs, rhymes, stories and games. At the Pants Factory, for example, kids can learn fun facts about famous inventions like the wheel or the computer. They can hunt for hidden numbers in the machine shop. Or they can run the See'em-Hear'em-Move'em-izer, a wild invention that lets kids select attributes to transform the ordinary (cats or hedgehogs, for example) into the extraordinary (like a glow-in-the-dark cat that meows like an electric guitar and moves like a rocket ship).

Parents will be pleased to know that amid all this madcap fun, kids are learning, too. Pantsylvania provides up-close, hands-on (and humorous)

experience with places like schools, factories, restaurants, and parks and their related cultural and social functions.

(Headbone Interactive, (800) 267-4709, Win/Mac CD-ROM, about $35)

ARTS & ANIMATION

Hard Hat
Age 5–10

Imagine Legos that change shape, color and design every time kids play. In *Hard Hat*, kids can manipulate more than 100 kinds of building materials, structural elements and tools to create skyscrapers, spaceships, cathedrals, bridges or whimsical constructions of their own design.

With this CD-ROM, building is as simple as clicking the mouse. First kids choose a site for their construction. Next, they construct the building's framework, selecting among beams and joists that can be stretched to fit into place. Then they select textures, from real-life bricks to colorful stripes, to cover the frame. Finally, they add windows, doors, columns, gargoyles and more. When the building is complete, kids discover surprise animations that hide behind doors or fly out of chimneys. And for kids who enjoy knocking down their creations as much as building them, *Hard Hat* offers a choice of imaginative demolition techniques.

By printing their buildings, kids get even more ways to extend their construction projects. They can try reassembling tall buildings (on the computer they can extend up to 4 screens high) on a closet door, transferring an alien city to a mural, or turning two-dimensional artwork into a three-dimensional milk carton town (which presents the spatial challenge of envisioning four sides of the same structure).

We don't suggest that computer construction should or could replace the hands-on pleasures of Legos, blocks or dirt. But for kids who love to build, *Hard Hat* offers a fun, new way to explore the process.

(Byron Preiss Multimedia, (800) 274-6800, Win/Mac CD-ROM, about $30)

TesselMania!
Ages 8 & Up

Tessellations are those fascinating patterns where a design repeats and interlocks and plays tricks on the eye, again and again. (Remember M.C. Escher's fish-into-birds-into-fish illustration?) They're widely used in schools to help kids develop visual perception and spatial awareness—both important mathematics skills—as well as an understanding of geometry. In *TesselMania!*, they make the leap from an exercise in spatial visualization to an art activity.

TesselMania! adapts MECC's popular school product, which focuses on the mathematics behind tessellations, into a creativity tool that focuses on the artistry of tessellations. It gives kids an art kit filled with colors, stamps and tools for creating a design. And then, with a click of the mouse, *TesselMania!* automatically transforms their design into a tessellation.

These patterns have an interesting life off the computer, as well as on-screen. Using the software's collection of cut-and-fold templates, kids can map their tessellations onto three-dimensional shapes, print them, cut them and fold them into pyramids, cubes, and the like. And by sending their artwork to outside vendors, kids can transfer their tessellations onto stationery, calendars, posters, banners, cards, T-shirts or other gift items.

The only thing missing: insights into the mathematics that make these visual tricks possible.

(MECC, (800) 685-6322, Win/Mac CD-ROM, about $40)

WORDPLAY & STORYTELLING

Top Secret Decoder
Ages 8–12

A suolubaf loot rof gnitaerc dna gnikcarc terces segassem!

Gibberish? No. It's a secret message, coded in one of more than a dozen inventive ciphers kids will find in *Top Secret Decoder*. (Just reverse the letters of each word: "A fabulous tool for creating and cracking secret messages!")

Coding messages is easy: Kids simply type in their message, select a code, click a button and their words are instantly transformed. The results range from pretty obvious to fairly devious to downright ingenious. On the easier end of the spectrum are pig Latin and "alphaglyph" codes, which represent each letter with an icon that begins with that letter (elephant = E). Then there are visual codes, crackable only by folding the paper on which they're printed, or holding them up to a mirror. And then there are substitution codes that need the "cypher wheel" to crack. And toughest of all: messages that utilize two or more codes!

Kids can click a button to get tips about codes and deciphering techniques. And they can write hints (which appear in very tiny type at the bottom of the page) when they print messages for friends. A great title for kids at that secretive, let's-start-a-club (or let's-stump-the-adults) stage.

(Houghton Mifflin Interactive, (800) 225-3362, Win/Mac CD-ROM, about $50)

Opening Night
Ages 8–16

An innovative theater simulation from the company that has created so many of the best computer simulations for kids. In *Opening Night*, kids play the roles of director, set designer, costumer, lighting designer and musical director to present their own on-screen production of a mystery play.

In each scene, kids place digitized actors—each with its own repertoire of emotions and gestures—against a background set. (The click-and-drag approach to assembling a scene is reminiscent of *Storybook Weaver*, also by this same publisher.) As kids move actors and props with the mouse, the software memorizes this "staging" and adds it to the script. Kids can alter or add words to the scripts and print them out. They can also choose costumes, props and sound effects, and control the lighting and music that accompanies the action on stage.

In another section of the software, kids can watch video interviews with theater professionals from the Children's Theater of Minneapolis, including actors, sound technicians, directors and others.

A wonderful way to let kids explore the complex decisions behind every performance.

(MECC, (800) 685-6322, Win/Mac CD-ROM, about $50)

Hollywood
Ages 9 & Up

A sophisticated, entertaining and instructive tool for creating animated stories. *Hollywood* inspires kids to write because they instantly see their words come alive on screen. Not only do their characters move, but they also speak the lines that kids write.

Twenty different backdrops inspire the action: a talk show set, a diner, a sports arena, a space ship. Kids can cast up to 10 offbeat characters in a show and develop their personalities by making choices about occupations (rock star or doctor, for example), hobbies (sky-diving or bowling, perhaps), moods (from paranoid to happy) and voices (whispery, commanding, and more). To move a character, kids simply click and drag it into position. An array of facial expressions, body language and actions (talking on the phone or eating pizza, for example) can be connected with a character. And, of course, kids can add sound effects and theme music.

Click any character and kids instantly become scriptwriters. *Hollywood*'s smartest feature: The software seems to "know" every character (as well as who they're with and where they are) and makes customized suggestions for story starters, plot twists and dialog any time kids want help. It automatically incorporates stage directions like entrances and exits as well as the narration and dialog kids write. Any change in the script is instantly reflected in the action, and any change in the action produces an instant update in the script. And during both the creative process and the performance, *Hollywood* lip-synchs the dialog and reads the characters' lines with one of the best text-to-speech voice generators we've heard.

Add-on story packs with new settings and characters extend the life of the software.

(Theatrix Interactive, (800) 955-TRIX, Win/Mac CD-ROM, about $40)

STORIES ON SCREEN

Curious George Comes Home
Ages 3–6

A surprisingly different kind of interactive storybook. Surprise number one: There are no printed words in this on-screen adventure. Surprise number two: Kids are genuine participants. They get to take Curious George on an outing—to the zoo or lake or music school. They get to choose whether to walk or take the bus or ride a bike. And when trouble presents itself—as it always does with Curious George—they get to choose what to do next. Not surprisingly, whatever choices kids make, George always complicates things further by getting too curious. But true to each of H.L. Rey's classic stories, everything turns out right in the end.

Now for Surprise number three: Every outing kids have with Curious George turns into a real book, with line drawings and the simple dialog and narrative kids heard during the adventure. Kids can print, color, read—or pretend to read—and collect their many adventures in a bright yellow book cover that comes with the software. Between making the simple choices during each adventure and enjoying the printed results, kids feel more like authors than just onlookers.

Curious George fans take note: This is the first product in a series called *Create Your Own Adventures with Curious George*. Check with the publisher for release dates of subsequent titles.

(Houghton Mifflin Interactive, (800) 225-3362, Win/Mac CD-ROM, about $50)

Chicka Chicka Boom Boom
Ages 3–6

As a book, *Chicka Chicka Boom Boom* is a rollicking alphabet rhyme that inspires kids to clap and chant their way to letter recognition. As a CD-ROM, it's a song-and-dance extravaganza. There are sound effects to click, animations to watch, songs to sing, dance routines to try, games to play, instruments to invent, new stories to hear.

In one activity, kids provide percussion for the *Chicka Chicka Boom Boom* song. They start by designing a noisemaker, clicking on a container (a tin can, perhaps) and something to put inside (beans or rice, for example). Naturally, each inside-outside combination produces a different sound. And kids can try them all as they accompany the song.

In an interesting touch, the CD-ROM features real but digitized children as guides to *Chicka Chicka Boom Boom*'s many activities. It also includes tips for parents and suggestions for playing musical ABC games off the computer. Make sure you like the *Chicka Chicka Boom Boom* song before you buy this CD-ROM; your kids are going to be singing it for a long time.

(Davidson, (800) 545-7677, Windows CD-ROM, about $40)

Polar Express
Ages 3–6

Chris Van Allsburg's Christmas classic is mysterious, heartwarming and bitter-sweet all at the same time. The CD-ROM version of *Polar Express* faithfully re-creates the book's darkly luminous artwork. It adds music and motion, gently animating the magical train on its northward journey; the wolves it passes, the pajama-clad children it carries, the elves they meet, Santa's reindeer, the falling snow and more.

As with many Stories on Screen, kids can hear the text read aloud. But they can't play inside *Polar Express* quite the way they can with other products. The software seems determined not to break the spell of this story with an abundance of hot spots or games or extensions to the storyline. This uninterrupted quality makes *Polar Express* closer to a TV video than other titles. Except that kids can go back to their favorite pages ... and hear the silvery jingle of the magical bell time and again.

(Houghton Mifflin Interactive, (800) 225-3362, Win/Mac CD-ROM, about $30)

Madeline and the Magnificent Puppet Show
Ages 4–8

A fun adventure for children who are mad about Madeline, and an appealing departure from the read-along style of interactive stories.

The story: Madeline's neighbor (along with his large and playful menagerie of animals) face eviction by a greedy landlord. So Madeline and her friends decide to raise money for him by putting on a puppet show. Your child's mission: Guide Madeline on a quest for all the things she'll need to make puppets, design invitations, create curtains and backdrops for a puppet theater and more. Along the way, there are pint-sized problems to solve (what, for example, can Madeline use as string for the puppets and where is it to be found?), lessons to learn (in French or Spanish) in Miss Clavell's classroom, and plenty of places to explore, both inside the school where Madeline lives and in her Parisian neighborhood.

The items kids need to find are in the same place every time they play. But happily, there's some variation in the adventure because they can use those same materials in different ways to accomplish their goals. For added longevity, there are three challenge levels for the games within the adventure.

The story is not one of Ludwig Bemelman's "real" Madeline adventures. The artwork and storyline, however, are pleasingly true to the gentle spirit of the originals. And the CD-ROM uses the same voice-overs as the Madeline series of videos and TV cartoons.

(Creative Wonders, (800) 543-9778, Windows CD-ROM, about $40)

MATH EXPLORATIONS

James Discovers Math
Ages 3–6

A spunky collection of early math activities that range from simple number recognition all the way to beginning addition and subtraction. With 10 activities, *James Discovers Math* offers kids more to do than most math programs for 3- to 6-year-olds. Especially nice touches: Colorful, hand-drawn artwork and a cute kid with an Australian accent to accompany children as they explore. Parents will enjoy the program's sense of humor as much as the kids do—maybe even more!

As soon as they master the mouse, little kids can click around in James's interactive story and singalong nursery rhymes (all about numbers, of course). Other games (and the math skills they encourage) include Picture and Boat Shapes (shape recognition), the Face Game (size comparison), Magic Carpet (patterns) and Fruit Shop (counting objects). Pencil Box is an inventive introduction to estimating and measuring, not with abstract measures like inches but familiar, everyday objects like pencils. In fact, whenever kids open James's pencil box, a different size pencil appears. And by clicking and dragging it, kids can figure out the length of animated creatures like a snail, an alligator and even a teacher! James's telling-time activity is one of the clearest we've seen for making sense of the hands on a clock and could, in fact, be useful for kids in the second or even third grade. Part of the Active Mind series covering reading, math, and science.

(Broderbund, (800) 521-6263, Win/Mac CD-ROM, about $40)

Where's Waldo? at the Circus
Ages 4–9

A playful combination of I-Spy activities and math challenges featuring Waldo in his signature red-striped cap and shirt. A good choice if you have a Waldo aficionado who could benefit from some time with math activities.

The story opens with the disappearance of the ringmaster's whistle and a plea for players to help find it. For starters, kids have to find Waldo. Next they have to find other things hidden in the crowded minutely detailed scenes so typical of the Waldo books. Then kids have to tackle special activities in clown alley, the lion cage, the bandstand and the midway.

The 6–10 activities in each area of the circus are math-related, featuring five levels of challenge and ranging from basic recognition skills (numerals, quantity, shapes, attributes) to some fairly challenging problems with weights and measurement, visualization, division and auditory discrimination. One bandstand game, for example, involves arranging band members by height. At the easy level, there are only a few instrumentalists. But when there are a dozen, with barely perceptible differences in height, it's quite a challenge.

One reservation about this product: kids compete against a clock in each math activity. At the easy level, kids get about two minutes to complete a task; at the hard level about a minute and 15 seconds. For kids who prefer to set their own pace, the time pressure may spoil the fun.

(WarnerActive, (800) 693-3253, Win/Mac CD-ROM, about $40)

Money Town
Ages 5–8

Even before they get to kindergarten, kids realize that money has value. That's why counting coins holds such special appeal. And *Money Town* is one of the only software programs designed to let kids play with money—and in the process learn how to count it, save it and spend it.

Money Town invites kids to the animated town where they help cartoon characters like Penny Bright and Small Change earn money to renovate and reopen the local park. As kids play puzzles and concentration-type games, they see their "deposits" accumulate. And then they decide how to spend their money: for grass and flowers, a statue or bird bath for the park. They also get practice in basic money math, including identifying and counting coins and making change.

Neale Godfrey, the author of several books about money for kids, helped developed *Money Town*, and she makes a video appearance on the CD-ROM with advice for parents.

(Davidson, (800) 545-7677, Windows CD-ROM, about $40)

Snootz Math Trek
Ages 6–10

Imaginative and challenging activities—featuring an odd but endearing pair of aliens known as Snootz—that encourage kids to discover problem-solving strategies and hone math thinking skills as they play. Kids who have outgrown *Millie's Math House* will be especially charmed by *Snootz Math Trek*. It's from the same development team and picks up at the skill level where *Millie's* leaves off.

The story of the Snootz has instant appeal. If these trumpet-nose creatures can hunt up all the items on their Big List, they can return to their home planet and play . . . for the rest of their lives. Players come to their aid by exploring the five activities where the items are hidden.

The activities include an addictive, two-player strategy game that dates back to ancient Mesopotamia; an inventive variation on hide and seek played on a grid of streets with map coordinates as clues; a set of more than 100 geometric puzzles; a musical pattern-recognition game; and an outfit-the-Snootz activity that looks easy at first but turns out to be a fiendish exercise in analyzing and constructing a complex set of attributes. Especially nice touches include a wealth of off-the-computer activities; a key to Snootian (along with a special Snootian font) that lets kids translate alien jokes that appear in speech balloons or codes messages for their friends; and a special section that tells kids about the math skills behind each activity, who uses them in real life and why they're worth mastering.

Part of *Space Cadet* series that also includes *Bumptz Science Carnival* (Page 228).

(Theatrix Interactive, (800) 955-TRIX, Win/Mac CD-ROM, about $35)

SKILLS & DRILLS

Radio Addition
Ages 5–8

The first of four *Radio Math* titles that feature country, rock and reggae "music videos" to present step-by-step lessons about basic math facts and concepts.

Radio Addition does a good job of explaining the process of addition, counting techniques, place value and regrouping. (In contrast, many Skills & Drills products focus more on practice and less on teaching.) Similar to the *Sound It Out Land* titles (Page 93) from the same publisher, *Radio Addition* is long on listening and watching and short on interactive discovery. Using *Radio Addition* is a lot like watching TV; kids are fairly passive for minutes at a time. Some children, accustomed to more constant and active involvement with their software, may become impatient. But for other children, sing-along instruction strikes just the right note.

These kids can't help but learn ... because they can't get the songs out of their heads.

Other planned titles in the series include *Radio Multiplication, Radio Subtraction* and *Radio Division*.

(Conexus, (800) 545-7677, Windows CD-ROM, about $35)

EXPLORATIONS FOR CURIOUS KIDS: ... AROUND THE WORLD

MayaQuest
Ages 10–16

An intriguing simulation from MECC (the *Oregon Trail* company) that casts kids both as modern-day adventurers bicycling through the Yucatan Peninsula and as historical detectives searching for clues to the collapse of the ancient Mayan civilization.

The unique thing about *MayaQuest* is the way it gives kids such an authentic sense of the sights and sounds of rain forests, ruins, people and places. It feels real because it is real: Its 1,500 photographs and video and audio clips were all taken during a 1994 bicycle expedition designed to shed light on Mayan geography, history and culture.

This high-tech trek was led by cyclist Dan Buettner, who responded daily to queries and suggestions from hundreds of students who followed his progress via the Internet. *MayaQuest* players get to tap into those communications as they retrace Buettner's expedition or venture onto alternate routes of their own. Or they can turn to an on-line forum where they can contact other *MayaQuest* players to exchange suggestions and theories.

And as with all MECC simulations, kids can delve into the product's ample reference materials to guide their decisions along the way and help them solve the mystery of the Mayan demise. In a new twist, kids can create a multimedia journal of their own quest using any of the photos, text or sounds on the CD-ROM.

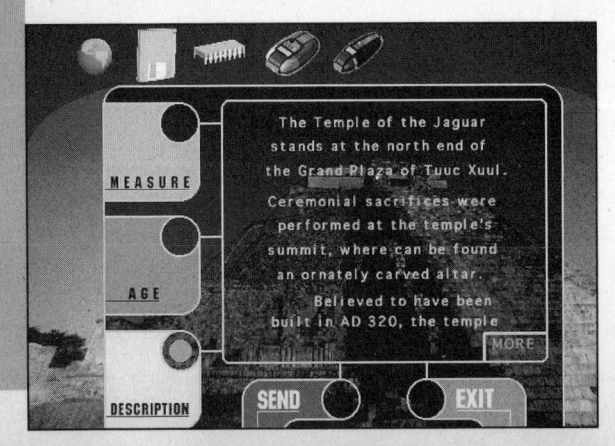

(MECC, (800) 685-6322, Win/Mac CD-ROM, about $50)

AfricaTrail
Ages 10–16

A modern-day Trail adventure designed to let kids interact with the diverse people across the African continent.

Like *MayaQuest, AfricaTrail* is based on a trek by cyclist Dan Buettner, this time from Tunisia to South Africa. Buettner made the trip in record time. And in order to retrace his progress southward, kids need to master a wealth of information about the different geographic regions on the itinerary and make appropriate decisions. Players get into the act in lots of ways: they control the budget for the trip, they buy supplies, they allocate the quantity of food for meals, they set the pace of travel, they obtain visas, they change money at every border crossing and more. Kids can even play native African games and experience road-rally action.

(MECC, (800) 685-6322, Win/Mac CD-ROM, about $50)

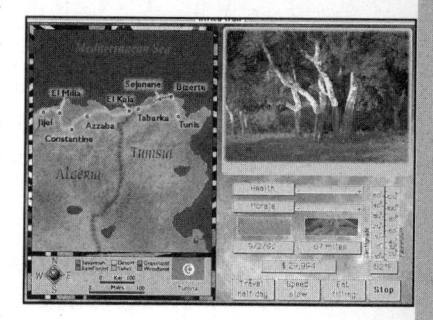

EXPLORATIONS FOR CURIOUS KIDS:
. . . BACK IN TIME

Louis Cat Orze
Ages 10 & Up

One minute, kids are bored tourists outside the gates of Versailles. The next minute, they're inside the court of Louis XIV in the year 1697 just in time to witness a shocking discovery: The Queen's necklace has been stolen. Everyone at court is suspect. And kids must ferret out the truth.

For older kids (and parents!) with a taste for historical intrigue, there's nothing else quite like *Louis Cat Orze*. With lavishly detailed illustrations and Baroque chamber music, this title looks and sounds great. And it's great fun to explore. Kids can eavesdrop on a secret conversation in the Orangerie . . . sneak into the Queen's bedchamber at midnight . . . see a glutinous monk arrested as a secret agent . . . or buy an audience with the King himself.

But it's tough to correctly finger the criminal unless players are committed to discovering—and remembering—a wealth of historical detail about 17th century France and the Sun King's entourage. To uncover useful information, players need to buy their way into different locations around Versailles. And to get money, they need to win big at the Palace Games.

These are not the card games that were so addictive for everyone else at Versailles. They're multiple-choice quizzes. And they may bring the adventure to a standstill for some players. After all, test-taking simply isn't as much fun as sleuthing. But with the visual delights of *Louis Cat Orze*, the fun of solving the mystery may well turn kids into *amis d'histoire*. To make things easier, consider playing *Louis Cat Orze* as a family, with older siblings and parents around to collaborate.

(IVI Publishing, (612) 996-6000, Win/Mac CD-ROM, about $50)

EXPLORATIONS FOR CURIOUS KIDS:
... INTO SCIENCE, NATURE AND BEYOND

Bumptz Science Carnival
Ages 6–10

Hundreds of inventive science puzzles, couched in a wacky and appealing story, introduce kids both to scientific principles—the properties of light, magnetism and buoyancy—and to the process of thinking scientifically.

Bumptz Science Carnival stars a busload of space aliens called Bumptz who have crash-landed at the Great Galaxies Amusement Park. They're round, wriggly critters, always getting waylaid somewhere between the entrance and exit of each carnival ride. The player's mission: Figure out the science needed to solve each ride's puzzles so the Bumptz can reach the exit, and then help them find the missing parts for their bus so they can blast off for home.

In the Photon-O-Tron ride, kids experiment with mirrors, color filters, lenses and prisms and use the properties of light to guide the Bumptz from entrance to exit. The Magnet-O-Whirl offers players a variety of wacky tools (such as ding dongers and boxing gloves) that embody some aspect of magnetism, gravity or other force that can be endlessly combined to give the Bumptz a wild ride. In Bubblearium, kids discover the scientific properties of propeller-nose sharks, inflator fish and squisher clams, and whether they make the Bumptz float or sink, and how to combine them so the Bumptz find their way out.

The software's best feature is its puzzle-construction mode. Not only can kids solve the puzzles in the carnival rides, they can also construct original rides for the Bumptz, and challenge friends, siblings or parents to come up with a solution. Other nice touches: Viewscope animations of how "real-world" properties of light, magnetism and buoyancy work and the "Experiment" button that lets kids print more than a dozen experiments to try off the computer.

Part of *Space Cadet* series that also includes *Snootz Math Trek*.

(Theatrix Interactive, (800) 955-TRIX, Win/Mac CD-ROM, about $35)

FUN & GAMES

Elroy Goes Bugzerk
Age 7–12

A great-looking interactive cartoon about the misadventures that befall an insect-crazy kid during a weekend on a farm after his dog eats a forbidden birthday cake.

The dilemma: Elroy needs to find an egg so he can bake a new cake, but he also wants to capture a rare "technoloptera" so he can defend his title in the 10th annual Insectathon. Players make choices that determine the twists and turns of the story. Make the wrong choices and the game ends pretty fast. Make the right choices and Elroy gets the bug and the egg. Along the way kids pick up fun facts about insects, which in turn can help them succeed.

Elroy Goes Bugzerk takes some getting used to, especially for kids who are accustomed to clicking everything on screen all the time. At first, kids can expect to spend a lot of time waiting and watching before they get to do something. But if they persist and advance deeper into the story, determined players will find there's progressively more and more to do. And their choices become more challenging, too.

If your kids go berserk for Elroy, watch for *Elroy Hits the Pavement*, the

next title in the *What the Heck Will Elroy Do Next?* series.
(Headbone Interactive, (800) 267-4709, Win/Mac CD-ROM, about $50)

The Lost Mind of Dr. Brain
Ages 9 & Up

One of the most challenging and addictive set of brain teasers to come along since *Myst*. Hundreds of word and logic puzzles, memory and strategy games, problem-solving adventures, visualization and musical challenges—each at three levels of difficulty—make playing *The Lost Mind of Dr. Brain* a great activity for everyone in the family.

The story is hokey but appealing: Dr. Brain has inadvertently transferred his mind into Rathbone, his laboratory rat. To reverse the brain drain—and win the game—players have to complete brain teasers in 10 different puzzle areas. In the Music Region, for example, kids have to unscramble mixed-up musical measures, flipping measures horizontally and vertically at the Expert and Genius levels of play. (For parents, it's a pleasure to hear substantial passages from classical composers in this musical memory game.) In the Motor Programming game, kids select a series of commands—and learn the rudiments of programming in the process—in order to maneuver around a maze.

With its stress on diverse intellectual challenges, Dr. Brain is a good companion to *Thinkin' Things Collection 2* (page 20) and *Thinkin' Things Collection 3* (Page 21). Dr. Brain addicts may also enjoy the earlier games in this series, *The Island of Dr. Brain* and *The Castle of Dr. Brain*. The newest title, however, features the best graphics, animation and music in the series.

(Sierra, (800) 757-7707, Win/Mac CD-ROM, $50)

Inside Magic
Ages 10 & Up

A how-to guide for aspiring magicians that reveals the sleight-of-hand illusions behind more than 40 magic tricks.

Peter Grand, a master magician and teacher, leads kids step-by-step through a variety of tricks with coins, cards, ropes, scarves and more.

His demonstrations are presented in video and animation sequences that kids can replay over and over—at full speed, half speed or in slow-motion. Best feature: Kids can view each trick from two perspectives, the audience view or the "back-stage" view that shows the techniques behind the illusions.

Inside Magic also includes tips for kids on how to create their own magic act and information about the origins of various magic tricks. The software comes with a magic kit, complete with all the props they'll need to perform the tricks they learn.

A good bet for any kid with an interest in magic. Beginners can quickly pick up the basics. Kids who've already mastered the basics can tackle the more complex techniques and polish their act with advice from a master.

(Houghton Mifflin Interactive, (800) 225-3362, Win/Mac CD-ROM, about $60)

Ascendancy
Ages 10 & Up

Be warned: This is the only product in the *Guide* where kids can declare war, make conquests and blow things up. But *Ascendancy*'s emphasis on exploration and strategic thinking—plus its intriguing visual challenges—overcame our objections . . . and may conquer yours, too.

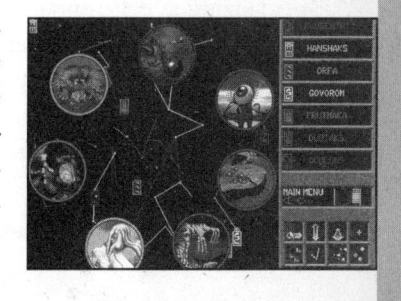

Players are in charge of an alien race, one of 21 species in an unknown galaxy. The goal: Gain ascendancy—either through alliance-building or conquest—over other races. In its beginning stages, this strategy game is somewhat like a *SimCity*. Kids need to figure out and build up the conditions necessary for entry into the space age: industry, scientific research, technological inventions. Next they design space ships for exploring and colonizing distant planets. Then they figure out how to chart a course through space and glean intelligence about potential allies and enemies. Of course, they can outfit their ships with weapons. But in this game knowledge and skill are often more powerful—and effective—than sheer might.

Excellent graphics give kids up-close views of their developing planet, their spacecraft and alien races as well as long-distance perspectives on vast star systems. Kids can play an hour- or a weekend-long game by adjusting the number of stars and the number of species in the galaxy, as well as by setting the playing "atmosphere" from peaceful to hostile. When violence erupts, by the way, it's fairly abstract: a burst of light and sound-effects from decimated spacecraft.

(Broderbund, (800) 521-6263, DOS CD-ROM, about $50)

INFORMATION, PLEASE!

Eyewitness Virtual Reality BIRD
Eyewitness Virtual Reality CAT
Ages 8 & Up

Two kid-friendly compendiums of fact that give young lovers of cats or birds an unusually vivid sense of being inside a wonderful hands-on museum. Kids wander through a three-dimensional space where they're free to explore, pull open specimen drawers and touch the exhibits.

Each of these titles takes kids to a different "floor" in the museum, one specializing in cats, one in birds. (Eventually there will be titles that create floors for reptiles, fish, sharks, horses, the jungle, dinosaurs, the rainforest and more.) Ringing the walls of each floor are "clickable" exhibits that present kids with more and more detail—in the form of beautifully displayed text, animations, still photography and video from the PBS series of the same name—with each successive click. Scattered throughout the exhibits are learning activities. In Beat the Cheetah, for example, kids can run a gazelle, race horse, athlete or sports car against the big cat and discover how they fare over different distances.

We like the fact that not all exhibits are strictly science. In *CAT*, kids can learn how cats figure in legend and myth, see their influence on ancient Egyptian culture and more. In a nice touch, kids can choose among several tours to guide them through the exhibits or create one of their own—a good way to show friends, parents or teachers what they've been up to on the computer—by selecting their favorite exhibits. A great family reference.

(DK Multimedia, (800) 225-3362, Windows CD-ROM, Macintosh version later, about $50)

Cartopedia
Ages 10 & Up

A sophisticated and beautifully designed atlas of the world. Best for adults and middle- to high-school aged kids with challenging homework assignments. Apart from its depth and distinctive DK looks, *Cartopedia* has some special features that distinguish it from the other atlases we recommend. Our favorite is the "compare" feature that automatically produces charts and graphs contrasting information on ethnic make-up, climate, health and scores of other topics for any two countries kids select.

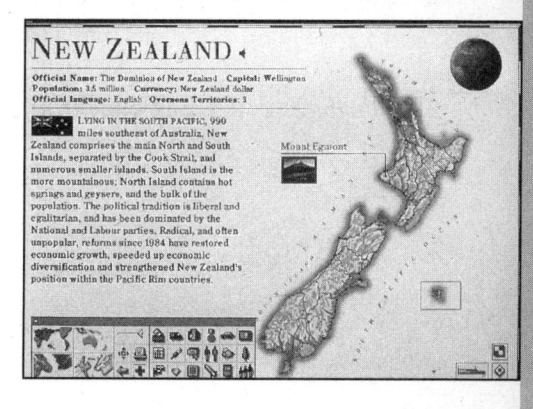

Which atlas to choose? Consider *PC Globe Maps 'N Facts* (Page 123) for basic school assignments. For visual excitement and informative narrative, try *3D Atlas* (Page 192). And for sophisticated research and a long-term family reference, *Cartopedia* is a good choice.

(DK Multimedia, (800) 225-3362, Win/Mac CD-ROM, $90)

Discovering Shakespeare
Ages 10 & Up

A good accompaniment to a child's first encounter with The Bard.

Discovering Shakespeare introduces kids to the life and times of the world's greatest playwright with a pleasing mix of illustrations, narration, text and short but absorbing movies. These video clips are among the product's best features. They give kids up-close looks at the gruesome make-up for the Weird Sisters in *Macbeth*, at a falconry demonstration (a sport often mentioned by Shakespeare), at landmarks that survive from Shakespeare's day and dozens more. And they're presented by such impassioned people—actors, make-up artists, historians of Elizabethan England, costumers and others—that kids can't resist being swept along by their enthusiasms.

Kids will also find a section that debunks a variety of myths about Shakespeare, a synopsis of every one of his plays, and an interactive timeline that lets them jump to movies about any topic highlighted in red. (This is how we discovered one of the product's many fun facts: potatoes were a new and strange and highly prized vegetable in Shakespeare's day!)

(IVI Publishing, (612) 996-6000, Win/Mac CD-ROM, about $50)

MORE BEST LISTS

THE BEST SIMULATION PROGRAMS

RATINGS	TITLES	AGES
★★★★	**The Oregon Trail II** (Page 134)	10-16
★★★★	**SimCity 2000** (Page 172)	10 & Up
★★★	**Klik & Play** (Page 180)	9-12
★★★	**Odell Down Under** (Page 156)	8-12
★★	**Widget Workshop** (Page 158)	10-12

THE MOST CHALLENGING PROGRAMS

RATINGS	TITLES	AGES
★★★★	Circus! (Page 10)	4-8
★★★★	Myst (Page 170)	9 & Up
★★★★	The Oregon Trail II (Page 134)	10-16
★★★★	SimCity 2000 (Page 172)	10 & Up
★★★	Thinkin' Things Collection 2 or 3 (Page 20)	6-12
★★	Widget Workshop (Page 158)	10-12

THE BEST VIDEO-GAME-MEETS-EDUCATION-PROGRAMS

RATINGS	TITLES	AGES
★★★	Klik & Play (Page 180)	9-12
★★	Troggle Trouble (Page 112)	6-12
★	The Math Blaster Series (Page 114)	6-12
★	The Muncher Series (Page 116)	6-12
★	Reading Blaster (Page 88)	7-10
★	The Treasure Series (Page 118)	5-9

THE BEST HOMEWORK HELPERS

RATINGS	TITLES	AGES
★★★	**Alien Tales** (Page 80)	8-12
★★★	**Encarta 1996** (Page 194)	11 & Up
★★★	**Davidson's Kid Phonics** (Page 82)	4-6
★★★	**Student Writing Center** (Page 202)	10 & Up
★★	**Adventures in Flight** (Page 104)	8-12
★★	**GeoSafari** (Page 186)	8-12

THE BEST PROGRAMS FOR KIDS & PARENTS TO USE TOGETHER

RATINGS	TITLES	AGES
★★★★	Kid Pix Studio (Page 34)	3-12
★★★★	Where in the World Is Carmen Sandiego? (Page 124)	8-12
★★★	3D Atlas (Page 192)	8 & Up
★★★	Davidson's Kid Works Deluxe (Page 62)	2-5
★★★	Travelrama USA (Page 130)	8-12
★★	Widget Workshop (Page 158)	10-12

THE BEST PROGRAMS FOR SIBLINGS TO SHARE

RATINGS	TITLES	AGES
★★★★	The Amazing Writing Machine (Page 52)	7-12
★★★★	Art Explorer (Page 40)	8-12
★★★★	Imagination Express (Page 54)	5-12
★★★★	Kid Pix Studio (Page 34)	3-12
★★★	Where in the World Is Carmen Sandiego? Junior Detective Edition (Page 128)	5-8
★★★	Zurk's Rainforest Lab (Page 16)	5-9

GLOSSARY

3-D graphics
Sophisticated visual effects that create the illusion of three-dimensional space.

Background
A backdrop or scenic illustration that children use as a canvas for their artwork.

CD-ROM
An optical disk that stores a software program; more and more kids' software is now delivered on CD-ROM, as opposed to floppy disks. The letters stand for Compact Disc Read-Only Memory.

Click
Literally, pressing the mouse button. Clicking initiates an action by the software.

Click and Drag
The sequence of actions used to place objects on the computer screen. Kids click an object (like a stamp) to select it, and with their finger still on the mouse button, drag it into position in their artwork.

Click Point
An area of the computer screen that is "live"; pressing a click point activates a sound effect, animation, video, or triggers a response of some sort. (See also, Hot Spot.)

Color Palette
Like an artist's palette, the choice of colors in a particular program.

Database
A collection of information, organized for quick search and retrieval.

Desktop
The on-screen environment created by a software program.

E-mail
Electronic mail; a message sent from one computer user to another via a network or on-line service.

Floppy Disk
A magnetic disk that stores a software program; this medium is being replaced by CD-ROMs.

Gameplay
The experience of playing a software program.

Graphics
The artwork used in software programs.

Hands-on Learning
A style of learning where kids make discoveries by asking questions, exploring, experimenting, creating.

Hot Spot
An area of the computer screen that is "live"; clicking a hot spot activates a sound effect, animation, video, or triggers a response of some sort. (See also, Click Point.)

Icon
A tiny picture on the computer screen; children's programs typically use icons in place of word commands to move from one part of the program to another or to save or print work.

Interactive
Interactive software opens a continual dialog between child and computer; the child's actions and choices determine the computer's response.

Internet
A vast international set of computer networks, commonly referred to as the information superhighway.

Menu

A list of options (like "open," "save," "print") used to tell a computer program what to do. Some menus "pull down" from the top of the screen. Others "pop up" into the workspace to offer options directly related to the child's activity.

Multimedia

Software that includes or combines narration, stereo-like sound, graphics, animation, photographic images, and/or video footage.

Network Service

A company that provides computer users with access to on-line resources.

On-line

Connection to a computer network through a modem and phone line. On-line services like CompuServe, America OnLine and Prodigy let you send and receive electronic mail and retrieve information from their databases.

Open-ended

An open-ended activity has no predetermined direction or right answer.

Photorealism

Images created from or closely resembling photographs.

Rebus

A riddle or puzzle in which pictures substitute for words or syllables; particularly instructive for beginning readers.

Screen Saver

A software program that fills the computer screen with special graphics whenever the computer is running but not being used.

Slide Show

A feature in some Art & Animation programs that links saved artwork and/or text and displays it sequentially to create a movie-like effect.

Stamps

Small pictures that children place in a program's workspace to create illustrated scenes; most often found in *Creative Pursuits* programs.

Storyboard

A pictorial outline used in planning stories, animations, slide shows or games.

Template

A model or blueprint, often used to given children guidance in writing projects.

Toolbar

A special pictorial menu depicting a software program's tools. Kids select a tool by clicking its picture.

Toolkit

A software program's collection of tools.

Tools

The computer equivalent of art supplies (stamps, backgrounds, erasers, brushes, effects and the like) that children use in *Creative Pursuits* programs.

Utility

A software program that helps manage tasks related to the computer or its system software.

Titles Index

3D Atlas (Page 192)
3-D Body Adventure (Page 166)
3-D Dinosaur Adventure (Page 166)
Adventures in Flight (Page 104)
The Adventures of Peter Rabbit & Benjamin Bunny (Page 214)
AfricaTrail (Page 227)
Alge-Blaster 3 (Page 114)
Alien Tales (Page 80)
Alphabet Blocks (Page 89)
AlphaBonk Farm (Page 12)
Amazing Animation (Page 42)
The Amazing Writing Machine (Page 52)
The Amazon Trail (Page 138)
Ancient Lands (Page 140)
Art Explorer (Page 40)
Arthur's Birthday (Page 70)
Arthur's Teacher Trouble (Page 70)
Ascendancy (Page 231)
At Bat (Page 178)
At Ease (Page 200)
Aviation Adventure (Page 166)
Baby ROM (Page 212)
The Backyard (Page 24)
Bailey's Book House (Page 60)
Beginning Reading (Page 90)
The Berenstain Bears Get in a Fight (Page 70)
Bug Adventure (Page 166)
Bumptz Science Carnival (Page 228)
Cartopedia (Page 233)

The Castle of Dr. Brain (Page 230)
Chicka Chicka Boom Boom (Page 220)
Circus! (Page 10)
Cosmic Osmo (Page 170)
Countdown (Page 102)
Counting on Frank (Page 106)
Crayola Amazing Art Adventure (Page 48)
Crayola Art Studio (Page 48)
Creative Writer (Page 64)
Curious George Comes Home (Page 220)
Dangerous Creatures (Page 160)
Davidson's Kid Keys (Page 210)
Davidson's Kid Phonics (Page 82)
Davidson's Kid Works 2 (Page 63)
Davidson's Kid Works Deluxe (Page 62)
Dinkytown Daycare Kids Story Pack (Page 59)
The Discis Kids Can Read Series (Page 76)
  Aesop's Fables (Page 77)
  Anansi: Three Tales (Page 77)
  Cinderella (Page 77)
  Heather Hits Her First Home Run (Page 77)
  Johnny Appleseed (Page 77)
  A Long Hard Day on the Ranch (Page 77)
  Moving Gives Me a Stomach Ache (Page 77)
  Mud Puddle (Page 77)

The Night Before Christmas (Page 77)
Northern Lights: The Soccer Trails (Page 77)
The Paper Bag Princess (Page 77)
Paul Bunyan (Page 77)
Pecos Bill (Page 77)
A Promise Is a Promise (Page 77)
Scary Poems for Rotten Kids (Page 77)
Somebody Catch My Homework (Page 77)
The Tale of Benjamin Bunny (Page 77)
The Tale of Peter Rabbit (Page 76)
Thomas' Snowsuit (Page 77)
Discovering Shakespeare (Page 233)
Dr. Seuss' ABCs (Page 70)
Eagle Eye Mysteries: In London (Page 184)
Eagle Eye Mysteries: The Original (Page 184)
Elroy Goes Bugzerk (Page 229)
Elroy Hits the Pavement (Page 229)
Encarta 1996 (Page 194)
Explorapedia: The World of Nature (Page 190)
Explorapedia: The World of People (Page 190)
Eyewitness Encyclopedia of History (Page 196)
Eyewitness Encyclopedia of Nature (Page 196)
Eyewitness Encyclopedia of Science (Page 196)
Eyewitness Virtual Reality BIRD (Page 232)
Eyewitness Virtual Reality CAT (Page 232)
Fine Artist (Page 47)
Flying Colors (Page 36)
Flying Colors Art Packs (Page 36)
Freddi Fish and the Case of the Missing Kelp Seeds (Page 174)
Freddi Fish and the Haunted House (Page 175)
Gahan Wilson's The Ultimate Haunted House (Page 182)
GeoSafari (Page 186)
Hard Hat (Page 216)
Harry and the Haunted House (Page 70)
Hollywood (Page 219)
Hollywood Hounds Story Pack (Page 59)
Imagination Express Destination: Castle (Page 55)
Imagination Express Destination: Neighborhood (Page 55)
Imagination Express Destination: Rainforest (Page 55)
Inside Magic (Page 230)
The Island of Dr. Brain (Page 230)
James Discovers Math (Page 222)
Junior Encyclopedias: The Airport (Page 215)
Junior Encyclopedias: The Farm (Page 214)
Junior Encyclopedias: The Jungle (Page 215)
Just Grandma and Me (Page 70)
Keroppi Day Hopper (Page 204)
Kid Cuts (Page 38)
Kid Pix 2 (Page 32)
Kid Pix Fun Pack (Page 32)
Kid Pix Studio (Page 34)
KidDesk (Page 200)
KidDesk Family Edition (Page 200)
KidMail Connection (Page 206)
Kid's Typing (Page 208)
Kids World (Page 46)
Klik & Play (Page 180)
Launch Pad (Page 200)
Leonardo the Inventor (Page 144)
Little Monster at School (Page 70)
The Lost Mind of Dr. Brain (Page 230)
Louis Cat Orze (Page 227)

INDEX • 247

Madeline and the Magnificent Puppet Show (Page 222)
The Magic School Bus Explores the Human Body (Page 164)
The Magic School Bus Visits the Solar System (Page 164)
Magic Theatre (Page 44)
Math Blaster: Episode 1—In Search of Spot (Page 114)
Math Blaster: Episode 2—Secret of the Lost City (Page 114)
Math Blaster Mystery: The Great Brain Robbery (Page 114)
Math Munchers Deluxe (Page 116)
Math Workshop (Page 98)
MayaQuest (Page 226)
Microsoft BOB (Page 201)
Millie's Math House (Page 100)
Money Town (Page 224)
My First Incredible Amazing Dictionary (Page 26)
Myst (Page 170)
The New Kid on the Block (Page 70)
Number Munchers (Page 116)
Odell Down Under (Page 156)
Opening Night (Page 218)
The Oregon Trail II (Page 134)
P.B. Bear's Birthday Party (Page 74)
PC Globe Maps 'N Facts (Page 123)
Pantsylvania (Page 215)
Peter Rabbit's 123 (Page 214)
Planetary Taxi (Page 152)
The Playroom (Page 22)
Polar Express (Page 221)
Print Artist (Page 31)
Print Shop Deluxe CD Ensemble (Page 31)
Putt-Putt Goes to the Moon (Page 176)
Putt-Putt Joins the Parade (Page 176)
Putt-Putt Saves the Zoo (Page 176)
Radio Addition (Page 225)
Radio Division (Page 226)
Radio Multiplication (Page 226)
Radio Subtraction (Page 226)
Reader Rabbit 1 (Page 84)
Reader Rabbit 2 (Page 84)
Reader Rabbit 3 (Page 84)
Reader Rabbit's Interactive Reading Journey (Page 86)
Reader Rabbit's Ready for Letters (Page 84)
Reading Blaster (Page 88)
Recess in Greece (Page 148)
Richard Scarry's How Things Work in Busytown (Page 28)
Safari (Page 157)
Sammy's Science House (Page 150)
Scavenger Hunt: Africa (Page 162)
Scavenger Hunt: Oceans (Page 162)
Science Adventure II (Page 166)
SimAnt (Page 173)
SimCity 2000 (Page 172)
SimCity Classic (Page 173)
SimEarth (Page 173)
SimFarm (Page 173)
SimIsle (Page 173)
SimTower (Page 172)
SimTown (Page 173)
Snootz Math Trek (Page 224)
Sound It Out Land 1, 2, 3 (Page 93)
Space Adventure II (Page 166)
Spider-Man Cartoon Maker (Page 45)
Star Act (Page 56)
Storybook Weaver Deluxe (Page 58)
Stowaway! (Page 146)
Student Writing Center (Page 202)
Super Munchers (Page 116)
Super Solvers Midnight Rescue! (Page 91)
Super Solvers OutNumbered! (Page 120)
Super Solvers Spellbound! (Page 91)
TesselMania! (Page 216)
Thinkin' Things Collection 1 (Page 18)

Thinkin' Things Collection 2 (Page 20)
Thinkin' Things Collection 3 (Page 21)
Top Secret Decoder (Page 217)
The Tortoise and the Hare (Page 70)
Travelrama USA (Page 130)
Treasure Cove! (Page 118)
Treasure Galaxy! (Page 118)
Treasure MathStorm! (Page 118)
Treasure Mountain! (Page 118)
Troggle Trouble (Page 112)
Trudy's Time & Place House (Page 213)
Undersea Adventure (Page 166)
What's the Secret? (Page 154)
Where's Waldo? at the Circus (Page 223)
Where in America's Past Is Carmen Sandiego? (Page 127)
Where in Europe Is Carmen Sandiego? (Page 127)
Where in Space Is Carmen Sandiego? (Page 127)
Where in Time Is Carmen Sandiego? (Page 127)
Where in the USA Is Carmen Sandiego? (Page 126)
Where in the World Is Carmen Sandiego? (Page 124)
Where in the World Is Carmen Sandiego? Junior Detective Edition (Page 128)
Widget Workshop (Page 158)
WiggleWorks Volume 1 (Page 92)
Word Munchers (Page 116)
Wrath of the Gods (Page 142)
The Yukon Trail (Page 136)
Zurk's Learning Safari (Page 14)
Zurk's Rainforest Lab (Page 16)

CD-ROM Titles Index

3D Atlas (Page 192)
3-D Body Adventure (Page 166)
3-D Dinosaur Adventure (Page 166)
Adventures in Flight (Page 104)
The Adventures of Peter Rabbit & Benjamin Bunny (Page 214)
AfricaTrail (Page 227)
Alge-Blaster 3 (Page 114)
Alien Tales (Page 80)
Alphabet Blocks (Page 89)
AlphaBonk Farm (Page 12)
Amazing Animation (Page 42)
The Amazing Writing Machine (Page 52)
The Amazon Trail (Page 138)
Ancient Lands (Page 140)
Art Explorer (Page 40)
Arthur's Birthday (Page 70)
Arthur's Teacher Trouble (Page 70)
Ascendancy (Page 231)
At Bat (Page 178)
Aviation Adventure (Page 166)
Baby ROM (Page 212)
Bailey's Book House (Page 60)
Beginning Reading (Page 90)
The Berenstain Bears Get in a Fight (Page 70)
Bug Adventure (Page 166)
Bumptz Science Carnival (Page 228)
Cartopedia (Page 233)
Chicka Chicka Boom Boom (Page 220)
Circus! (Page 10)
Cosmic Osmo (Page 170)
Countdown (Page 102)
Counting on Frank (Page 106)
Crayola Amazing Art Adventure (Page 48)
Crayola Art Studio (Page 48)
Creative Writer (Page 64)
Curious George Comes Home (Page 220)
Dangerous Creatures (Page 160)
Davidson's Kid Phonics (Page 82)
Davidson's Kid Works Deluxe (Page 62)
The Discis Kids Can Read Series (Page 76)
  Aesop's Fables (Page 77)
  Anansi: Three Tales (Page 77)
  Cinderella (Page 77)
  Heather Hits Her First Home Run (Page 77)
  Johnny Appleseed (Page 77)
  A Long Hard Day on the Ranch (Page 77)
  Moving Gives Me a Stomach Ache (Page 77)
  Mud Puddle (Page 77)
  The Night Before Christmas (Page 77)
  Northern Lights: The Soccer Trails (Page 77)
  The Paper Bag Princess (Page 77)
  Paul Bunyan (Page 77)

Pecos Bill (Page 77)
A Promise Is a Promise (Page 77)
Scary Poems for Rotten Kids (Page 77)
Somebody Catch My Homework (Page 77)
The Tale of Benjamin Bunny (Page 77)
The Tale of Peter Rabbit (Page 76)
Thomas' Snowsuit (Page 77)
Discovering Shakespeare (Page 233)
Dr. Seuss' ABCs (Page 70)
Eagle Eye Mysteries: In London (Page 184)
Eagle Eye Mysteries: The Original (Page 184)
Elroy Goes Bugzerk (Page 229)
Elroy Hits the Pavement (Page 229)
Encarta 1996 (Page 194)
Explorapedia: The World of Nature (Page 190)
Explorapedia: The World of People (Page 190)
Eyewitness Encyclopedia of History (Page 196)
Eyewitness Encyclopedia of Nature (Page 196)
Eyewitness Encyclopedia of Science (Page 196)
Eyewitness Virtual Reality BIRD (Page 232)
Eyewitness Virtual Reality CAT (Page 232)
Fine Artist (Page 47)
Flying Colors (Page 36)
Freddi Fish and the Case of the Missing Kelp Seeds (Page 174)
Freddi Fish and the Haunted House (Page 175)
Gahan Wilson's The Ultimate Haunted House (Page 182)
GeoSafari (Page 186)
Hard Hat (Page 216)
Harry and the Haunted House (Page 70)
Hollywood (Page 219)
Imagination Express Destination: Castle (Page 55)
Imagination Express Destination: Neighborhood (Page 55)
Imagination Express Destination: Rainforest (Page 55)
Inside Magic (Page 230)
James Discovers Math (Page 222)
Junior Encyclopedias: The Airport (Page 215)
Junior Encyclopedias: The Farm (Page 214)
Junior Encyclopedias: The Jungle (Page 215)
Just Grandma and Me (Page 70)
Keroppi Day Hopper (Page 204)
Kid Pix Studio (Page 34)
KidMail Connection (Page 206)
Kid's Typing (Page 208)
Launch Pad (Page 200)
Leonardo the Inventor (Page 144)
Little Monster at School (Page 70)
The Lost Mind of Dr. Brain (Page 230)
Louis Cat Orze (Page 227)
Madeline and the Magnificent Puppet Show (Page 222)
The Magic School Bus Explores the Human Body (Page 164)
The Magic School Bus Visits the Solar System (Page 164)
Magic Theatre (Page 44)
Math Blaster: Episode 1—In Search of Spot (Page 114)
Math Blaster: Episode 2—Secret of the Lost City (Page 114)
Math Blaster Mystery: The Great Brain Robbery (Page 114)
Math Munchers Deluxe (Page 116)
Math Workshop (Page 98)
MayaQuest (Page 226)
Millie's Math House (Page 100)
Money Town (Page 224)

My First Incredible Amazing Dictionary (Page 26)
Myst (Page 170)
The New Kid on the Block (Page 70)
Opening Night (Page 218)
The Oregon Trail II (Page 134)
P.B. Bear's Birthday Party (Page 74)
PC Globe Maps 'N Facts (Page 123)
Pantsylvania (Page 215)
Peter Rabbit's 123 (Page 214)
Planetary Taxi (Page 152)
The Playroom (Page 22)
Polar Express (Page 221)
Print Shop Deluxe CD Ensemble (Page 31)
Putt-Putt Goes to the Moon (Page 176)
Putt-Putt Joins the Parade (Page 176)
Putt-Putt Saves the Zoo (Page 176)
Radio Addition (Page 225)
Radio Division (Page 226)
Radio Multiplication (Page 226)
Radio Subtraction (Page 226)
Reader Rabbit 1 (Page 84)
Reader Rabbit 2 (Page 84)
Reader Rabbit 3 (Page 84)
Reader Rabbit's Interactive Reading Journey (Page 86)
Reading Blaster (Page 88)
Recess in Greece (Page 148)
Richard Scarry's How Things Work in Busytown (Page 28)
Safari (Page 157)
Sammy's Science House (Page 150)
Scavenger Hunt: Africa (Page 162)
Scavenger Hunt: Oceans (Page 162)
Science Adventure II (Page 166)
SimIsle (Page 173)
SimTown (Page 173)
Snootz Math Trek (Page 224)

Sound It Out Land 1, 2, 3 (Page 93)
Space Adventure II (Page 166)
Spider-Man Cartoon Maker (Page 45)
Star Act (Page 56)
Storybook Weaver Deluxe (Page 58)
Stowaway! (Page 146)
Student Writing Center (Page 202)
Super Solvers Spellbound! (Page 91)
TesselMania! (Page 216)
Thinkin' Things Collection 1 (Page 18)
Thinkin' Things Collection 2 (Page 20)
Thinkin' Things Collection 3 (Page 21)
Top Secret Decoder (Page 217)
The Tortoise and the Hare (Page 70)
Travelrama USA (Page 130)
Treasure Cove! (Page 118)
Treasure Galaxy! (Page 118)
Treasure MathStorm! (Page 118)
Treasure Mountain! (Page 118)
Troggle Trouble (Page 112)
Trudy's Time & Place House (Page 213)
Undersea Adventure (Page 166)
What's the Secret? (Page 154)
Where in the USA Is Carmen Sandiego? (Page 126)
Where in the World Is Carmen Sandiego? (Page 124)
Where in the World Is Carmen Sandiego? Jr. Detective Edition (Page 128)
Where's Waldo? at the Circus (Page 223)
WiggleWorks Volume 1 (Page 92)
Wrath of the Gods (Page 142)
The Yukon Trail (Page 136)
Zurk's Learning Safari (Page 14)
Zurk's Rainforest Lab (Page 16)

Floppy Titles Index

3-D Body Adventure (Page 166)
3-D Dinosaur Adventure (Page 166)
Alge-Blaster 3 (Page 114)
Alphabet Blocks (Page 89)
Amazing Animation (Page 42)
The Amazing Writing Machine (Page 52)
The Amazon Trail (Page 138)
Art Explorer (Page 40)
At Ease (Page 200)
The Backyard (Page 24)
Bailey's Book House (Page 60)
Beginning Reading (Page 90)
Cosmic Osmo (Page 170)
Crayola Amazing Art Adventure (Page 48)
Crayola Art Studio (Page 48)
Creative Writer (Page 64)
Davidson's Kid Keys (Page 210)
Davidson's Kid Works 2 (Page 63)
Dinkytown Daycare Kids Story Pack (Page 59)
Eagle Eye Mysteries: In London (Page 184)
Eagle Eye Mysteries: The Original (Page 184)
Fine Artist (Page 47)
Flying Colors (Page 36)
Flying Colors Art Packs (Page 36)
Hollywood Hounds Story Pack (Page 59)
Keroppi Day Hopper (Page 204)
Kid Cuts (Page 38)
Kid Pix 2 (Page 32)
Kid Pix Fun Pack (Page 32)
KidDesk (Page 200)
KidDesk Family Edition (Page 200)
KidMail Connection (Page 206)
Kids World (Page 46)
Klik & Play (Page 180)
Launch Pad (Page 200)
Magic Theatre (Page 44)
Math Blaster: Episode 1—In Search of Spot (Page 114)
Math Blaster: Episode 2—Secret of the Lost City (Page 114)
Microsoft BOB (Page 201)
Millie's Math House (Page 100)
Number Munchers (Page 116)
Odell Down Under (Page 156)
The Playroom (Page 22)
Print Artist (Page 31)
Reader Rabbit 1 (Page 84)
Reader Rabbit 2 (Page 84)
Reader Rabbit 3 (Page 84)
Reader Rabbit's Ready for Letters (Page 84)
Reading Blaster (Page 88)
Richard Scarry's How Things Work in Busytown (Page 28)
Sammy's Science House (Page 150)
SimAnt (Page 173)
SimCity 2000 (Page 172)
SimCity Classic (Page 173)
SimEarth (Page 173)
SimFarm (Page 173)
SimTower (Page 172)

Storybook Weaver (Page 58)
Student Writing Center (Page 202)
Super Munchers (Page 116)
Super Solvers Midnight Rescue! (Page 91)
Super Solvers OutNumbered! (Page 120)
Super Solvers Spellbound! (Page 91)
Thinkin' Things Collection 1 (Page 18)
Thinkin' Things Collection 2 (Page 20)
Treasure Cove! (Page 118)
Treasure Galaxy! (Page 118)
Treasure MathStorm! (Page 118)
Treasure Mountain! (Page 118)
Troggle Trouble (Page 112)
Undersea Adventure (Page 166)
Where in America's Past Is Carmen Sandiego? (Page 127)
Where in Europe Is Carmen Sandiego? (Page 127)
Where in Space Is Carmen Sandiego? (Page 127)
Where in Time Is Carmen Sandiego? (Page 127)
Where in the USA Is Carmen Sandiego? (Page 126)
Where in the World Is Carmen Sandiego? (Page 124)
Widget Workshop (Page 158)
Word Munchers (Page 116)
The Yukon Trail (Page 136)
Zurk's Learning Safari (Page 14)

Publishers Index

3M (612) 737-3249
  What's the Secret? (Page 154)

Adobe/Aldus (800) 888-6293
  Art Explorer (Page 40)

Apple (800) 776-2333 x5924
  At Ease (Page 200)
  WiggleWorks Volume 1 (Page 92)

Berkeley Systems (510) 540-5535
  Launch Pad (Page 200)

Big Top Productions (415) 978-5363
  Keroppi Day Hopper (Page 204)

Bit Jugglers (415) 968-3908
  Kids World (Page 46)

Broderbund (800) 521-6263
  Alien Tales (Page 80)
  The Amazing Writing Machine (Page 52)
  Ascendancy (Page 231)
  The Backyard (Page 24)
  Cosmic Osmo (Page 170)
  James Discovers Math (Page 222)
  Kid Cuts (Page 38)
  Kid Pix 2 (Page 32)
  Kid Pix Fun Pack (Page 32)
  Kid Pix Studio (Page 34)
  Math Workshop (Page 98)
  Myst (Page 170)
  The Playroom (Page 22)
  PC Globe Maps 'N Facts (Page 123)
  Print Shop Deluxe CD Ensemble (Page 31)
  Where in America's Past Is Carmen Sandiego? (Page 127)
  Where in Europe Is Carmen Sandiego? (Page 127)
  Where in Space Is Carmen Sandiego? (Page 127)
  Where in Time Is Carmen Sandiego? (Page 127)
  Where in the USA Is Carmen Sandiego? (Page 126)
  Where in the World Is Carmen Sandiego? (Page 124)
  Where in the World Is Carmen Sandiego? Jr. Detective Edition (Page 128)

Byron Preiss Multimedia (800) 274-6800
  Baby ROM (Page 212)
  Hard Hat (Page 216)

Claris (800) 325-2747
  Amazing Animation (Page 42)

Conexus (800) 545-7677
  Radio Addition (Page 225)
  Radio Division (Page 226)
  Radio Multiplication (Page 226)

Radio Subtraction (Page 226)
Sound It Out Land 1 (Page 93)
Sound It Out Land 2 (Page 93)
Sound It Out Land 3 (Page 93)

ConnectSoft (800) 234-9497
KidMail Connection (Page 206)

Creative Wonders (800) 543-9778
3D Atlas (Page 192)
Counting on Frank (Page 106)
Eagle Eye Mysteries: In London (Page 184)
Eagle Eye Mysteries: The Original (Page 184)
Madeline and the Magnificent Puppet Show (Page 222)

DK Multimedia (800) 225-3362
Cartopedia (Page 233)
Eyewitness Encyclopedia of History (Page 196)
Eyewitness Encyclopedia of Nature (Page 196)
Eyewitness Encyclopedia of Science (Page 196)
Eyewitness Virtual Reality BIRD (Page 232)
Eyewitness Virtual Reality CAT (Page 232)
My First Incredible Amazing Dictionary (Page 26)
P.B. Bear's Birthday Party (Page 74)
Stowaway! (Page 146)

Davidson (800) 545-7677
Alge-Blaster 3 (Page 114)
Chicka Chicka Boom Boom (Page 220)
Davidson's Kid Keys (Page 210)
Davidson's Kid Phonics (Page 82)
Davidson's Kid Works Deluxe (Page 62)
Flying Colors (Page 36)

Math Blaster: Episode 1—In Search of Spot (Page 114)
Math Blaster: Episode 2—Secret of the Lost City (Page 114)
Math Blaster Mystery: The Great Brain Robbery (Page 114)
Money Town (Page 224)
Reading Blaster (Page 88)

Discis (800) 567-4321
Aesop's Fables (Page 77)
Anansi: Three Tales (Page 77)
Cinderella (Page 77)
Heather Hits Her First Home Run (Page 77)
Johnny Appleseed (Page 77)
A Long Hard Day on the Ranch (Page 77)
Moving Gives Me a Stomach Ache (Page 77)
Mud Puddle (Page 77)
The Night Before Christmas (Page 77)
Northern Lights: The Soccer Trails (Page 77)
The Paper Bag Princess (Page 77)
Paul Bunyan (Page 77)
Pecos Bill (Page 77)
A Promise Is a Promise (Page 77)
Scary Poems for Rotten Kids (Page 77)
Somebody Catch My Homework (Page 77)
The Tale of Benjamin Bunny (Page 77)
The Tale of Peter Rabbit (Page 76)
Thomas' Snowsuit (Page 77)

Edmark (800) 691-2985
Bailey's Book House (Page 60)
Imagination Express Destination: Castle (Page 55)
Imagination Express Destination: Neighborhood (Page 55)

Imagination Express Destination: Rainforest (Page 55)
KidDesk (Page 200)
KidDesk Family Edition (Page 200)
Millie's Math House (Page 100)
Sammy's Science House (Page 150)
Thinkin' Things Collection 1 (Page 18)
Thinkin' Things Collection 2 (Page 20)
Thinkin' Things Collection 3 (Page 21)
Trudy's Time and Place House (Page 213)

Educational Insights (800) 526-2947
GeoSafari (Page 186)

Future Vision (800) 472-8777
Leonardo the Inventor (Page 144)

Headbone Interactive (800) 267-4709
AlphaBonk Farm (Page 12)
Elroy Goes Bugzerk (Page 229)
Elroy Hits the Pavement (Page 229)
Pantsylvania (Page 215)

Houghton Mifflin Interactive (800) 225-3362
Curious George Comes Home (Page 220)
Inside Magic (Page 230)
Polar Express (Page 221)
Top Secret Decoder (Page 217)

Humongous (206) 485-1212
Freddi Fish and the Case of the Missing Kelp Seeds (Page 174)
Freddi Fish and the Haunted House (Page 175)

Junior Encyclopedias: The Airport (Page 215)
Junior Encyclopedias: The Farm (Page 214)
Junior Encyclopedias: The Jungle (Page 215)
Putt-Putt Goes to the Moon (Page 176)
Putt-Putt Joins the Parade (Page 176)
Putt-Putt Saves the Zoo (Page 176)

IVI Publishing (800) 432-1332
Discovering Shakespeare (Page 233)
Louis Cat Orze (Page 227)

JAmbone (604) 739-7281
At Bat (Page 178)

Knowledge Adventure (800) 542-4240
3-D Body Adventure (Page 166)
3-D Dinosaur Adventure (Page 166)
Aviation Adventure (Page 166)
Bug Adventure (Page 166)
Magic Theatre (Page 44)
Science Adventure II (Page 166)
Space Adventure II (Page 166)
Spider-Man Cartoon Maker (Page 45)
Undersea Adventure (Page 166)

Living Books (800) 521-6263
Arthur's Birthday (Page 70)
Arthur's Teacher Trouble (Page 70)
The Berenstain Bears Get in a Fight (Page 70)
Dr. Seuss' ABCs (Page 70)
Harry and the Haunted House (Page 70)
Just Grandma and Me (Page 70)

Little Monster at School (Page 70)
The New Kid on the Block (Page 70)
The Tortoise and the Hare (Page 70)

Luminaria (415) 284-6464
Wrath of the Gods (Page 142)

Maxis (800) 526-2947
Klik & Play (Page 180)
Print Artist (Page 31)
SimAnt (Page 173)
SimCity 2000 (Page 172)
SimCity Classic (Page 173)
SimEarth (Page 173)
SimFarm (Page 173)
SimIsle (Page 173)
SimTower (Page 172)
SimTown (Page 173)
Star Act (Page 56)
Widget Workshop (Page 158)

MECC (800) 685-6322
AfricaTrail (Page 227)
The Amazon Trail (Page 138)
Math Munchers Deluxe (Page 116)
MayaQuest (Page 226)
Number Munchers (Page 116)
Odell Down Under (Page 156)
Opening Night (Page 218)
The Oregon Trail II (Page 134)
Storybook Weaver Deluxe (Page 58)
  Dinkytown Daycare Kids Story Pack (Page 59)
  Hollywood Hounds Story Pack (Page 59)
Super Munchers (Page 116)
TesselMania! (Page 216)
Troggle Trouble (Page 112)
Word Munchers (Page 116)
The Yukon Trail (Page 136)

Medio (800) 788-3866
Safari (Page 157)

Micrografx (800) 676-3110
Crayola Amazing Art Adventure (Page 48)
Crayola Art Studio (Page 48)

Microsoft (800) 228-6270
Ancient Lands (Page 140)
Creative Writer (Page 64)
Encarta 1996 (Page 194)
Explorapedia: The World of Nature (Page 190)
Explorapedia: The World of People (Page 190)
Fine Artist (Page 47)
Gahan Wilson's The Ultimate Haunted House (Page 182)
The Magic School Bus Explores the Human Body (Page 164)
The Magic School Bus Visits the Solar System (Page 164)
Microsoft BOB (Page 201)

Mindscape (800) 234-3088
The Adventures of Peter Rabbit & Benjamin Bunny (Page 214)
Peter Rabbit's 123 (Page 214)

Morgan Interactive (415) 693-9596
Recess in Greece (Page 148)

Sanctuary Woods (800) 872-3518
Adventures in Flight (Page 104)

Sierra (800) 757-7707
Alphabet Blocks (Page 89)
Beginning Reading (Page 90)
The Castle of Dr. Brain (Page 230)
The Island of Dr. Brain (Page 230)
Kid's Typing (Page 208)
The Lost Mind of Dr. Brain (Page 230)

INDEX • 259

Soleil (415) 494-0114
   Zurk's Learning Safari (Page 14)
   Zurk's Rainforest Lab (Page 16)

Swede (800) 545-7677
   Scavenger Hunt: Africa (Page 162)
   Scavenger Hunt: Oceans (Page 162)

The Learning Company (800) 852-2255
   Reader Rabbit 1 (Page 84)
   Reader Rabbit 2 (Page 84)
   Reader Rabbit 3 (Page 84)
   Reader Rabbit's Interactive Reading Journey (Page 86)
   Reader Rabbit's Ready for Letters (Page 84)
   Student Writing Center (Page 202)
   Super Solvers Midnight Rescue! (Page 91)
   Super Solvers OutNumbered! (Page 120)
   Super Solvers Spellbound! (Page 91)
   Treasure Cove! (Page 118)
   Treasure Galaxy! (Page 118)
   Treasure MathStorm! (Page 118)
   Treasure Mountain! (Page 118)

Theatrix Interactive (800) 955-8749
   Bumptz Science Carnival (Page 228)
   Hollywood (Page 219)
   Snootz Math Trek (Page 224)

Viacom New Media (800) 469-2539
   Richard Scarry's How Things Work in Busytown (Page 28)

Voyager (800) 446-2001
   Circus! (Page 10)
   Countdown (Page 102)
   Planetary Taxi (Page 152)

WarnerActive (800) 693-3253
   Where's Waldo? at the Circus (Page 223)

Zenda Studios (800) 872-3518
   Travelrama USA (Page 130)

Titles by Age Index

Under Age 2
Baby ROM (Page 212)

Age 2
At Ease (Page 200)
Baby ROM (Page 212)
Bailey's Book House (Page 60)
Davidson's Kid Works 2 (Page 63)
Davidson's Kid Works Deluxe (Page 62)
Junior Encyclopedias: The Airport (Page 215)
Junior Encyclopedias: The Farm (Page 214)
Junior Encyclopedias: The Jungle (Page 215)
Just Grandma and Me (Page 70)
KidDesk (Page 200)
KidDesk Family Edition (Page 200)
Launch Pad (Page 200)
Little Monster at School (Page 70)
Millie's Math House (Page 100)
My First Incredible Amazing Dictionary (Page 26)
P.B. Bear's Birthday Pary (Page 74)
The Playroom (Page 22)
Zurk's Learning Safari (Page 14)

Age 3
3-D Body Adventure (Page 166)
The Adventures of Peter Rabbit & Benjamin Bunny (Page 214)
Alphabet Blocks (Page 89)
AlphaBonk Farm (Page 12)
Arthur's Birthday (Page 70)
Arthur's Teacher Trouble (Page 70)
At Ease (Page 200)
Baby ROM (Page 212)
The Backyard (Page 24)
Bailey's Book House (Page 60)
The Berenstain Bears Get in a Fight (Page 70)
Bug Adventure (Page 166)
Chicka Chicka Boom Boom (Page 220)
Crayola Amazing Art Adventure (Page 48)
Curious George Comes Home (Page 220)
Davidson's Kid Keys (Page 210)
Davidson's Kid Works 2 (Page 63)
Davidson's Kid Works Deluxe (Page 62)
The Discis Kids Can Read Series (Page 76)
Dr. Seuss' ABCs (Page 70)
Freddi Fish and the Case of the Missing Kelp Seeds (Page 174)
Freddi Fish and the Haunted House (Page 175)
James Discovers Math (Page 222)
Junior Encyclopedias: The Airport (Page 215)
Junior Encyclopedias: The Farm (Page 214)
Junior Encyclopedias: The Jungle (Page 215)

Just Grandma and Me (Page 70)
Kid Cuts (Page 38)
Kid Pix 2 (Page 32)
Kid Pix Fun Pack (Page 32)
Kid Pix Studio (Page 34)
KidDesk (Page 200)
KidDesk Family Edition (Page 200)
Launch Pad (Page 200)
Little Monster at School (Page 70)
Millie's Math House (Page 100)
My First Incredible Amazing Dictionary (Page 26)
The New Kid on the Block (Page 70)
P.B. Bear's Birthday Party (Page 74)
Peter Rabbit's 123 (Page 214)
The Playroom (Page 22)
Polar Express (Page 221)
Putt-Putt Goes to the Moon (Page 176)
Putt-Putt Joins the Parade (Page 176)
Putt-Putt Saves the Zoo (Page 176)
Reader Rabbit's Ready for Letters (Page 84)
Richard Scarry's How Things Work in Busytown (Page 28)
Sammy's Science House (Page 150)
Thinkin' Things Collection 1 (Page 18)
The Tortoise and the Hare (Page 70)
Trudy's Time & Place House (Page 213)
WiggleWorks Volume 1 (Page 92)
Zurk's Learning Safari (Page 14)

Age 4
3-D Body Adventure (Page 166)
The Adventures of Peter Rabbit & Benjamin Bunny (Page 214)
Alphabet Blocks (Page 89)
AlphaBonk Farm (Page 12)
Arthur's Birthday (Page 70)
Arthur's Teacher Trouble (Page 70)
At Ease (Page 200)
Baby ROM (Page 212)
The Backyard (Page 24)
Bailey's Book House (Page 60)
The Berenstain Bears Get in a Fight (Page 70)
Bug Adventure (Page 166)
Chicka Chicka Boom Boom (Page 220)
Circus! (Page 10)
Crayola Amazing Art Adventure (Page 48)
Curious George Comes Home (Page 220)
Davidson's Kid Keys (Page 210)
Davidson's Kid Phonics (Page 82)
Davidson's Kid Works 2 (Page 63)
Davidson's Kid Works Deluxe (Page 62)
The Discis Kids Can Read Series (Page 76)
Dr. Seuss' ABCs (Page 70)
Freddi Fish and the Case of the Missing Kelp Seeds (Page 174)
Freddi Fish and the Haunted House (Page 175)
Harry and the Haunted House (Page 70)
James Discovers Math (Page 222)
Junior Encyclopedias: The Airport (Page 215)
Junior Encyclopedias: The Farm (Page 214)
Junior Encyclopedias: The Jungle (Page 215)
Just Grandma and Me (Page 70)
Kid Cuts (Page 38)
Kid Pix 2 (Page 32)
Kid Pix Fun Pack (Page 32)
Kid Pix Studio (Page 34)
KidDesk (Page 200)
KidDesk Family Edition (Page 200)
Launch Pad (Page 200)
Little Monster at School (Page 70)

Madeline and the Magnificent Puppet Show (Page 222)
Millie's Math House (Page 100)
My First Incredible Amazing Dictionary (Page 26)
The New Kid on the Block (Page 70)
P.B. Bear's Birthday Party (Page 74)
Pantsylvania (Page 215)
Peter Rabbit's 123 (Page 214)
The Playroom (Page 22)
Polar Express (Page 221)
Putt-Putt Goes to the Moon (Page 176)
Putt-Putt Joins the Parade (Page 176)
Putt-Putt Saves the Zoo (Page 176)
Reader Rabbit 1 (Page 84)
Reader Rabbit's Interactive Reading Journey (Page 86)
Reader Rabbit's Ready for Letters (Page 84)
Richard Scarry's How Things Work in Busytown (Page 28)
Sammy's Science House (Page 150)
Sound It Out Land 1, 2, 3 (Page 93)
Thinkin' Things Collection 1 (Page 18)
The Tortoise and the Hare (Page 70)
Trudy's Time & Place House (Page 213)
Where's Waldo? at the Circus (Page 223)
WiggleWorks Volume 1 (Page 92)
Zurk's Learning Safari (Page 14)

Age 5

3-D Body Adventure (Page 166)
The Adventures of Peter Rabbit & Benjamin Bunny (Page 214)
AlphaBonk Farm (Page 12)
Amazing Animation (Page 42)
Arthur's Birthday (Page 70)
Arthur's Teacher Trouble (Page 70)
At Ease (Page 200)
The Backyard (Page 24)
Bailey's Book House (Page 60)
Beginning Reading (Page 90)
The Berenstain Bears Get in a Fight (Page 70)
Bug Adventure (Page 166)
Chicka Chicka Boom Boom (Page 220)
Circus! (Page 10)
Countdown (Page 102)
Crayola Amazing Art Adventure (Page 48)
Curious George Comes Home (Page 220)
Davidson's Kid Keys (Page 210)
Davidson's Kid Phonics (Page 82)
Davidson's Kid Works 2 (Page 63)
Davidson's Kid Works Deluxe (Page 62)
Dinkytown Daycare Kids Story Pack (Page 59)
The Discis Kids Can Read Series (Page 76)
Dr. Seuss' ABCs (Page 70)
Flying Colors (Page 36)
Freddi Fish and the Case of the Missing Kelp Seeds (Page 174)
Freddi Fish and the Haunted House (Page 175)
Hard Hat (Page 216)
Harry and the Haunted House (Page 70)
Hollywood Hounds Story Pack (Page 59)
Imagination Express Destination: Castle (Page 55)
Imagination Express Destination: Neighborhood (Page 55)
Imagination Express Destination: Rainforest (Page 55)
James Discovers Math (Page 222)
Junior Encyclopedias: The Airport (Page 215)

Junior Encyclopedias: The Farm (Page 214)
Junior Encyclopedias: The Jungle (Page 215)
Just Grandma and Me (Page 70)
Kid Cuts (Page 38)
Kid Pix 2 (Page 32)
Kid Pix Fun Pack (Page 32)
Kid Pix Studio (Page 34)
KidDesk (Page 200)
KidDesk Family Edition (Page 200)
KidMail Connection (Page 206)
Kids World (Page 46)
Launch Pad (Page 200)
Little Monster at School (Page 70)
Madeline and the Magnificent Puppet Show (Page 222)
Math Workshop (Page 98)
Millie's Math House (Page 100)
Money Town (Page 224)
The New Kid on the Block (Page 70)
Pantsylvania (Page 215)
Peter Rabbit's 123 (Page 214)
Polar Express (Page 221)
Putt-Putt Goes to the Moon (Page 176)
Putt-Putt Joins the Parade (Page 176)
Putt-Putt Saves the Zoo (Page 176)
Radio Addition (Page 225)
Radio Division (Page 226)
Radio Multiplication (Page 226)
Radio Subtraction (Page 226)
Reader Rabbit 1 (Page 84)
Reader Rabbit's Interactive Reading Journey (Page 86)
Richard Scarry's How Things Work in Busytown (Page 28)
Sammy's Science House (Page 150)
Sound It Out Land 1, 2, 3 (Page 93)
Storybook Weaver Deluxe (Page 58)
Thinkin' Things Collection 1 (Page 18)

The Tortoise and the Hare (Page 70)
Treasure Cove! (Page 118)
Treasure Galaxy! (Page 118)
Treasure MathStorm! (Page 118)
Treasure Mountain! (Page 118)
Trudy's Time & Place House (Page 213)
Undersea Adventure (Page 166)
Where in the World Is Carmen Sandiego? Junior Detective Edition (Page 128)
Where's Waldo? at the Circus (Page 223)
WiggleWorks Volume 1 (Page 92)
Zurk's Learning Safari (Page 14)
Zurk's Rainforest Lab (Page 16)

Age 6

3-D Body Adventure (Page 166)
The Adventures of Peter Rabbit & Benjamin Bunny (Page 214)
Amazing Animation (Page 42)
Arthur's Birthday (Page 70)
Arthur's Teacher Trouble (Page 70)
At Ease (Page 200)
Beginning Reading (Page 90)
The Berenstain Bears Get in a Fight (Page 70)
Bug Adventure (Page 166)
Bumptz Science Carnival (Page 228)
Chicka Chicka Boom Boom (Page 220)
Circus! (Page 10)
Countdown (Page 102)
Crayola Amazing Art Adventure (Page 48)
Curious George Comes Home (Page 220)
Davidson's Kid Keys (Page 210)
Davidson's Kid Phonics (Page 82)
Davidson's Kid Works Deluxe (Page 62)

INDEX

Dinkytown Daycare Kids Story Pack (Page 59)
The Discis Kids Can Read Series (Page 76)
Dr. Seuss' ABCs (Page 70)
Explorapedia: The World of Nature (Page 190)
Explorapedia: The World of People (Page 190)
Flying Colors (Page 36)
Freddi Fish and the Case of the Missing Kelp Seeds (Page 174)
Freddi Fish and the Haunted House (Page 175)
Hard Hat (Page 216)
Harry and the Haunted House (Page 70)
Hollywood Hounds Story Pack (Page 59)
Imagination Express Destination: Castle (Page 55)
Imagination Express Destination: Neighborhood (Page 55)
Imagination Express Destination: Rainforest (Page 55)
James Discovers Math (Page 222)
Kid Cuts (Page 38)
Kid Pix 2 (Page 32)
Kid Pix Fun Pack (Page 32)
Kid Pix Studio (Page 34)
KidDesk (Page 200)
KidDesk Family Edition (Page 200)
KidMail Connection (Page 206)
Kid's Typing (Page 208)
Kids World (Page 46)
Launch Pad (Page 200)
Madeline and the Magnificent Puppet Show (Page 222)
The Magic School Bus Explores the Human Body (Page 164)
The Magic School Bus Visits the Solar System (Page 164)
Magic Theatre (Page 44)
Math Blaster: Episode 1—In Search of Spot (Page 114)
Math Blaster: Episode 2—Secret of the Lost City (Page 114)
Math Workshop (Page 98)
Money Town (Page 224)
The New Kid on the Block (Page 70)
Pantsylvania (Page 215)
Peter Rabbit's 123 (Page 214)
Polar Express (Page 221)
Radio Addition (Page 225)
Radio Division (Page 226)
Radio Multiplication (Page 226)
Radio Subtraction (Page 226)
Reader Rabbit 1 (Page 84)
Reader Rabbit 2 (Page 84)
Reader Rabbit 3 (Page 84)
Reader Rabbit's Interactive Reading Journey (Page 86)
Snootz Math Trek (Page 224)
Sound It Out Land 1, 2, 3 (Page 93)
Spider-Man Cartoon Maker (Page 45)
Storybook Weaver Deluxe (Page 58)
Thinkin' Things Collection 1 (Page 18)
Thinkin' Things Collection 2 (Page 20)
The Tortoise and the Hare (Page 70)
Treasure Cove! (Page 118)
Treasure Galaxy! (Page 118)
Treasure MathStorm! (Page 118)
Treasure Mountain! (Page 118)
Troggle Trouble (Page 112)
Trudy's Time & Place House (Page 213)
Undersea Adventure (Page 166)
Where in the World Is Carmen Sandiego? Junior Detective Edition (Page 128)
Where's Waldo? at the Circus (Page 223)
Word Munchers (Page 116)
Zurk's Rainforest Lab (Page 16)

Age 7

3-D Body Adventure (Page 166)
Amazing Animation (Page 42)
The Amazing Writing Machine (Page 52)
Arthur's Birthday (Page 70)
Arthur's Teacher Trouble (Page 70)
At Bat (Page 178)
At Ease (Page 200)
Beginning Reading (Page 90)
Bug Adventure (Page 166)
Bumptz Science Carnival (Page 228)
Circus! (Page 10)
Countdown (Page 102)
Crayola Art Studio (Page 48)
Creative Writer (Page 64)
Davidson's Kid Keys (Page 210)
Davidson's Kid Works Deluxe (Page 62)
Dinkytown Daycare Kids Story Pack (Page 59)
The Discis Kids Can Read Series (Page 76)
Eagle Eye Mysteries: In London (Page 184)
Eagle Eye Mysteries: The Original (Page 184)
Elroy Goes Bugzerk (Page 229)
Elroy Hits the Pavement (Page 229)
Explorapedia: The World of Nature (Page 190)
Explorapedia: The World of People (Page 190)
Flying Colors (Page 36)
Hard Hat (Page 216)
Hollywood Hounds Story Pack (Page 59)
Imagination Express Destination: Castle (Page 55)
Imagination Express Destination: Neighborhood (Page 55)
Imagination Express Destination: Rainforest (Page 55)
Keroppi Day Hopper (Page 204)
Kid Cuts (Page 38)
Kid Pix 2 (Page 32)
Kid Pix Fun Pack (Page 32)
Kid Pix Studio (Page 34)
KidDesk (Page 200)
KidDesk Family Edition (Page 200)
KidMail Connection (Page 206)
Kid's Typing (Page 208)
Kids World (Page 46)
Launch Pad (Page 200)
Madeline and the Magnificent Puppet Show (Page 222)
The Magic School Bus Explores the Human Body (Page 164)
The Magic School Bus Visits the Solar System (Page 164)
Magic Theatre (Page 44)
Math Blaster: Episode 1—In Search of Spot (Page 114)
Math Blaster: Episode 2—Secret of the Lost City (Page 114)
Math Workshop (Page 98)
Money Town (Page 224)
The New Kid on the Block (Page 70)
Pantsylvania (Page 215)
Planetary Taxi (Page 152)
Radio Addition (Page 225)
Radio Division (Page 226)
Radio Multiplication (Page 226)
Radio Subtraction (Page 226)
Reader Rabbit 2 (Page 84)
Reader Rabbit 3 (Page 84)
Reading Blaster (Page 88)
Recess in Greece (Page 148)
Safari (Page 157)
Scavenger Hunt: Africa (Page 162)
Scavenger Hunt: Oceans (Page 162)
Snootz Math Trek (Page 224)
Spider-Man Cartoon Maker (Page 45)
Storybook Weaver Deluxe (Page 58)
Super Solvers Midnight Rescue! (Page 91)

INDEX • 267

Super Solvers OutNumbered! (Page 120)
Super Solvers Spellbound! (Page 91)
Thinkin' Things Collection 1 (Page 18)
Thinkin' Things Collection 2 (Page 20)
The Tortoise and the Hare (Page 70)
Treasure Cove! (Page 118)
Treasure Galaxy! (Page 118)
Treasure MathStorm! (Page 118)
Treasure Mountain! (Page 118)
Troggle Trouble (Page 112)
Undersea Adventure (Page 166)
What's the Secret? (Page 154)
Where in the World Is Carmen Sandiego? Junior Detective Edition (Page 128)
Where's Waldo? at the Circus (Page 223)
Word Munchers (Page 116)
Zurk's Rainforest Lab (Page 16)

Age 8

3D Atlas (Page 192)
3-D Body Adventure (Page 166)
Adventures in Flight (Page 104)
Alien Tales (Page 80)
Amazing Animation (Page 42)
The Amazing Writing Machine (Page 52)
Ancient Lands (Page 140)
Art Explorer (Page 40)
Arthur's Birthday (Page 70)
Arthur's Teacher Trouble (Page 70)
At Bat (Page 178)
At Ease (Page 200)
Aviation Adventure (Page 166)
Bug Adventure (Page 166)
Bumptz Science Carnival (Page 228)
Circus! (Page 10)
Countdown (Page 102)

Counting on Frank (Page 106)
Crayola Art Studio (Page 48)
Creative Writer (Page 64)
Dangerous Creatures (Page 160)
Davidson's Kid Keys (Page 210)
Dinkytown Daycare Kids Story Pack (Page 59)
The Discis Kids Can Read Series (Page 76)
Eagle Eye Mysteries: In London (Page 184)
Eagle Eye Mysteries: The Original (Page 184)
Elroy Goes Bugzerk (Page 229)
Elroy Hits the Pavement (Page 229)
Explorapedia: The World of Nature (Page 190)
Explorapedia: The World of People (Page 190)
Eyewitness Virtual Reality BIRD (Page 232)
Eyewitness Virtual Reality CAT (Page 232)
Fine Artist (Page 47)
Flying Colors (Page 36)
Gahan Wilson's The Ultimate Haunted House (Page 182)
GeoSafari (Page 186)
Hard Hat (Page 216)
Hollywood Hounds Story Pack (Page 59)
Imagination Express Destination: Castle (Page 55)
Imagination Express Destination: Neighborhood (Page 55)
Imagination Express Destination: Rainforest (Page 55)
Keroppi Day Hopper (Page 204)
Kid Cuts (Page 38)
Kid Pix 2 (Page 32)
Kid Pix Fun Pack (Page 32)
Kid Pix Studio (Page 34)
KidDesk (Page 200)
KidDesk Family Edition (Page 200)
KidMail Connection (Page 206)
Kid's Typing (Page 208)

Kids World (Page 46)
Launch Pad (Page 200)
Leonardo the Inventor (Page 144)
Madeline and the Magnificent Puppet Show (Page 222)
The Magic School Bus Explores the Human Body (Page 164)
The Magic School Bus Visits the Solar System (Page 164)
Magic Theatre (Page 44)
Math Blaster: Episode 1—In Search of Spot (Page 114)
Math Blaster: Episode 2—Secret of the Lost City (Page 114)
Math Munchers Deluxe (Page 116)
Math Workshop (Page 98)
Money Town (Page 224)
The New Kid on the Block (Page 70)
Number Munchers (Page 116)
Odell Down Under (Page 156)
Opening Night (Page 218)
Pantsylvania (Page 215)
Planetary Taxi (Page 152)
Radio Addition (Page 225)
Radio Division (Page 226)
Radio Multiplication (Page 226)
Radio Subtraction (Page 226)
Reader Rabbit 2 (Page 84)
Reader Rabbit 3 (Page 84)
Reading Blaster (Page 88)
Recess in Greece (Page 148)
Safari (Page 157)
Scavenger Hunt: Africa (Page 162)
Scavenger Hunt: Oceans (Page 162)
Science Adventure II (Page 166)
SimTown (Page 173)
Snootz Math Trek (Page 224)
Space Adventure II (Page 166)
Spider-Man Cartoon Maker (Page 45)
Star Act (Page 56)
Storybook Weaver Deluxe (Page 58)
Stowaway! (Page 146)

Super Munchers (Page 116)
Super Solvers Midnight Rescue! (Page 91)
Super Solvers OutNumbered! (Page 120)
Super Solvers Spellbound! (Page 91)
TesselMania! (Page 216)
Thinkin' Things Collection 2 (Page 20)
Thinkin' Things Collection 3 (Page 21)
Top Secret Decoder (Page 217)
The Tortoise and the Hare (Page 70)
Travelrama USA (Page 130)
Treasure Cove! (Page 118)
Treasure Galaxy! (Page 118)
Treasure MathStorm! (Page 118)
Treasure Mountain! (Page 118)
Troggle Trouble (Page 112)
Undersea Adventure (Page 166)
What's the Secret? (Page 154)
Where in America's Past Is Carmen Sandiego? (Page 127)
Where in Europe Is Carmen Sandiego? (Page 127)
Where in Space Is Carmen Sandiego? (Page 127)
Where in Time Is Carmen Sandiego? (Page 127)
Where in the USA Is Carmen Sandiego? (Page 126)
Where in the World Is Carmen Sandiego? (Page 124)
Where's Waldo? at the Circus (Page 223)
Word Munchers (Page 116)
Zurk's Rainforest Lab (Page 16)

Age 9
3D Atlas (Page 192)
3-D Body Adventure (Page 166)
Adventures in Flight (Page 104)
Alien Tales (Page 80)
Amazing Animation (Page 42)

The Amazing Writing Machine (Page 52)
Ancient Lands (Page 140)
Art Explorer (Page 40)
At Bat (Page 178)
At Ease (Page 200)
Aviation Adventure (Page 166)
Bumptz Science Carnival (Page 228)
The Castle of Dr. Brain (Page 230)
Countdown (Page 102)
Counting on Frank (Page 106)
Crayola Art Studio (Page 48)
Creative Writer (Page 64)
Dangerous Creatures (Page 160)
Dinkytown Daycare Kids Story Pack (Page 59)
Eagle Eye Mysteries: In London (Page 184)
Eagle Eye Mysteries: The Original (Page 184)
Elroy Goes Bugzerk (Page 229)
Elroy Hits the Pavement (Page 229)
Explorapedia: The World of Nature (Page 190)
Explorapedia: The World of People (Page 190)
Eyewitness Virtual Reality BIRD (Page 232)
Eyewitness Virtual Reality CAT (Page 232)
Fine Artist (Page 47)
Flying Colors (Page 36)
Gahan Wilson's The Ultimate Haunted House (Page 182)
GeoSafari (Page 186)
Hard Hat (Page 216)
Hollywood (Page 219)
Hollywood Hounds Story Pack (Page 59)
Imagination Express Destination: Castle (Page 55)
Imagination Express Destination: Neighborhood (Page 55)
Imagination Express Destination: Rainforest (Page 55)
The Island of Dr. Brain (Page 230)
Keroppi Day Hopper (Page 204)
Kid Pix 2 (Page 32)
Kid Pix Fun Pack (Page 32)
Kid Pix Studio (Page 34)
KidDesk (Page 200)
KidDesk Family Edition (Page 200)
KidMail Connection (Page 206)
Kids World (Page 46)
Klik & Play (Page 180)
Launch Pad (Page 200)
Leonardo the Inventor (Page 144)
The Lost Mind of Dr. Brain (Page 230)
The Magic School Bus Explores the Human Body (Page 164)
The Magic School Bus Visits the Solar System (Page 164)
Magic Theatre (Page 44)
Math Blaster: Episode 1—In Search of Spot (Page 114)
Math Blaster: Episode 2—Secret of the Lost City (Page 114)
Math Munchers Deluxe (Page 116)
Math Workshop (Page 98)
Myst (Page 170)
Number Munchers (Page 116)
Odell Down Under (Page 156)
Opening Night (Page 218)
Pantsylvania (Page 215)
Planetary Taxi (Page 152)
Reading Blaster (Page 88)
Recess in Greece (Page 148)
Safari (Page 157)
Scavenger Hunt: Africa (Page 162)
Scavenger Hunt: Oceans (Page 162)
Science Adventure II (Page 166)
SimTown (Page 173)
Snootz Math Trek (Page 224)
Space Adventure II (Page 166)
Spider-Man Cartoon Maker (Page 45)
Star Act (Page 56)
Storybook Weaver Deluxe (Page 58)

Stowaway! (Page 146)
Super Munchers (Page 116)
Super Solvers Midnight Rescue! (Page 91)
Super Solvers OutNumbered! (Page 120)
Super Solvers Spellbound! (Page 91)
TesselMania! (Page 216)
Thinkin' Things Collection 2 (Page 20)
Thinkin' Things Collection 3 (Page 21)
Top Secret Decoder (Page 217)
Travelrama USA (Page 130)
Treasure Cove! (Page 118)
Treasure Galaxy! (Page 118)
Treasure MathStorm! (Page 118)
Treasure Mountain! (Page 118)
Troggle Trouble (Page 112)
Undersea Adventure (Page 166)
What's the Secret? (Page 154)
Where in America's Past Is Carmen Sandiego? (Page 127)
Where in Europe Is Carmen Sandiego? (Page 127)
Where in Space Is Carmen Sandiego? (Page 127)
Where in Time Is Carmen Sandiego? (Page 127)
Where in the USA Is Carmen Sandiego? (Page 126)
Where in the World Is Carmen Sandiego? (Page 124)
Where's Waldo? at the Circus (Page 223)
Word Munchers (Page 116)
Wrath of the Gods (Page 142)
Zurk's Rainforest Lab (Page 16)

Age 10

3D Atlas (Page 192)
3-D Body Adventure (Page 166)
Adventures in Flight (Page 104)
AfricaTrail (Page 227)
Alien Tales (Page 80)
Amazing Animation (Page 42)
The Amazing Writing Machine (Page 52)
The Amazon Trail (Page 138)
Ancient Lands (Page 140)
Art Explorer (Page 40)
Ascendancy (Page 231)
At Bat (Page 178)
At Ease (Page 200)
Aviation Adventure (Page 166)
Bumptz Science Carnival (Page 228)
Cartopedia (Page 233)
The Castle of Dr. Brain (Page 230)
Countdown (Page 102)
Counting on Frank (Page 106)
Crayola Art Studio (Page 48)
Creative Writer (Page 64)
Dangerous Creatures (Page 160)
Discovering Shakespeare (Page 233)
Eagle Eye Mysteries: In London (Page 184)
Eagle Eye Mysteries: The Original (Page 184)
Elroy Goes Bugzerk (Page 229)
Elroy Hits the Pavement (Page 229)
Explorapedia: The World of Nature (Page 190)
Explorapedia: The World of People (Page 190)
Eyewitness Virtual Reality BIRD (Page 232)
Eyewitness Virtual Reality CAT (Page 232)
Fine Artist (Page 47)
Flying Colors (Page 36)
Gahan Wilson's The Ultimate Haunted House (Page 182)
GeoSafari (Page 186)
Hard Hat (Page 216)
Hollywood (Page 219)
Imagination Express Destination: Castle (Page 55)
Imagination Express Destination: Neighborhood (Page 55)

Imagination Express Destination: Rainforest (Page 55)
Inside Magic (Page 230)
The Island of Dr. Brain (Page 230)
Keroppi Day Hopper (Page 204)
Kid Pix 2 (Page 32)
Kid Pix Fun Pack (Page 32)
Kid Pix Studio (Page 34)
KidDesk (Page 200)
KidDesk Family Edition (Page 200)
KidMail Connection (Page 206)
Kids World (Page 46)
Klik & Play (Page 180)
Launch Pad (Page 200)
Leonardo the Inventor (Page 144)
The Lost Mind of Dr. Brain (Page 230)
Louis Cat Orze (Page 227)
The Magic School Bus Explores the Human Body (Page 164)
The Magic School Bus Visits the Solar System (Page 164)
Magic Theatre (Page 44)
Math Blaster: Episode 1—In Search of Spot (Page 114)
Math Blaster: Episode 2—Secret of the Lost City (Page 114)
Math Blaster Mystery: The Great Brain Robbery (Page 114)
Math Munchers Deluxe (Page 116)
Math Workshop (Page 98)
MayaQuest (Page 226)
Myst (Page 170)
Number Munchers (Page 116)
Odell Down Under (Page 156)
Opening Night (Page 218)
Planetary Taxi (Page 152)
Reading Blaster (Page 88)
Recess in Greece (Page 148)
Safari (Page 157)
Scavenger Hunt: Africa (Page 162)
Scavenger Hunt: Oceans (Page 162)
Science Adventure II (Page 166)
SimAnt (Page 173)
SimCity 2000 (Page 172)
SimCity Classic (Page 173)
SimEarth (Page 173)
SimFarm (Page 173)
SimIsle (Page 173)
SimTower (Page 172)
SimTown (Page 173)
Snootz Math Trek (Page 224)
Space Adventure II (Page 166)
Spider-Man Cartoon Maker (Page 45)
Star Act (Page 56)
Stowaway! (Page 146)
Student Writing Center (Page 202)
Super Munchers (Page 116)
Super Solvers Midnight Rescue! (Page 91)
Super Solvers OutNumbered! (Page 120)
Super Solvers Spellbound! (Page 91)
TesselMania! (Page 216)
Thinkin' Things Collection 2 (Page 20)
Thinkin' Things Collection 3 (Page 21)
Top Secret Decoder (Page 217)
Travelrama USA (Page 130)
Troggle Trouble (Page 112)
Undersea Adventure (Page 166)
What's the Secret? (Page 154)
Where in America's Past Is Carmen Sandiego? (Page 127)
Where in Europe Is Carmen Sandiego? (Page 127)
Where in Space Is Carmen Sandiego? (Page 127)
Where in Time Is Carmen Sandiego? (Page 127)
Where in the USA Is Carmen Sandiego? (Page 126)
Where in the World Is Carmen Sandiego? (Page 124)
Widget Workshop (Page 158)
Word Munchers (Page 116)
Wrath of the Gods (Page 142)
The Yukon Trail (Page 136)

Age 11

3D Atlas (Page 192)
3-D Body Adventure (Page 166)
Adventures in Flight (Page 104)
AfricaTrail (Page 227)
Alien Tales (Page 80)
Amazing Animation (Page 42)
The Amazing Writing Machine (Page 52)
The Amazon Trail (Page 138)
Ancient Lands (Page 140)
Art Explorer (Page 40)
Ascendancy (Page 231)
At Bat (Page 178)
At Ease (Page 200)
Aviation Adventure (Page 166)
Cartopedia (Page 233)
The Castle of Dr. Brain (Page 230)
Countdown (Page 102)
Counting on Frank (Page 106)
Crayola Art Studio (Page 48)
Creative Writer (Page 64)
Dangerous Creatures (Page 160)
Discovering Shakespeare (Page 233)
Elroy Goes Bugzerk (Page 229)
Elroy Hits the Pavement (Page 229)
Encarta 1996 (Page 194)
Eyewitness Encyclopedia of History (Page 196)
Eyewitness Encyclopedia of Nature (Page 196)
Eyewitness Encyclopedia of Science (Page 196)
Eyewitness Virtual Reality BIRD (Page 232)
Eyewitness Virtual Reality CAT (Page 232)
Fine Artist (Page 47)
Flying Colors (Page 36)
Gahan Wilson's The Ultimate Haunted House (Page 182)
GeoSafari (Page 186)
Hollywood (Page 219)
Imagination Express Destination: Castle (Page 55)
Imagination Express Destination: Neighborhood (Page 55)
Imagination Express Destination: Rainforest (Page 55)
Inside Magic (Page 230)
The Island of Dr. Brain (Page 230)
Keroppi Day Hopper (Page 204)
Kid Pix Studio (Page 34)
KidDesk (Page 200)
KidDesk Family Edition (Page 200)
KidMail Connection (Page 206)
Klik & Play (Page 180)
Launch Pad (Page 200)
Leonardo the Inventor (Page 144)
The Lost Mind of Dr. Brain (Page 230)
Louis Cat Orze (Page 227)
Magic Theatre (Page 44)
Math Blaster: Episode 1—In Search of Spot (Page 114)
Math Blaster: Episode 2—Secret of the Lost City (Page 114)
Math Blaster Mystery: The Great Brain Robbery (Page 114)
Math Munchers Deluxe (Page 116)
Math Workshop (Page 98)
MayaQuest (Page 226)
Myst (Page 170)
Number Munchers (Page 116)
Odell Down Under (Page 156)
Opening Night (Page 218)
The Oregon Trail II (Page 134)
Planetary Taxi (Page 152)
Recess in Greece (Page 148)
Scavenger Hunt: Africa (Page 162)
Scavenger Hunt: Oceans (Page 162)
Science Adventure II (Page 166)
SimAnt (Page 173)
SimCity 2000 (Page 172)
SimCity Classic (Page 173)
SimEarth (Page 173)
SimFarm (Page 173)
SimIsle (Page 173)
SimTower (Page 172)
SimTown (Page 173)

Space Adventure II (Page 166)
Spider-Man Cartoon Maker (Page 45)
Star Act (Page 56)
Stowaway! (Page 146)
Student Writing Center (Page 202)
Super Munchers (Page 116)
Super Solvers Spellbound! (Page 91)
TesselMania! (Page 216)
Thinkin' Things Collection 2 (Page 20)
Thinkin' Things Collection 3 (Page 21)
Top Secret Decoder (Page 217)
Travelrama USA (Page 130)
Troggle Trouble (Page 112)
Undersea Adventure (Page 166)
What's the Secret? (Page 154)
Where in America's Past Is Carmen Sandiego? (Page 127)
Where in Europe Is Carmen Sandiego? (Page 127)
Where in Space Is Carmen Sandiego? (Page 127)
Where in Time Is Carmen Sandiego? (Page 127)
Where in the USA Is Carmen Sandiego? (Page 126)
Where in the World Is Carmen Sandiego? (Page 124)
Widget Workshop (Page 158)
Word Munchers (Page 116)
Wrath of the Gods (Page 142)
The Yukon Trail (Page 136)

Age 12
3D Atlas (Page 192)
3-D Body Adventure (Page 166)
Adventures in Flight (Page 104)
AfricaTrail (Page 227)
Alge-Blaster 3 (Page 114)
Alien Tales (Page 80)
Amazing Animation (Page 42)
The Amazing Writing Machine (Page 52)
The Amazon Trail (Page 138)
Ancient Lands (Page 140)
Art Explorer (Page 40)
Ascendancy (Page 231)
At Bat (Page 178)
At Ease (Page 200)
Aviation Adventure (Page 166)
Cartopedia (Page 233)
The Castle of Dr. Brain (Page 230)
Countdown (Page 102)
Counting on Frank (Page 106)
Crayola Art Studio (Page 48)
Creative Writer (Page 64)
Dangerous Creatures (Page 160)
Elroy Goes Bugzerk (Page 229)
Elroy Hits the Pavement (Page 229)
Encarta 1996 (Page 194)
Eyewitness Encyclopedia of History (Page 196)
Eyewitness Encyclopedia of Nature (Page 196)
Eyewitness Encyclopedia of Science (Page 196)
Eyewitness Virtual Reality BIRD (Page 232)
Eyewitness Virtual Reality CAT (Page 232)
Fine Artist (Page 47)
Flying Colors (Page 36)
Gahan Wilson's The Ultimate Haunted House (Page 182)
GeoSafari (Page 186)
Hollywood (Page 219)
Imagination Express Destination: Castle (Page 55)
Imagination Express Destination: Neighborhood (Page 55)
Imagination Express Destination: Rainforest (Page 55)
Inside Magic (Page 230)
The Island of Dr. Brain (Page 230)
Keroppi Day Hopper (Page 204)
Kid Pix Studio (Page 34)
KidDesk (Page 200)
KidDesk Family Edition (Page 200)
KidMail Connection (Page 206)

Klik & Play (Page 180)
Launch Pad (Page 200)
Leonardo the Inventor (Page 144)
The Lost Mind of Dr. Brain (Page 230)
Louis Cat Orze (Page 227)
Magic Theatre (Page 44)
Math Blaster: Episode 1—In Search of Spot (Page 114)
Math Blaster: Episode 2—Secret of the Lost City (Page 114)
Math Blaster Mystery: The Great Brain Robbery (Page 114)
Math Munchers Deluxe (Page 116)
Math Workshop (Page 98)
MayaQuest (Page 226)
Myst (Page 170)
Number Munchers (Page 116)
Odell Down Under (Page 156)
Opening Night (Page 218)
The Oregon Trail II (Page 134)
Planetary Taxi (Page 152)
Recess in Greece (Page 148)
Safari (Page 157)
Scavenger Hunt: Africa (Page 162)
Scavenger Hunt: Oceans (Page 162)
Science Adventure II (Page 166)
SimAnt (Page 173)
SimCity 2000 (Page 172)
SimCity Classic (Page 173)
SimEarth (Page 173)
SimFarm (Page 173)
SimIsle (Page 173)
SimTower (Page 172)
SimTown (Page 173)

Space Adventure II (Page 166)
Spider-Man Cartoon Maker (Page 45)
Star Act (Page 56)
Stowaway! (Page 146)
Student Writing Center (Page 202)
Super Munchers (Page 116)
Super Solvers Spellbound! (Page 91)
TesselMania! (Page 216)
Thinkin' Things Collection 2 (Page 20)
Thinkin' Things Collection 3 (Page 21)
Top Secret Decoder (Page 217)
Travelrama USA (Page 130)
Troggle Trouble (Page 112)
Undersea Adventure (Page 166)
What's the Secret? (Page 154)
Where in America's Past Is Carmen Sandiego? (Page 127)
Where in Europe Is Carmen Sandiego? (Page 127)
Where in Space Is Carmen Sandiego? (Page 127)
Where in Time Is Carmen Sandiego? (Page 127)
Where in the USA Is Carmen Sandiego? (Page 126)
Where in the World Is Carmen Sandiego? (Page 124)
Widget Workshop (Page 158)
Word Munchers (Page 116)
Wrath of the Gods (Page 142)
The Yukon Trail (Page 136)

Titles by Rating Index

★★★★

AlphaBonk Farm (Page 12)
The Amazing Writing Machine (Page 52)
The Amazon Trail (Page 138)
Art Explorer (Page 40)
Arthur's Birthday (Page 70)
Arthur's Teacher Trouble (Page 70)
At Bat (Page 178)
At Ease (Page 200)
The Berenstain Bears Get in a Fight (Page 70)
Circus! (Page 10)
Dr. Seuss' ABCs (Page 70)
Flying Colors (Page 36)
Freddi Fish and the Case of the Missing Kelp Seeds (Page 174)
Harry and the Haunted House (Page 70)
Imagination Express (Page 54)
Just Grandma and Me (Page 70)
Kid Cuts (Page 38)
Kid Pix 2 (Page 32)
Kid Pix Fun Pack (Page 32)
Kid Pix Studio (Page 34)
KidDesk (Page 200)
Launch Pad (Page 200)
Little Monster At School (Page 70)
Math Workshop (Page 98)
Millie's Math House (Page 100)
Myst (Page 170)
The New Kid on the Block (Page 70)
The Oregon Trail II (Page 134)
Planetary Taxi (Page 152)
Putt-Putt Saves the Zoo (Page 176)
Sammy's Science House (Page 150)
SimCity 2000 (Page 172)
Star Act (Page 56)
The Tortoise and the Hare (Page 70)
What's the Secret? (Page 154)
Where in the USA Is Carmen Sandiego? (Page 126)
Where in the World Is Carmen Sandiego? (Page 124)
The Yukon Trail (Page 136)

★★★

3D Atlas (Page 192)
Alien Tales (Page 80)
Bailey's Book House (Page 60)
Countdown (Page 102)
Davidson's Kid Phonics (Page 82)
Davidson's Kid Works Deluxe (Page 62)
Encarta 1996 (Page 194)
Explorapedia: The World of Nature (Page 190)
Explorapedia: The World of People (Page 190)
Eyewitness Encyclopedia of History (Page 196)
Eyewitness Encyclopedia of Nature (Page 196)
Eyewitness Encyclopedia of Science (Page 196)

Gahan Wilson's The Ultimate Haunted House (Page 182)
Klik & Play (Page 180)
Odell Down Under (Page 156)
Storybook Weaver Deluxe (Page 58)
Student Writing Center (Page 202)
Thinkin' Things Collection 1 (Page 18)
Thinkin' Things Collection 2 (Page 20)
Travelrama USA (Page 130)
Where in the World Is Carmen Sandiego? Junior Detective Edition (Page 128)
Zurk's Learning Safari (Page 14)
Zurk's Rainforest Lab (Page 16)

★★

Adventures in Flight (Page 104)
Amazing Animation (Page 42)
Ancient Lands (Page 140)
The Backyard (Page 24)
Counting on Frank (Page 106)
Creative Writer (Page 64)
Dangerous Creatures (Page 160)
Davidson's Kid Keys (Page 210)
The Discis Kids Can Read Series (Page 76)
The Eagle Eye Mysteries Series (Page 184)
GeoSafari (Page 186)
Keroppi Day Hopper (Page 204)
KidMail Connection (Page 206)
Kid's Typing (Page 208)
Kids World (Page 46)
Leonardo the Inventor (Page 144)
Magic Theatre (Page 44)
  Spider-Man Cartoon Maker (Page 45)
My First Incredible Amazing Dictionary (Page 26)
P.B. Bear's Birthday Party (Page 74)
The Playroom (Page 22)

Putt-Putt Joins the Parade (Page 176)
Putt-Putt Goes to the Moon (Page 176)
Reader Rabbit 1 (Page 84)
Reader Rabbit 2 (Page 84)
Reader Rabbit's Interactive Reading Journey (Page 86)
Safari (Page 157)
The Scavenger Hunt Adventure Series (Page 162)
Troggle Trouble (Page 112)
Widget Workshop (Page 158)
Wrath of the Gods (Page 142)

★

Alge-Blaster 3 (Page 114)
Alphabet Blocks (Page 89)
Beginning Reading (Page 90)
Crayola Amazing Art Adventure (Page 48)
Crayola Art Studio (Page 48)
Fine Artist (Page 47)
The Knowledge Adventure Series (Page 166)
The Magic School Bus Explores the Human Body (Page 164)
The Magic School Bus Visits the Solar System (Page 164)
Math Blaster: Episode 1—In Search of Spot (Page 114)
Math Blaster: Episode 2—Secret of the Lost City (Page 114)
Math Blaster Mystery: The Great Brain Robbery (Page 114)
Math Munchers Deluxe (Page 116)
Number Munchers (Page 116)
Reader Rabbit 3 (Page 84)
Reader Rabbit's Ready for Letters (Page 84)
Reading Blaster (Page 88)
Recess in Greece (Page 148)
Richard Scarry's How Things Work in Busytown (Page 28)
Sound It Out Land 1, 2, 3 (Page 93)
Stowaway! (Page 146)

Super Munchers (Page 116)
Super Solvers Midnight Rescue! (Page 91)
Super Solvers OutNumbered! (Page 120)
Super Solvers Spellbound! (Page 91)

Treasure Cove! (Page 118)
Treasure Galaxy! (Page 118)
Treasure MathStorm! (Page 118)
Treasure Mountain! (Page 118)
WiggleWorks Volume 1 (Page 92)
Word Munchers (Page 116)

Titles by Subject

ARTS & ANIMATION
Freehand art, coloring, design, painting, animation, crafts, slide shows

★★★★ Kid Pix 2 & Kid Pix Fun Pack (Page 32) 3–10
★★★★ Kid Pix Studio (Page 34) 3–12
★★★★ Flying Colors (Page 36) 5–12
★★★★ Kid Cuts (Page 38) 3–8
★★★★ Art Explorer (Page 40) 8–12
★★ Amazing Animation (Page 42) 5–12
★★ Magic Theatre (Page 44) & Spider-Man Cartoon Maker (Page 45) 6–12
★★ Kids World (Page 46) 5–10
★ Fine Artist (Page 47) 8–12
★ Crayola Amazing Art Adventure (Page 48) 3–6
★ Crayola Art Studio (Page 48) 6–9

EXPLORATIONS FOR CURIOUS KIDS: AROUND THE WORLD
Geography, map reading, reasoning

★★★★ Where in the USA Is Carmen Sandiego? (Page 126) 8–12
★★★★ Where in the World Is Carmen Sandiego? (Page 124) 8–12
★★★ Where in the World Is Carmen Sandiego? Junior Detective Edition (Page 128) 5–8
★★★ Travelrama USA (Page 130) 8–12

EXPLORATIONS FOR CURIOUS KIDS: BACK IN TIME
History, mythology, simulations

★★★★ The Oregon Trail II (Page 134) 10–16
★★★★ The Yukon Trail (Page 136) 10–16
★★★★ The Amazon Trail (Page 138) 10–16
★★ Ancient Lands (Page 140) 6 & Up
★★ Leonardo the Inventor (Page 144) 6 & Up
★★ Wrath of the Gods (Page 142) 9 & Up
★ Stowaway! (Page 146) 8–12
★ Recess in Greece (Page 148) 7–12

EXPLORATIONS FOR CURIOUS KIDS: INTO SCIENCE, NATURE & BEYOND
Life sciences, outer space, wildlife, & more

★★★★ Sammy's Science House (Page 150) 3–5
★★★★ Planetary Taxi (Page 152) 7–12
★★★★ What's the Secret? (Page 154) 7–12
★★★ Odell Down Under (Page 156) 8–12
★★ Widget Workshop (Page 158) 10–12
★★ Safari (Page 157) 6 & Up
★★ Dangerous Creatures (Page 160) 6 & Up
★★ The Scavenger Hunt Adventure Series (Page 162) 7–12
★ The Magic School Bus Series (Page 164) 6–10
★ The Knowledge Adventure Series (Page 166) 3–12

FUN & GAMES
Adventures, quests, simulations, strategy & problem-solving

★★★★ Myst (Page 170) 9 & Up
★★★★ SimCity 2000 (Page 172) 10 & Up
  SimTower (Page 172) 10 & Up
  SimIsle (Page 173) 10 &Up
  SimAnt (Page 173) 10 &Up
  SimEarth (Page 173) 10 & Up
  SimFarm (Page 173) 10 & Up
  SimCity Classic (Page 173) 10 & Up
  SimTown (Page 173) 8–12
★★★★ The Freddi Fish Series (Page 174) 3–6
★★★★ At Bat (Page 178) 7–12
★★★★ Putt-Putt Saves the Zoo (Page 176) 3–5
★★★ Klik & Play (Page 180) 9–12
★★★ Gahan Wilson's The Ultimate Haunted House (Page 182) 8–12
★★ Putt-Putt Goes to the Moon (Page 176) 3–5
★★ Putt-Put Joins the Parade (Page 176) 3–5
★★ The Eagle Eye Mysteries Series (Page 184) 7–10
★★ GeoSafari (Page 186) 8–12

INFORMATION, PLEASE!
Interactive reference tools

★★★ Explorapedia: The World of Nature (Page 190) 6–10
★★★ Explorapedia: The World of People (Page 190) 6–10
★★★ 3D Atlas (Page 192) 8 & Up
★★★ Encarta 1996 (Page 194) 11 & Up
★★★ The Eyewitness Encyclopedia Series (Page 196) 11 & Up

MATH EXPLORATIONS
Discovering concepts and developing strategies for solving mathematical problems

★★★★ Math Workshop (Page 98) 5–12
★★★★ Millie's Math House (Page 100) 2–5
★★★ Countdown (Page 102) 5–12

★★ Adventures in Flight (Page 104) 8–12
★★ Counting on Frank (Page 106) 8–12

PLAYING TO LEARN
Early Learning titles for ages 2–5 including ABCs, counting & more

★★★★ Circus! (Page 10) 4–8
★★★★ AlphaBonk Farm (Page 12) 3–5
★★★ Zurk's Learning Safari (Page 14) 2–5
★★★ Zurk's Rainforest Lab (Page 16) 5–9
★★★ Thinkin' Things Collection 1 (Page 18) 3–8
★★★ Thinkin' Things Collection 2 (Page 20) 6–12
★★ The Playroom (Page 22) 3–4
★★ The Backyard (Page 24) 3–5
★★ My First Incredible Amazing Dictionary (Page 26) 2–4
★ Richard Scarry's How Things Work in Busytown (Page 28) 3–5

PRODUCTIVITY
Typing, e-mail, word processing, organizers & utilities

★★★★ KidDesk (Page 200) All
★★★★ KidDesk Family Edition (Page 200) All
★★★★ At Ease (Page 200) All
★★★★ Launch Pad (Page 200) All
★★★ Student Writing Center (Page 202) 10 & Up
★★ Keroppi Day Hopper (Page 204) 7–12
★★ KidMail Connection (Page 206) 8–12
★★ Kid's Typing (Page 208) 6–8
★★ Davidson's Kid Keys (Page 210) 3–8

READING BASICS
Exercises in phonics, spelling & reading comprehension

★★★ Alien Tales (Page 80) 8–12
★★★ Davidson's Kid Phonics (Page 82) 4–6
★★ Reader Rabbit 1 (Page 84) 4–6
★★ Reader Rabbit 2 (Page 84) 5–8
★★ Reader Rabbit's Interactive Reading Journey (Page 86) 4–6
★ Reader Rabbit 3 (Page 84) 6–8
★ Reader Rabbit's Ready for Letters (Page 84) 3–5
★ Reading Blaster (Page 88) 7–10
★ Alphabet Blocks (Page 89) 3–4
★ Beginning Reading (Page 90) 5–7
★ Super Solvers Spellbound! (Page 91) 7–10
★ Super Solvers Midnight Rescue! (Page 91) 7–10
★ WiggleWorks Volume 1 (Page 92) 3–5
★ Word Munchers (Page 116) 6–10
★ The Sound It Out Land Series (Page 93) 4–6

SKILLS & DRILLS
Exercises in addition, subtraction, multiplication, division & other math basics

★★ Troggle Trouble (Page 112) 6–12

★ The Math Blaster Series (Page 114) 6–12
★ The Muncher Series (Page 116) 8–12
★ The Treasure Series (Page 118) 5–9
★ Super Solvers OutNumbered! (Page 120) 5–9

STORIES ON SCREEN
Interactive books & poetry

★★★★ Just Grandma and Me (Page 70) 2–5
★★★★ Dr. Seuss' ABCs (Page 70) 3–7
★★★★ Arthur's Teacher Trouble (Page 70) 3–8
★★★★ Arthur's Birthday (Page 70) 3–8
★★★★ The New Kid on the Block (Page 70) 3–8
★★★★ The Tortoise and the Hare (Page 70) 3–8
★★★★ Little Monster At School (Page 70) 2–5
★★★★ Harry and the Haunted House (Page 70) 4–6
★★★★ The Berenstain Bears Get in a Fight (Page 70) 3–6
★★ P.B. Bear's Birthday Party (Page 74) 2–4
★★ The Discis Kids Can Read Series (Page 76) 2–6

WORDPLAY & STORYTELLING
Creative writing, poems, plays, journals, cards & storybooks

★★★★ The Amazing Writing Machine (Page 52) 7–12
★★★★ Imagination Express (Page 54) 5–12
★★★★ Star Act (Page 56) 8–12
★★★ Bailey's Book House (Page 60) 2–5
★★★ Storybook Weaver Deluxe (Page 58) 5–9
★★★ Davidson's Kid Works Deluxe (Page 62) 2–5
★★ Creative Writer (Page 64) 7–12